"Wickedly funny and deeply harrowing. . . . Darkly ironic. . . . Novakovich knows how to tell a story, and his prose has an easy, elegant velocity. . . . Strange, lyrical beauty abounds here."

—Maud Casey, *New York Times Book Review*

"Like a modern-day Çandide of the Balkans, Ivan Dolinar, the antihero of this laugh-while-you-grimace novel, bumbles his way through life, wars, and love. . . . Novakovich chronicles his character's journey through a world whose patent absurdity is almost impossible to exaggerate. He writes with dark wit, and a touching sympathy for the lost soul that Ivan represents."

—*Newsweek International*

"Like Aleksandar Hemon and Ha Jin . . . Novakovich manages the feat of writing vibrantly and inventively in a second language, shaping English to the dictates of his satiric, folk-tinged storytelling." —*Publishers Weekly*

"[Dolinar] is a fully rounded character, the type of protagonist . . . that we rarely find in fiction." —*Chicago Tribune*

"A forlorn and frequently hilarious novel. . . . Dolinar is a marvelous creation, equal parts bumbling philosopher and resigned victim of fate. . . . Novakovich tempers his descriptions of the horrors of war with black humor and moments of grace. . . . Disturbing and frequently beautiful. . . . The novel is a sort of Balkan conflation of Louis-Ferdinand Céline, Gogol's *Dead Souls,* and [Vonnegut's] *Slaughterhouse-Five.*"

—*Minneapolis Star Tribune*

"An ambitious first novel . . . The magic realism of the final sections is exemplary; Novakovich has found his groove."

—*Washington Post*

"Both humorous and horrifying as it traces one man's misadventures as he tries to love a dictator and fight on both sides of the war between Croatia and Serbia."   —*USA Today*

"*April Fool's Day* is a wonder. . . . [It] has an economy of style and narrative that all good readers will relish."

—Keith Botsford, *The Republic of Letters*

"A heartfelt novel about the war-torn Balkans that's actually quite funny . . . and touching."   —*GQ*

"Novakovich's book, rife with dark humor, is notable for its witty reflections on politics, literature, and the vicissitudes of the human heart."   —*San Diego Union-Tribune*

"[An] eccentric first novel from one of the more interesting and unusual contemporary writers. . . . Novakovich's understatements work superbly in the closing chapters, when Ivan's inquisitive ghost achieves a harmony with his surroundings that had been denied him throughout his life."

—*Kirkus Reviews* (starred review)

"Delightfully neurotic. . . . Novakovich brings a deft touch to his ambitious and unconventional first novel."

—*Columbus Dispatch*

Infidelities

Books by Josip Novakovich

NOVELS
April Fool's Day

SHORT FICTION
Infidelities: Stories of War and Lust
Salvation and Other Disasters
Yolk

ESSAYS
Plum Brandy: A Croatian Journey
Apricots from Chernobyl

AS EDITOR
Stepmother Tongue: Stories in English as a Second Language
(with Robert Shapard)

Infidelities

Stories
of War
and Lust

JOSIP NOVAKOVICH

HARPER **PERENNIAL**

HARPER ● PERENNIAL

HarperCollins books may be purchased for educational, business, or sales promotional use. For information please write: Special Markets Department, HarperCollins Publishers, 10 East 53rd Street, New York, NY 10022.

FIRST EDITION

Designed by Jaime Putorti

Library of Congress Cataloging-in-Publication Data

Novakovich, Josip.

Infidelities : stories of war and lust / Josip Novakovich.— 1st Harper Perennial ed.

p. cm.

ISBN-10: 0-06-058399-1
ISBN-13: 978-0-06-058399-6

1. Balkan Peninsula—Emigration and immigration—Fiction. 2. World War, 1914–1918—Bosnia and Hercegovina—Fiction. 3. Sarajevo (Bosnia and Hercegovina)—Fiction. 4. Croatian Americans—Fiction. 5. Immigrants—Fiction. I. Title.

PS3564.O914I54 2005

813'.54—dc22

2004065068

05 06 07 08 09 ❖/RRD 10 9 8 7 6 5 4 3 2 1

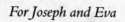

For Joseph and Eva

Contents

Acknowledgments

These stories have appeared in the following publications:
"Spleen" in *The Paris Review*, May 2003, and in the anthology
  Wild East: Stories from the Last Frontier.
"The Stamp" in *Ploughshares*, December 2002.
"Night Guests" in *Antioch Review*, September 2001.
"Neighbors" in *TriQuarterly*, January 2000.
"Hail" in *TriQuarterly*, January 2003.
"Snow Powder" in *Other Voices*, April 2003, and in a shorter
  form in *Powder*, December 2002.
"Tchaikovsky's Bust" in *Fiction*, June 2002.
"The Bridge Under the Danube" in *Boulevard*, June 2002.
"59th Parallel" in *The Sun*, January 2003.
"Ribs" in *Tin House*, July 2001.
"A Purple Story" appears for the first time in this volume.

I'm enormously grateful to Terry Karten for her wonderful edit-
ing and steadfast support, and I'm thanking—for encouragement and feedback—Francine Prose, Anne Edelstein, Danny
Mulligan, Emilie Stewart, Jeanette Novakovich, Richard Bur-
gin, Andrew Proctor, Carol Keeley, Larry Goldstein, Don Lee,

and Mark Mirsky, and gracias to the institutions which helped by granting me time in the guise of money: the National Endowment for the Arts, the New York Public Library's Dorothy B. Cullman Center for Scholars and Writers, the Yaddo Corporation, the Guggenheim Foundation, and the Tennessee Williams Fellowship at the University of the South.

Infidelities

Spleen

When I found out that a Bosnian family had moved into our neighborhood, just across from my place, I was thrilled. I had left Bosnia seven years before, and I hardly ever saw anybody from there.

To me now it didn't matter whether the neighbors were Muslims, Croats, or Serbs from Bosnia; the main thing was that they were Bosnian, that they spoke the language I loved and hadn't heard in a while, but when I learned that they were a Croatian family from Bugojno, I was all the more delighted. And nostalgic. Perhaps I could have gone home, but I didn't trust it: my hometown was in Republika Srpska. Under the NATO supervision, it was already possible to go back, and probably nothing bad would have happened, but I still

couldn't see sleeping there without streetlights around. I recalled the events before my departure. Some people had already fled from my hometown because they'd heard the Serb
army was coming, but I didn't believe they would bother me.
If they were targeting people ethnically, I thought I was safe,
since I was half Serb, half Croat. Then, one night, somebody
knocked on the door and shouted, Open up! Police.

I looked through the door and saw two men with masks
over their heads.

That's not what you'd expect police to look like. What
would police need to talk to me about anyway?

I went to the kitchen, took a sharp, midsized knife, put it in
my sleeve and waited while they tore the door down. I hid in a
clothes cabinet. The two thugs went through the house, over-
turning the tables, smashing the china, and they shouted for
me to come out. One walked into the basement, and the other
opened the toilet. At that moment, I sneaked out of the closet,
walking softly, barefoot. But he saw me and ran after me and
knocked me down. The knife slid out of my sleeve and fell on
the floor but he must not have heard it because he'd knocked
down a pile of plates on the way, and they crashed on the floor.
He tore my clothes off. Meanwhile, the man—or should I say,
beast—downstairs kept smashing the jars of jam and pickled
peppers; suddenly he quieted because probably he'd found the
wine bottles.

The thug pinned me to the floor and as I tried to throw
him off my body, he whacked my head against the boards. I
am pretty strong, and I think I could have thrown him off if he
hadn't whacked my head each time I moved. It hurt terribly. I
thought migraines were the worst headache you could have,

but this was worse, it hurt deeper inside, and I was dizzy, as though my brain had turned around in my skull and was now loose and wobbling.

He slid a little lower and sat on my thighs. You must help me to get it hard, he said.

I don't want to.

You must. Here, take it into your hand.

I did with one hand.

It's awkward like that, can I sit up, I asked.

Sure, no problem.

I sat up sideways, felt on the floor for the knife, grabbed its handle, and without hesitation stuck the knife into him. I wanted to get him in the middle of his abdomen but I missed and stuck it to the side, the left side. I did not think it went deep.

He shrieked and didn't react when I leaped to the side and ran straight out of doors. And so I ran into the hills, naked, in the cold November night. I nearly froze, turned blue, and didn't know where to hide, except in the Benedictine monastery on top of the hill. I broke into the chapel in the middle of matins, five in the morning now, still dark. The poor men crossed themselves, hid their faces, prayed in Latin, and I heard one word, which I liked, *misericordia*. But one of them, said, Brothers, don't be silly. Help her! He took off his brown garment, put it over me, and stood there in his striped shirt and long johns.

The monks gave me hot water and coffee, and when I stopped shivering, I wanted to run away. I told them what had happened and advised them to run away as well. The one who had intervened for me drove me west, to Mostar. As he drove he wanted to hold hands with me. No harm, I thought. And indeed, what harm was it? This fifty-year-old man, holding hands. He did not ask for anything more. I think he just loved some female creature comfort. I did not wait for further developments. I stole a bicycle in Mostar, and rode it all the way into Croatia, to Metkovic. That was not hard since the road mostly goes downhill. And in Croatia, I appealed to Caritas, where they gave me papers and let me go abroad, to the States. Now that was more adventure than I had hoped to get.

I've always wanted to be a homebody. I never got the joy of travel, wanderlust. Nearly the only aspect of travel I enjoyed as a kid was the homecoming. I'd rush to the side of the train as it crested the hill before my hometown, and seeing the first glimpse of the church steeples and the minaret and the old castle made me happy. So it's all the more miraculous to me that I have become a world traveler, an American.

And my workplace, a bank, is nice. Next to it, there's a restaurant, Dubrovnik. I don't need to go into it, but just knowing it's there comforts me; it's a bit of homeland. And just recently, I did go into it with my fellow bank teller, a Polish woman named Maria. We walked up the stairs into the restaurant and entered a tobacco cloud. The guests in the stinging smoke gave me an impression that a group of angels was noisily resting in the cloud. Since I couldn't make out many details I saw only the silhouettes blowing smoke from their cigarettes, feeding their blue cloud, as if the moment the cloud vanished, they would all fall to earth. I liked to imagine that the gathering was a choir of smoked angels but I knew it was unlikely that any of them were angels; most were recent immigrants from Herzegovina and Croatia, and some had participated in the war.

As I savored soft chicken *paprikash,* Maria said, You know, a Bosnian family moved into our neighborhood, right next door to you. Have you met them?

No. I had no idea that anybody moved in.

They are having a grill next Saturday. They invited me, and I can bring along anybody I want. Would you like to come along?

Maria wiped her shiny lips and cheeks with a napkin from her lap, and added, They are quite handsome.

Her napkin turned red.

THE GREEN BACKYARD of my new neighbors was enveloped in the grill smoke; I enjoyed the smell of coal.

That is one aspect of American culture we from the Balkans quickly adapt to, grilling cutlets and sausages, although we add our variant to it, *chevapi,* spicy mixed meat. The boombox on the windowsill played folk music, the kind that used to bore and bother me, but now made me feel at home. You know, accordion, bass, and a wailing voice.

The bald host wore a green outfit as though he were in a hospital, and when I asked him whether he was a doctor, he said, I work at Mercy Hospital as an X-ray technician.

That's a good job, isn't it? How many hours a week counts as full time?

Twenty-four.

So you have lots of free time. Nice.

It could be nicer. I studied to be a doctor in Sarajevo, did very well, but wasn't very wise: I participated in a protest against Tito, had to go to prison, and couldn't go back to the university afterward. I had no choice but to emigrate.

Have you met my nephew yet? He pointed out a man who was facing away from us. The man turned around, balding like his uncle, with a wide bony face, and teeth unusually white for someone from our parts—they were also wide-spaced and maybe that's what saved them.

He looked familiar, but the more I looked at him, the more I was sure that I was wrong. That is just it—many people from my native region can give me that feeling of familiarity even without my ever having met them. In my hometown, they'd all be strangers to me, but the familiar kind of stranger, and that is what I imagined I was responding to.

He came over to me and asked where I was from and what I did, the kind of questions you would not expect from someone from our native region, but from an American.

When I told him I worked for a bank, he grew wildly enthusiastic. I need to buy a house, he said. Can you get me a mortgage? What's the best rate you can offer?

That depends on your credit rating.

Credit rating, phew. How would I have any? But I have a refugee status, and a Lutheran church backing me. And I just got a job, as an electrician.

You must be smart then. A dumb electrician would be dangerous.

You are right about that. But maybe I am a dumb and brave electrician.

Have you ever gotten a good shock?

Of course, who hasn't. Even you have an electrical shock story.

True.

Bank, he said. Isn't it boring to work there?

Not in the least. There are many Croats and Slovenes there but not Bosnians.

So it must be boring!

It's always interesting with our people—they are still to my mind our people. One day a man paid for his entire new house in cash. He opened a brown suitcase—it was full of ten-dollar bills. Nothing but ten-dollar bills.

Why don't you write a check? I asked him.

Can't trust checks, he said.

And why only ten-dollar bills?

Can't trust no hundret-dollar bills, he said. Too many Italians here. They are all Mafioso, and that's what they do, they print fake bills. Ten dollar is the best.

He was an old Croatian car dealer. The motto of his dealership was, Honest Cars for Honest Cash. You wouldn't imagine that someone completely stuck in the cash economy could become rich, but that man did, bringing half a million dollars just like that. I wonder how he dared walk in the streets, alone, with all the cash.

Dragan laughed.

Our people are such hopeless hicks! All of us are peasants.

He kept standing closer and closer, and I moved a little away from him, and so we kept moving around the yard. I was keenly aware of it, and he apparently wasn't, or didn't mind. Perhaps I had adopted the American subconscious concept of personal space, which is about an arm's length, so nobody can touch you or hit you without your getting a chance to duck; it's also convenient because at that distance anybody's bad

breath would dissolve in the air and you wouldn't have to suffer it and likewise, you wouldn't have to worry that if you had
morning breath, you'd make people uncomfortable breathing
in your free-floating bacteria. I like this Anglo-Saxon personal
space, but naturally, a fresh arrival from Bosnia wouldn't understand the space and would find it cold and standoffish.

But after a while it occurred to me that he was not so much
after a house and mortgage as after me.

In the meanwhile, his uncle was retelling Bosnian jokes to
Maria, who rewarded him with her booming laughter.

We ate *chevapi* then. I looked forward to the taste, but the
meat was overgrilled. Our hosts were too eager to talk and so
they forgot the meat. Actually, since we didn't use to have re-
frigerators in the Balkans, we customarily overgrilled meat, to
make sure to kill all the bacteria. Only here did I for the first
time see people eating bloody meat, calling it rare and medium
rare. With us, there was only one way: well-done. At any rate,
while I loved the smell of grilled meat, I couldn't eat the charcoal crusts to get to the meat. Instead, I drank the red wine
Dragan offered—and it was spectacular, Grgich, deep red and
purple, tasting of plums, for some reason. Now both he and I
relaxed, and he told me his repertoire of Bosnian jokes.
Strangely, though I found many of them funny, now I can't remember any.

Anyway, I agreed to get together with this man, Dragan—
for no serious reason, other than that I loved speaking Bosnian. I guess that's a serious enough reason. We met in our
neighborhood beer hall. That's one thing about Cleveland—it
has many ethnic neighborhoods, and this was the German
contribution.

You know, he said, my uncle is a funny cat. At night, he sometimes dresses like a doctor and pretends to be one, and visits patients in the clinic, even offering them new diagnoses and advising them to undergo surgery; he loves to advise heart patients to get transplants. He was caught impersonating a doctor and fired, but then, there was such a shortage of nurses and medical technicians that they let him come back. He suffers on the job because he imagines he knows much more than his superiors. He is so absorbed in his status struggle that he neglects other aspects of his life. He lent his life savings to a friend of his from Bosnia, forty thousand dollars, without a security note, just on the honorable word. The friend disappeared, and that was that for life savings. What an idiot my uncle is!

How can you speak so badly of him? He takes care of you.

I am not speaking badly of him. Everybody knows what he's done. It's funny.

Mostly sad. He lost so much money. And he pretends to be what he's not. Does that run in the family?

What do you mean? Crazy generosity? Well . . .

No, pretending.

I don't pretend anything.

I did not say you did. I simply wonder whether what he's doing is a family trait.

Is that how you talk for fun?

Yes, I continue a theme, a thread. So he's your uncle.

And so? What are you getting at? (He sat up from his chair.)

My God, I thought you had a sense of humor.

Yes, I had it.

Okay, mellow out. Have a beer.

Good idea. Two Guinnesses please, he asked the waitress, and turned his head. The waitress wore a short skirt and black stockings that went only a few inches above her knees, so there was a stretch of thighs between the hem of the skirt and the stockings.

Good body, I said.

Guinness has lots of body.

She has a good body.

You noticed?

I noticed you noticing.

Oh, here we go again. You are catching me or something?

No.

I noticed her style. I don't know whether she has a good body, but the style's—

Sexy?

I forgot how difficult our women can be. Now I feel right at home.

Same goes for me and our men. I do feel at home. That's the point, I wanted to feel like I was home.

And that's why you agreed to come out with me?

Yes.

It doesn't matter what I am like, the main thing is I'm from over there?

It matters what people are like.

The beer was foamy and cool, and left a creamy edge on his lips, which he never wiped off right away, but talked like that, with the foam on his upper lip.

The second round of ale got to my head. The American bars are dark. We kissed in that darkness under the spell of dark ale, or under the excuse of it. He tasted of unfiltered cigarettes, and I liked that, it reminded me of home. Yes, I had kissed a few Americans, and nonsmoking immigrants, who before the kiss, regularly chewed mints, so their mouths were cool, slightly antiseptic. Well, the three, four times I had kissed they went to the bathroom to floss their teeth, no doubt, and to brush them, so you'd get a refurbished mouth. But this was a European kiss, old style, with a nicotine bite to it, and an undertone of hot peppers—he must have had *feferonki* somewhere. The kiss was hotly reminiscent of the old continent, so I closed my eyes and floated into the smoky spaces with Turkish coffee poured from *dzezva,* coppery vessels, and heavy dregs on the bottom, from which old peasant women read fortunes. Upon drinking a cup, you'd have a few coffee grains left in your mouth, to chew on, to chase around your mouth with your tongue, and that is what the kiss now felt, like a grainy chase. A gritty and biting kiss. I stretched my neck and he kissed it, his five o'clock whiskers scratching me like a rasping paper, raw, but I liked that sensation of hurt.

We went to my home and continued our erotic pursuits so impatiently that we had not fully undressed. I still had my skirt on, and he had his shirt and tie, though everything else was off. I pulled him to me by his red tie, and the tightening grip of his collar, plus the labor of lust, made his face all red, and blue veins popped on his forehead and kept changing their courses, like overflowing tributaries of a river, seeking the most urgent way to the sea.

I wondered why this man trusted me and let me pull the tie. I felt a sudden impulse to strangle him, inexplicable but tempting. Instead, I let go of the tie and loosened it. He panted with his mouth open, baring his teeth, and again he kissed my neck, and bit it, perhaps playfully, but still that shot a wave of fright through my blood. I bit his ear. We kept biting each other, as though we were two wolves, steadying each other in the playful grip of teeth. Our lust affected our bones, and came from our bones, and flesh was in the way. The bones of our love made us both sharp, not dreamy and sleepy as I used to be in lovemaking, not floating in the delicacy of sensations, but aggressively alert. It was as though we wanted to destroy each other—and that did result in a sensation, the kind you have when your life is in question, jumping off a cliff into a deep azure bay, skiing downhill and hitting a bump that suspends you in the air.

There was an extraordinary undercurrent of hatred in our sex, and it shocked me. I was shuddering, at first I thought in the premonition of an orgasm, but no, from the cold fright. He let go of my neck, and his tie tickled my stomach and breasts as he rocked back and forth. I was nearly strangling him again, holding on to his tie, like a friar to the church bell, while he was smashing his pubic bone into mine in the rhythm of a church bell, and I did indeed hear the ringing in my ears. If the bones were to break, I wasn't sure it would be mine that would give first. Love and lust aren't synonyms, as everybody knows, and hate and lust aren't antonyms, as I found out. Love is usually safe, someone there who can help you, who can spread his arms to keep you from falling, and in that sense, it's antithetical to that sensation of total collapse and abandon that the most intense orgasms are made of. Hatred, however, helps along that delicious sensation of destruction and self-destruction. That is what I realized as I was coming in this sea, not of joy, but terror. I would not have thought like that if we had not been making love and hate in our sex, and if hate had not prevailed.

I slid my hands under his shirt, and touched his stomach. His stomach twitched like a horse's flank when bitten by a horsefly. His skin was smooth and soft. That surprised me because his neck's hairs stuck out above the collar of his shirt. When my hands roamed further, he gripped them and put them back. That tickles, he said.

So? Tickling is good. You can tickle me, if you like.

I touched him again, and he twitched, and lost his erection. That was just as well; we had survived several hours of passion, and both of us sighed perhaps with relief, perhaps with the contemplation of the unsettling nature of our collision.

Even after he was gone, I sat in amazement at what had transpired and the animosity which hung mustily in the air as a war of different body vapors, his sweat and my sweat, his garlicky, mine olivey, his sugary, mine salty.

After he was gone, I wondered why he had kept his shirt on, and that is how I went to sleep. I woke up, certain I had had an enlightening dream, like that biochemist who had a vision of a snake eating its own tail, which was the solution for the circular structure of benzene or whatever it was and is forever, of course. Now, in my dream, Dragan appeared in a black T-shirt. I asked him, why don't you take it off?

I can't.

I will make love to you only if you take it off.

I'd rather not.

So I undressed and teased him, and when he took off his T-shirt, I saw a brown scar on his left side, under the ribs, in the spleen area. The scar paled, then blushed, and became angry red. Drops of blood slid out of it and went down his flank. Give me back my shirt, he said, right away! I had thrown it behind the bed. I don't know where it is, I said.

Find it! He said. Blood now gushed.

By the time I took mercy on him, though I thought I had no reason to do it, and wanted to hand him his shirt, he fell on the floor, in an oily red puddle. Blood kept coming out of him, and furniture floated, and my bed turned into a sinking boat. I shrieked, and woke up with the echo of it, from the attic and the basement, the whole house was empty with the aftermath of my shriek.

I went to the bathroom. The floor was dry. I brushed my teeth. My gums weren't bleeding. I looked into my eyes. They weren't bloodshot.

I had believed in my dreams, but I also doubted them—I had had all sorts of dreams, in some I had lost all my teeth and when I woke up they were still fast in my jaws.

We were supposed to meet again the following evening after my work. I dreaded it. I would not answer the door. I would turn all the lights off and pretend I was not there.

When eight o'clock approached, I grew terrified that the man would not come, that he would know I had figured him out.

SUDDENLY THREE POLICE CARS screeched to the house, their lights flashing. Ha, I thought, they must have the evidence. Once they got him out in handcuffs, I would run out and tell them what I had to add. I put my Nikes on and tightened them, remembering that Nike comes from Greek for Victoria,

female winner. Soon the cops escorted the familiar bald silhouette, which wore green. It was the poor pretend-doctor.
The nephew showed up on the doorstep and smoked a cigarette. Of course, it was possible that he yawned because he'd
had too much sex. Still, why wouldn't he at least talk to the
cops, why wouldn't he be upset? Maybe he liked it this way,
maybe he'd even turned his uncle in, to have more space to
himself. Now he wouldn't need to buy a house. But what did I
know what had happened there? I went back to the kitchen
and prepared some cappuccino, letting it hiss and spit like an
angry cat, although it would be hard to imagine a cat being that
angry with milk.

Soon the doorbell rang. I let Dragan in. This time he was
not formal; he wore a black T-shirt, just like in my dream. He
brought in red carnations and a bottle of Eagle Peak merlot. I
turned on the music, Mahler's Fifth. Some of the funeral
chords in Mahler's music give me chills, so this was masochis-
tic of me, in all the redness and blackness to have these jarring
notes in minor keys.

You like that music? he asked.

Love it.

Why not play some real folk music?

Later. This is good for a slow start.

We have been anything but slow and we are way past a
start.

I've never heard a man complaining about getting to bed
too quickly.

I'm not complaining. But then, maybe I could if you let
others sleep with you so quickly. How many were there before
me?

Oh, nobody else has been so special to me. (My voice sounded more cynical than I wanted. Yes, indeed, nobody was so special, I had to admit to myself. And, I went on talking.) Poor uncle of yours. Why did they take him?

How do you know?

I am the good kind of neighbor, I look out the window.

God spare us from watchful neighbors. Seriously though, my uncle is totally insane. He went around the kidney ward, injecting morphine into the patients. He kept repeating, There's too much pain in the world, too much pain.

He's right about that. That's kind of charming.

It would be if the drugs weren't an additional stress on the kidneys. If he'd done it in the orthopedic ward, maybe nobody would have complained, but what he did was dangerous, criminal. I am ashamed of him.

But he meant well, and probably the patients were in pain, and felt better afterward. Maybe he knows better about it all than we and the cops do. I think it's touching.

He chuckled. That gave me the creeps. Or maybe a particularly well-placed dissonance in Mahler gave me a chill, and if it didn't, it catalyzed it. As though he understood precisely what went on in my spine, he repeated, You sure you like that music?

He smiled, sitting in a slouchy posture. He didn't look dangerous, but almost amiable, low-key, not like an alpha dog, but a beta, sitting at a fireplace with his tail curled.

Above his T-shirt and inside it, he massaged his pectoral muscle, slowly, sensually. It seemed strange to me that a man would caress himself like that—it was surprising and slightly erotic.

Out of nervousness, I drank half the bottle, and soon we

were kissing on my queen-sized bed. I grew excited, partly because this had a forbidden quality to it: I had forbidden it to myself, and now I was transgressing. I had of course planned to get to bed, to check out his scar, but I had not wanted to be aroused, and here I was.

Under the pillow I had a kitchen knife, just in case. I know, that sounds like some praying mantis kind of thing, and if so, maybe the man should have his last wish, without knowing it was his last, to make love. I didn't mind the idea; in a way, I almost wanted him to become aggressive and dangerous so I could do it. Not that I wanted to do it, but the temptation flashed in my mind.

As we made out, I slid my hand under his T-shirt, to his navel.

He pushed my hand away, and said, I'm ticklish.

Yes, I know you said that, but you don't mind being touched elsewhere.

Only my feet and my stomach are ticklish.

I touched his neck and slid my hands downward, but the T-shirt was too tight from my angle to go further.

What are you trying to do? He asked. You like collar bones?

Collar bones are my weakness. Why won't you take off your shirt?

Out of vanity. I don't want you to see how my stomach sags, how my chest hairs are getting gray, and how deep my innie is.

Now that you have told me all that, what's there to hide? I know what to expect, it can get only better. Let's fully undress. Isn't it funny, we haven't been naked yet. We have screwed each other's daylights, and haven't seen each other naked.

All right, but turn off the light then.

I thought about that. I wanted the light to examine him. But I could examine him anyway, I would let my fingers do it. I turned off the overhead light.

Good, that will be romantic, I said. I'll light the candles then.

I took out half a dozen candles and lit them.

He pulled off the T-shirt, his red underwear, and his soccer-style socks, which went almost to his knees. For his age, he was in good shape; his stomach didn't sag. He had lied. I had candlelight coming from all the corners of the room, and bathroom light came through a crack and spread wider and wider on the floor onto the wall, but that was not enough to see his scar. So as he lay down, I put my hand on his flank. He shrank, and his stomach twitched.

Just let go, I said.

All right, I guess you know a technique.

I felt all around, touched his ribs, below them, and I could not believe my fingers. There was no scar. What? Could my dreams have been wrong? It was horrible to think that I had found that man and that he was under my fingertips, but suddenly it was more horrible to think that this was not the man, and the other one was at large, who knew where, if he was not dead. How would I find him? Why should I want to find him? Why didn't I feel relief? I could've been overjoyed to be with a man who made love so vigorously—I could have a boyfriend, maybe even a new family, that wouldn't have been outlandish at my age, midthirties.

I was in such a state of shock that right away I quit the foreplay. I can't do it, I said.

Why not?

Dark thoughts have crossed my mind and they won't go away.

What are your dark thoughts?

And I told him, in detail, the attempted rape, and how I fled, except I didn't tell him about the knife and the wound. I said I knocked the guy down with a candelabra.

That is admirable, that you had so much courage to do that, he said. But why would you think of that right now?

Why admirable? What choice did I have?

Do you know what happened to the guy?

No, and I don't think I want to know. Do you?

Why would I? What a question!

I have no idea.

Did you think that even before?

I did not answer. I decided not to worry about anything. (I could worry; yes, I was tempted. It flashed in my mind that if this was not the first man, this could be the second man, the one who went to the basement to drink wine. But then, how did I know that one drank wine? Simply because he grew quiet? Well, this one certainly liked wine. But then, what's so unusual about that? Oh, no, I decided, I shouldn't keep having paranoid thoughts. They had to stop somewhere. I was wrong once, I could keep being wrong.) We drank more Eagle Peak; he'd brought two bottles, it turned out, and kept one in his laptop briefcase.

Let's shower together, I said. Maybe we'll make love, maybe not, but let's shower.

He obeyed and followed me. I soaped up our bodies, and so in foam, in hot water, we washed, our hairs dripping, our eyes stinging from soap, gasping from exhaustion and lack of air in the steamy cubicle, in the trapped cloud of our own making. He tried to grip me, and I clasped him, but we kept slipping out of each other's hold; the evasive slipperiness of our bodies made me lose the sense of balance so much that I enjoyed the illusion of exquisitely falling through the clouds.

The Stamp

I sought vengeance, and now I dream of forgiveness. My friends, let me explain how this came about. I want to lay it all out. I hope this last journal of mine will reach you, so you can be with me, with my thoughts, as long as it takes you to read it, and I can be with you as long as it takes me to write it, and beyond, though I am not sure there is much beyond.

On St. Vitus Day, a sunny day early in the summer, it was muggy, with all the steam and coal smoke from trains sitting in the valley. I sweated as I rushed to a photo shop so my friends and historians would have an image of me after I was gone; maybe it was vain of me to imagine they needed anything like that, but on the other hand, I had friends and a sister who loved me, so who was I to think that they would not want my photo? It would be selfish of me not to leave them a part of myself. I paid extra to have the picture done in an hour in several copies; it was expensive, but soon I would not need money, so I didn't care. I marveled that it could be done so quickly. Who knows what else soon could be speedily done in this world of ours—I regretted getting ready to depart it without seeing the technological miracles to come. Maybe one day letters would be sent without our having to lick stamps. Now I chuckled as I licked the backs of the dull images of sagging Franz Josef with mustaches fit for a walrus for the letters and humorless Franz Ferdinand for the postcards. Sure, soon there won't be any need for these images one way or another, I would help that. I sat down at a park bench a few blocks away from the river Miljacka and wrote to my friends—and I wanted to say good-bye to my sister, Jovanka, and to a girl I loved, Jelena. I varied what I said; to my sister I wrote, I must go far away. Good-bye. We will never see each other again. I wept when I wrote that.

To a friend I wrote: Tomorrow I will not be alive anymore; I am dying of an unspeakable pulmonary illness. I loved our walks. (I hadn't imagined at the time how true that would be; I thought I was lying when I wrote that about the illness. I had expected execution, maybe being shot on the spot without a trial, but here I am, while recalling all this, afflicted with a bloody cough, shivering from TB, but let that not distract me from recalling that day.) I had not imagined I would be so emotional about saying good-bye. My dog, Vuk, followed me everywhere as though he knew we wouldn't see each other again. I petted him, even pulled out a fat dark tick from his ear and crushed it with my leather sole on the cobbles, and heard it pop. He licked the reddened cobblestone, finding his own blood tasty, and then he licked my chin. Although I would have preferred a different sequence, first my chin, then the tick, I let him. I did not need to fear disease now, and why be disgusted? I was not a Viennese or Parisian noble or burgher to indulge squeamishness, though I was tempted to yield to it, such is the power of culture and slavish indoctrination that we provincials adopted. Vuk gave me the last lick and then shadowed me down the street. I shouted at him to go back, and he pretended to, after curling his tail, but when I rounded the next corner, there he was. I carried him back, and as I was closing the wooden gate, he still managed to get out, so I pushed him back in and kicked him hard in the chest. I could hear him even a kilometer away, howling. I felt miserable. I was tempted to go back and give up the business of making history. What good would a place in history books be compared with the real life and love of such a creature as a German shepherd? I didn't blame him for being called a German, though I hated everything German; he had nothing to do with them, he only had that name, poor soul, they managed to colonize even animals. Now I didn't like the idea of never again. But no, this would not be the matter of personal feelings, I should be able to transcend those.

I had expected crowds to throng along the river boulevard, Appel Quay, awaiting the archduke's parade, and they did, but where I stood, next to a gas lamppost, there was plenty of space. In my sagging jacket, my hands were getting clammy and cold, and the grenade metal was warmer than they were. I wished I had a Browning like the rest of them; that would have been more straightforward, but I proved to be such a bad shot, and I skipped practices. My hand always trembles a little, which makes it hard to concentrate. Now, that is not a problem when I swing something like a stone or a grenade. As a child in Trebinje I loved throwing stones. I could do it for hours, aiming at trees and lampposts, and I was the best thrower in my street. Even now as an adult in late-night walks in Belgrade in Kalemegdan Park, I would for no reason at all pick up stones and throw them at lampposts. I was an atheist, yet I admired the story of David and Goliath. After reading it in my grandmother's crumbly Bible in Cyrillic, I walked out and filled up my pockets with stones, and challenged the biggest bully in the neighborhood. He ran after me. I turned around, and aimed at his head, released the stone, and hit him in the middle of his forehead. For years later he had the scar. I feared that one day he would beat the hell out of me, but he did not. He had ceased to be a bully. So I chose the grenade, thinking I would be a kind of David, but all of a sudden my hand shook too much. Actually, I should have felt privileged to have the bomb. A couple of days before, when I chatted on a train with strangers, Gavrilo, who thought I was being indiscreet, took my bomb away. I could have strangled him for that; I was no doubt stronger than he, but he had the support of our group, and they all gave me hell for talking too much. Only a few hours before standing in the street did I get back the bomb from my arrogant and bossy friend, in a sweets shop. We didn't drink, but we all loved cream pies. I don't even know how I managed to still consider him a friend.

Now I couldn't back out. What would my friends think of me? Gavrilo would laugh. Well, now I thought I was cowardly, but nobody else must know it. And what if I didn't do it? Suppose that in fact I went over to a gendarme and told him about the whole plot. I could save the future monarch. I would have wanted to save his wife, who was a Czech, and at least she should be spared, but she was married to him, so she was a traitor as well, and if she went, so be it.

I imagined the monarch would continue to oppress Bosnia, and all the Slavs in it. Everybody who wanted to advance would still have to study in German, and bow to the pasty and cheesy Germans as though they were higher beings. I'd have to bow even to the drunken Hungarian slobs. Anyway, if I told a policeman of the plot, I would get no credit, but would be jailed for being a conspirator. It would be a different matter if they gave me a nice apartment in Paris and a pension for the rest of my life. But of course, they wouldn't do that, they would jail me. Even if they gave me an apartment, what kind of life would that be? Somebody from the Black Hand or Mlada Bosna would kill me as a traitor.

And what if I just quietly slunk away, walked over the bridge to the other side of the river, and up the mountain all the way to Pale, to enjoy the fresh air, the beautiful views? Who was to say that the other comrades could actually kill the archduke? I had no confidence in the whole lot. So if I didn't do it, who could?

However, if I succeeded, wouldn't I be sorry to die? I have never made love, nothing that would count, anyway; I have not yet finished reading *Crime and Punishment.* But so what? What kind of life do I have to wait for? Work, and shrieking children who'll be starving to death, while I slave twelve hours a day in some miserable printing press outfit, sorting out letters and poisoning myself with lead, and if I get tired of that, what else could I do? Go into coal mines to feed the Austrian trains, so the gentlemen and the soft women with garters could frolic all over our rails? Plus, what's left in the novel—I got stuck in the middle, and suddenly it grew boring with all the conspiracies and confessions and weeping.

But now was no time to get lost in thought. The six cars were glimmering, reflecting shafts of prickly sunlight, so it looked like thin swords flying at me. What if I didn't notice the archduke in time? What if I mistook the general Potiorek for him; the general was imitating the duke. I looked around. There was a gendarme some ten paces away from me. Did he notice I was looking at him? Should I have been scared of him? Well, now that I glared at him, he would be aware of me, and the best way then was not to be stealthy. I was tempted to tell him what I was about to do, just to amaze him. I wasn't that foolish, though. I walked up to him, and said, Sir, could you please tell me in what car His Highness is?

Oh, yes, in the second one, over there. He pointed out the shiniest car.

Thank you for the directions, I said.

Oh, don't mention it. We are all excited—such an incredible privilege to see the next emperor right here!

I moved away from the gendarme, and noticed the peacocky feathers above the duke's head. I tore off the bomb cap. It was louder than I expected. I saw the driver in the approaching first car shrink back and look over and accelerate. Did he suspect what it was? Now it would definitely go off. I was stuck. What should I do with the bomb now? Throw it in the river behind? What would that do? Kill a few fish feeding on an Austrian clerk's dung? How long could the bomb wait in my hands? Ten seconds, I knew that. I squeezed the bomb tightly in my pocket. My teeth chattered as though cold winter winds had suddenly begun to blow through my thin clothes.

The second car was close, approaching from my left, slowly, some twenty paces away. Very few policemen stood at the sidewalk. I had expected more of them; maybe there were many undercover agents around? But maybe not. The archduke boasted that he did not need high security; he wanted to appear brave. Maybe he was brave. It was easy to be brave with so much army at your command, even if the army was away.

Eight seconds. It looked unbelievably easy. I would never have such an opportunity again. Maybe just one strike, and I could liberate the Serbs—Austrians might get the message that they were not wanted, or there would be war, but at any rate, freedom from foreigners would come sooner or later. Maybe many people would die, but then the rest would live. Now, nobody lived.

Six seconds? The car was twelve yards or so from me. The duchess smiled, basking in the hazy sunshine. She had moist lips, gleaming teeth, looked fresh, that's what having underlings does for you. I knew that she hardly ever took trips with her husband, and she never rode with him in parades in Vienna because she was not of royal birth and therefore was not allowed to, but this time she must have done him a favor, or he had perhaps told her of the quaint beauties of the Balkans, and she could not resist the tourist temptations. She looked comfortable, pleasant, but what right did she have to her happiness?

I pulled out the bomb, with maybe three seconds left, still sort of hiding it with my palm. At that moment the archduke shot me a glance, a steady, cold glance. For a second our eyes were locked, and I hated that calm, the superiority in his gaze, which analyzed me as though I were a specimen in a zoo. I thought he could read all my intentions, and that he derided me, convinced that I couldn't do it, that he was so much above me that I was fit only to crawl at his feet and lick the shoe polish off his boots, and that even that would be a great favor to me. You will pay for this, I thought, and lifted my arm high and flung toward those eyes. But I had been too eager, and the metal slid from my clammy skin a little too soon. The bomb was flying in an arc above the archduke's head. The duke, obviously understanding the bomb was flying at his wife on the other side of him, lifted his arm, and the bomb deflected from it, hit the car roof cloth, which was drawn back for the good weather, bounced off it, and fell on the pavement under the third car, where it exploded, with shrapnel whistling, and then ensued the screams of the struck pedestrians. The second car sped away, and a dozen men were running toward me. I took cyanide, wrapped in a newspaper, from my left pocket and stuffed it into my mouth, together with a bit of the wrapping, so I wouldn't spill the powder, more than enough to kill me, but my throat was so dry I could not swallow. I pulled out the paper, and tried to make spittle in my mouth to swallow. By no means did I want to be caught by the police; now I'd have to die. I jumped over the fence and into the river, into the shallow water, which trickled among the rocks. I sprained my ankle, but no matter, why worry about that now?

A dozen civilians and policemen jumped after me into the river. I did not run away, did not resist, but threw myself prostrate into the cold water. The policemen grabbed me, pulled

me up, twisted my arms, hit me with their clubs over the head. I felt a trickle of warm urine in my pants—even if I thought I was not afraid, I was afraid, but didn't have enough mind to pay attention to it; something in my body was afraid. Why did I have so much water down there, and so little in my mouth? My throat was still choking dry. The hits blazed in my head, they were hot.

Don't bother beating me, I said. I've taken poison and have only a minute to live. So don't waste your time!

As they dragged me away, I felt nauseated. The poison is working, I thought. Am I ready to die? Yes, I am ready. That'll be easier than dealing with the police and the trials, and they'd kill me, anyway. How? Would they hang me on the gallows, in a public performance? Would they shoot me with my eyes covered in black cloth? Would a crowd gather? Would they all cheer, even those who hated the Austrians, would even they cheer, so they would not be suspected of wanting the end of Austria? Would they cheer the loudest? Would mothers bring along their children, so they would learn to obey and fear the authorities? Would Jovanka come out, and die from grief?

I felt like vomiting, but could not vomit.

Who are you? What is your name? a short policeman shouted into my nose, as though it were my nose that should have been able to listen, his breath stinking from rotten teeth and plum brandy.

I am a Serbian hero! I shrieked. And that was true, at that moment I realized it was true; my words worked faster than my mind. It felt good to say that. Now everything seemed worth it. I even straightened up, and my head and spine and shins all tingled—from a mixture of pain and pride.

Name, what is your name?

What's in a name? I told you. Names come from fathers, but a heroic deed from deep inside. (I was thinking it wasn't such a bad throw—I was just a second off, and considering I didn't have a stopwatch, and didn't really count, that was not bad; actually, the car would have been past me in a second or two—so I did pretty well. They certainly knew they were not welcome!)

Name! the officer said, and kicked me below the kneecap, so I suddenly lost balance as my muscles jerked.

They gave me blows as we went along. Old men with walking sticks jabbed at me. People hollered, spat. Blood flowed down my head and glued my eyes. I did not mind that warm feeling on my face; it felt as though it were enveloping me, protecting me, healing me. As long as there was blood on me, I felt safe. It doesn't make any sense, but what can I tell you, that is how I felt. Actually, I even felt happy. I had done my job. I was free now. They could jail me, kill me, but I had done what I had set out to do. I had not believed I could do it. I smiled from joy. No matter what they did to me, they could not take away my heroic deed. I didn't need to accomplish anything anymore. This was it. This was better than getting a doctorate or an Olympic medal.

I don't know how much time elapsed in a dark room in the military barracks, where I sprawled on a wooden bench along the wall, or whether the room was dark or only my vision failing. Several officers came in and interrogated me during the day, and again they came at night, and kept repeating the same questions, to try to catch me lying. I was lying at first, but later, it made no difference, except I did not want to give them any names, such as where I slept, because I knew that could get the people I knew into trouble. It seemed to me they were gullible, and I could tell them anything, and they would write it down and believe it. So, when they asked me whether I worked alone or with an organization, such as Black Hand, more for a joke than anything else, I said, I am working for the International Free Masons.

I knew nothing about the Free Masons, except that Catholic Austrians were scared of them and believed in all sorts of conspiracy theories involving the Masons. I told them we were trying to create a world without monarchs, monarchies, and countries, just one peaceful world.

Strange enough, they believed this and, from what I heard later on, kept bringing it up for months, in courts, in the newspapers—just one little joke threw them off so much. I wish I had given them more silly lies, but they kept harping on this one so much, without ever getting it, that I grew bored. They were not a fun bunch at all.

The lamplight was right in front of me on the table, so I saw nothing beyond it, and the police voices came from behind it, from the dark. Not that I wanted to look at the ugly men, but having voices like that just coming at me was spooky.

Who worked with you?

Nobody, I answered.

But that is not true, we know it is not true. Several men after you drew their guns and took shots at the crown prince. He is dead. Are you glad?

I did not know what to think. I was glad, and I was not glad. So, someone else managed to do it! I thought I was the only one who could, and just trying was good enough, but someone actually did it, on His Majesty's way back on the Quay.

Did they kill anybody else? I asked.

Yes, His Majesty's wife.

Who killed them?

Gavrilo Princip. You know him?

I knew of him. But I didn't know he planned to do this.

Strange to say, I felt jealous of Princip. I'd never expected him to succeed. So, he would be glorious, he would be a Serbian saint, and I would die in obscurity. But I was happy, too. I had many emotions, as much as I could in my dazed state. The tyrant was gone. We did it. After all, it was a beautiful plan, to have several men, one after another, shoot, and maybe none of them would have, if I hadn't started it all, showed how possible it was. But how did the archduke even get the idea to drive again down the Quay? My bomb must have confused everybody and made the real assassination possible.

The interrogations went on interminably. Sometimes they had to repeat a question two or three times because I just could not think and concentrate. They thought I was spiteful, and they pulled my ears as though I were a schoolboy, but they no longer hit.

They manipulated me and toyed with my emotions. Don't lie, a policeman said, we know Gavrilo is one of your best friends. But do you know what? He confessed he was tempted to shoot you after you threw your bomb and failed to kill yourself. He said if you hadn't been so far he would have shot you and then himself, so nobody would find out about the plot, how do you like that?

Of course, I didn't like that. Just to think of it, the gall that boy had. He certainly made better friends with ideas than with people. Any moment, if he became a political leader, he'd shoot off his friends, if he thought the ideas called for it. I was disgusted. I guess he had what it took to become a great leader. But maybe they had lied to me.

Are you sorry for what you did? They repeated that question many times.

I certainly was not, and if I was, it had to do only with my failure to accomplish the deed. And I felt sorry for all the pedestrians I wounded. They were now in the hospitals, bleeding, maybe feverish, and considering our health care system, which was not ours, of course, but Austrian, some of them might get gangrene and die slowly, painfully, all because of my imprecision. I should have controlled my emotions better: I had thrown too hard in my zeal and rashness. Just one more second of aiming and self-control would have done it. I was a second or two too fast for history, or history was too slow for my nervous temperament.

I was sick for a couple of days, vomiting. I could not keep any food down. The cyanide was working, to some extent, enough to burn my throat. I think it was old and stale. It would have been better if the explosive had been too old, and the poison fresh. I still hoped to die, but could not die. I was too weak to die. In my room, I slept terribly; my throat and nose burned. I shivered, though it was not cold, but then, my health was never robust. Whenever I turned in sleep, the chains clanked and clattered and rang dull. They were cold and heavy. Still, I managed to move around during the day. There was terrible shrieking and wailing coming out of the yard. I peeped through the window and saw the police clubbing dozens of men, Serbs. It was sunny and hot, and those who were not beaten were forced to look at the sun; many of them had their mouths open from all the heat and no water. There weren't that many people who had anything to do with us. This mass beating was totally arbitrary and irrational. The wailing, the pain, echoed from the walls, grew stronger, and the echoes and the original screams mixed up in a dizzying, pulsating sorrow. There, we wanted freedom for our people, but this was a far cry from it. Some of the men doubling over were old, some weren't men at all but children. I didn't know what to do about it—clearly, I could do nothing but look. And I couldn't even do that. When the gallows were raised, and men were being hanged—for what? for who they were?—a gendarme shot at me. He narrowly missed. The glass above my head shattered, one fragment cut into my cheek, and others splashed on the floor in smithereens. So now I could not watch, but I could hear even better through the broken glass.

After the hangings, the following day, more beatings went on for hours. I was sorry for causing this grief, but at the same time this strengthened my hatred for the monarchy, and I wished I had managed to kill the monarch and the general.

It was terribly lonely in the cell. I could not talk to my friends. I did come up with a system of messages—I wrote at the bottom of my plate, and the plates went from one room to another. Princip and Ilic caught on, and we exchanged drawings, jokes, and so on. We also tapped messages through the wall, with sharp and dull thuds—we had learned the code for each letter beforehand, we had got ready for this part; that had been my idea, from a Russian manual. One day I tapped a code into Ilic's wall, but he did not respond. I was sure he had hanged himself. So I tapped the message to Princip, who tapped back that he was saddened by the news. The next day Ilic tapped to me—I was overjoyed that he was alive, and so was Princip when I communicated the news to him. I had certainly jumped to conclusions too easily; I was so nervous and jumpy. But communicating through the wall in code was not good enough for me to have a sense of community, and I was lonely. If nothing else, I knew that tapping for a while would bring an angry Austrian guard, who would shout at me to stop. After he went, I continued, and then he'd come in again and shout. I was amazed that they could not decipher our code— maybe they didn't even know we were communicating.

WE WERE ALL GATHERED for the trial in the court and examined and cross-examined sometime in October. By now we all had small beards, goatees, from not shaving. None of us had firm black beards, we all looked Chekhovian. This was the first time I saw my friends since the end of June, so for a while I didn't pay any attention to what the judge was saying. I giggled from happiness at being with my friends. After all we were just boys; and if only we had stuck to being boys. It felt like we were ignoring a lesson at school, and the fat judge's bad temper made it only all the more entertaining.

Princip was proud and belligerent. His nose was broader than before from the beatings he got in the streets upon his arrest, but he spoke clearly, in a strong and sonorous manner. I wondered where he had strength for such a voice. I was much bigger than him, yet my voice was weak, it could never ring.

What hurt me most was that I heard that a kind man, with a large family, who had let us sleep in his house on our way to

Sarajevo, was executed. I did not let them have his name, maybe Princip did. What bad luck for him. He did not even know what we were up to, and now his children would have to grow up without him. The prosecutor used that as an example of how we should not get off easy if a man like that had to die for what we did. For that I was truly sorry.

And my sorrow deepened when the prosecutor said, Do you know what the archduke's last words were? "Sophie, dear, please do not die. Our children need you."

Can you imagine that? You orphaned three children! You certainly deserve to die, underage or not.

I had not known that the archduke had children. And that as he was dying he thought of his children, as no doubt did his wife, that did something to me. I was totally unprepared for this, and for my reaction. Maybe it was the last blow in the accumulation of sorrowful news. I am sure my father wouldn't bother to think of me. Those children had been lucky to have parents who loved them, but they were also unlucky to have us.

The prosecutor showed us the pictures of the lovely children. One boy had thick black hair, wavy, shiny, it was parted just like mine, from right to left, with a thick wave; the older one had short hair and a serious look, the same angle of brows as mine, almost the same mirthless expression as mine, as though he had been posing for history as well. If you took the two boys and mixed up their features, you would get me in my boyhood; I felt a strong kinship with them. How could they look like me? How did they get stuck in the royal family? The girl, with a white bow on her pate, had wonderfully rich hair draped over her shoulder into her lap, and she, too, looked serious and beautiful. They all looked at the camera, but the mother, from whom they must have inherited the beauty, looked at them, mostly at her daughter, in a posture of pride and worry, as though she had a premonition. Nobody was smiling here. And why not? Shouldn't children be happy? Maybe they had never been happy. I felt sorry for them that they had such a father. Maybe that's why they could not laugh although they were just children. Maybe they would grow up to be monsters, maybe not. They were pretty and soulful, that must have been their Slavic side.

Sophie, dear, please do not die. That line kept sounding in my head, and I could not stop it. It was driving me insane. I could not listen to the interrogation after this, and I jumped out of my seat and shouted, We are sorry for what we did, we are sorry that we orphaned children. . . . I know I gave a whole speech, but now I don't remember what exactly I said, except that everybody listened to me for a while. Damn it, I was a good speaker.

Speak for yourself, Princip cut in. I am not sorry. They have orphaned many of our children, why aren't you sorry for them! Don't ever talk in my name!

I am deeply sorry. I am surprised he isn't. I . . . I—At that point my voice choked from tears that went backward, not down my nose, but into my throat. Only if I'd had that salty liquid when I had tried to swallow cyanide—maybe I wouldn't have had to face what I did to these children, wouldn't have had to quarrel in court with Gavro.

He just wants mercy, Gavrilo said.

You stay quiet, I said. What do you know about me? What do you know about people? You know only books and ideas.

No, I don't want mercy. In fact, I want punishment. All I want before I die is that the children forgive me. But how can they forgive me? No, it's better that they not forgive me.

Sophie, dear, our children need you. Please don't die. I imagined the children next to the casket, trying to reach for their mama, to kiss her; they couldn't, maybe they would be struck by fear of death, maybe disgust, maybe they would not be allowed. That must have already happened. What did they do? Did they break down and cry out, in shrill screams, the world breaking down in shafts of cathedral light, through stained glass, full of vermilion, lit up by their tears? Or did they stay quiet, stunned, with the grief too deep for tears, their voices subdued, muffled; perhaps they could not utter a word; maybe they could not breathe. Maybe they felt pretty much the way I did, when the police showered me with blows to the head and groin? Maybe they lost control, wetted, from terror and grief, lost the feel of their bodies?

I could not control my emotions. I wept right there in the court for the family I had attempted to kill. I did not care what people thought. And the fact that I was the only one in our group weeping made me think I should weep even more, for the hard-heartedness of my comrades.

I would not have minded just wasting their father. In fact, I think that would have been a favor to them. I had hated my father, and he'd hated me; he beat me daily. And when I grew bigger and stronger, and he couldn't easily subdue me, he had me jailed once when I had a quarrel with our maid; he'd come home with a gendarme. I'd asked her to undress for me, and she refused, and shouted at me to get out. I hadn't even touched her. I don't know why that made such a big impression on my father. Maybe he'd been interested in the maid, and he thought we competed. I would not be surprised if she'd been his mistress; the bastard had no moral backbone. He'd sent me to apprentice as a blacksmith because he did not like my grades at school. And there, the master blacksmith, just for fun, put a hot iron to the back of my neck. I still have a scar there. The back of my neck is pretty hairy, but nothing grows in the diagonal of the burn. That's all because of my father, I am sure; I don't think anybody liked him. He ran a tavern, and since he couldn't pass up on opportunities to make money, he'd become a police informant. What better job for an informant than to ply guests with brandy? He was a regular spy for the Austrians, and he adored the Hapsburgs. I even played a joke with him; I had got an Austrian flag to put on our house on the day of the assassination, so people would not suspect me for being an assassin. Anyway, if for nothing else, I wanted to kill the emperor to get at the father. I don't know, I just couldn't bring myself to kill my father, that would have been too personal, but killing the emperor, well, the archduke was to be emperor, that would have been perfect. Without my father's odious influence on me, I would not have become a member of such a subversive group. I was glad about dead fathers. However, that their mother was killed, that was terrible. Maybe it was even terrible that their father was killed; maybe they liked him, maybe he was even a good father. I am not the one to judge that, the children only could.

I could no longer listen to the trial. I was imagining three children, spoiled, true, but children, and children are so pure that even if they are spoiled they can't be held responsible for that, they are still innocent. . . . So these children would not see their parents again, they would not sit on their laps and listen to bedtime stories, Red Riding Hood and Robin Hood. . . . Well, maybe they would not have heard the Robin Hood story. Probably not. They will hear the story of the assassination, however. They will hate Princip and me. They could never forgive us.

IF THEY LIKED to drink hot chocolate with their mother, they will not drink it again.

The judge surprised me by ordering us to be imprisoned rather than executed because we were not twenty years old yet. Several people who were over twenty, even though they had hardly anything to do with the conspiracy, were to be executed, hanged, and several already were, in our yard, and in Trebinje, my native town. In a way, I would have preferred summary execution. Now I would spend years in prison, I would not even be allowed to read the newspapers. If I could follow the course of the war in prison, that would be a different matter, I would not have minded it that much, especially if the Allies won. Then whatever we had aspired for, the collapse of the Hapsburgs, the emancipation of the south Slavs, would happen; then it would have been worth it. We were transferred to the prison in Theresienstadt, three of us: Princip, Grabez, and I. That was a miserable journey in the cold train; we were chained to our benches, our bones were rattled and, after all the clanking, felt broken.

In Theresienstadt, the bed was hard, flea-infested, cold. There was no heat at night, and I was chained in shackles and chains weighing over ten kilograms, which conducted all the heat out of my body. The water in the jug sometimes froze overnight. If it hadn't, I would not have known whether it was all my imagination that it was cold, but there was no doubt, it was. It took me several months to realize that if I put the ball, which I could barely lift, under covers, together with the chains, that I would lose less heat and wouldn't be so cold. By then, I had got the chronic chills, so it did not matter anymore that I had figured out a way of protecting my heat.

I got TB somehow. I found out that Gavrilo also had it. Maybe we all had TB even before the assassination. I know Princip said he probably had it, and Grabez thought he might have it, and maybe that is why they were willing to die. I coughed every winter, but it did not mean I had TB. I believed I did not have it. How could we all have TB? I think the Austrians gave it to us, intentionally; they gave us contaminated food and stale water, I am sure, in prison. They were not allowed to execute us by law, but they would do it stealthily by implanting disease in us. I am quite certain that they did it. Once they found out we had TB, they did nothing to save us. They could have sent us to the mountains. They could have heated our rooms. They did not. That was their way of killing us.

I haven't had much will to live lately. The walls in the prison are so thick I cannot tap codes to Gavro and Grabez. I am terribly lonely, so lonely that I even accept visits by a priest. The priest can be a bore; he wants me to confess, to pray with him, and he doesn't know any jokes. I told him one, and he did not laugh. It was the only decent joke I knew. Two Montenegrins stand on the pier and notice a boat sinking and hear men screaming for help.

One Montenegrin says, Look at that, men are drowning, and we are just standing.

You are right about that, says the other. Let's sit down.

Instead of laughing at the joke, the priest wanted to pray with me. And so we prayed. I meant it all, and still do. I pray with him for forgiveness for what I have done to the three children.

And just today, it seems the prayers are working. The priest has brought me a letter in a beautiful handwriting. *Dear Ned-jeljko: We forgive you. We feel sorry for you that you have to suffer so much. We know you were misguided. May God forgive you, too, and bless you. We know you are a good soul, you have repented.*

THAT WAS A LETTER from the archduke's children! I did not know how to react; I was purely amazed. I kept rereading the letter, admiring every curl and slant in the calligraphically drawn letters. I had always loved letters—it was no accident that I'd become a typesetter—but none were quite as beautiful as these. I smell the page—it smells of lilac and ink. I am swooning as I inhale. Maybe I would be swooning, anyway. I am not even aware when the priest left. Maybe he has not left. Maybe he is here to bury me. Maybe I am dying. Is that a real letter? I ask. Suddenly I doubt. I need to see the envelope. If it doesn't have a stamp, how will I know where it came from? Maybe the priest wrote it. Maybe that was one little benevolent lie he came up with out of compassion for me, but I doubt it; he isn't capable of such beauty, such handwriting. I feel around the table with my fingers, and pick up a fine beige envelope. There is a blue seal, which says, Wien. So it's true, it's a letter from them, the beautiful souls whom I have injured. Suddenly, I notice Franz Ferdinand is gazing from the envelope, from under the green feathers of his hat, with his cold, hateful concentration, looking straight into me, just the way he did at the moment I was flinging the grenade at him, in that awful contemptuous manner! I don't want to look at the image. Is this a ghost? I cover the image with my thumb, and feel the fine wavy ribs of the stamp. No, I won't let him lurk like this. I am tearing the stamp and his image into small pieces, and I am eating it, relishing the glue and ink in my throat.

This confession in the form of a letter, apparently written in the authentic trembling hand of Nedjeljko Cabrinovic in his prison cell in Theresienstadt in January 1916, was recently found in the loft of a long-deceased priest, N.M., before his house was to be torn down in order to create expansion space for the world-famous beer brewery in Plzen. For a while, D.M., the CEO of the brewery, kept the letter and reread it to various dinner guests as a prize, but when he read it to Sacerby, the Bosnian minister demanded that the letter be given over to the Bosnian govern-ment in Sarajevo for the archives. Whether the letter had been destroyed in the Sarajevo siege, or whether it still exists in some private hands, or in public hands, remains a mystery, and the confession above is a reconstruction, done by a dozen brewery guests, as the closest possible approximation to the original.

The writing ceases here, at the bottom of the mouse-chipped page of the vanished original. The story, or rather, the history, does not end here, nor for that matter with the addendum, which follows:

The Sarajevo police department demanded from the There-sienstadt military prison that Cabrinovic's corpse be beheaded and his skull sent to Sarajevo, where it would be preserved and kept in a museum, in a jar, for future generations. After a lengthy exchange of letters among various departments of the Austrian government, it was decided that Cabrinovic's corpse should be left intact. Many people schemed to get his and Princip's bones; it would not have been the first case of a missing skull. The skull of Bogdan Zerajic, who had attempted to assassinate a provincial governor in Bosnia in 1910, was displayed in the Sarajevo Criminal Museum. The chief police inspector in Sarajevo occasionally used Zerajic's skull as an inkpot to threaten those he interrogated, saying that unless they confessed everything, their skulls would serve the same letter-writing purpose. In 1919 Zerajic's skull was put back together with his body, but in 1920 when the body was exhumed to be placed in a common grave, the skull was missing again, and thus his headless body was placed with those of Princip (whose corpse was whole, except for a missing arm, which TB of the bones had destroyed), Grabez, and several other conspirators, including Cabrinovic, in the common grave.

Night Guests

A loud knocking. I stumbled out of bed and to the door. I lived in Wayne National Forest in Ohio, near a little-traveled road, with the nearest neighbor half a mile away, and I should have had the policy of not answering the door or of having a gun handy. But that was the risk I usually took, to answer the door, with no bad consequences except a lot of boring conversations with the Mormons, who, of course, visited only during the day, in the most beautiful, heavenly weather.

But now it was terribly dark out there. The silhouettes in the door, I thought, looked familiar; it was probably Mimi with John, my former house sitters, who might have needed something. My dog didn't bark but sniffed their crotches; maybe they had been somewhere interesting. They were giggling. I opened the door, and a splash of cold air and the images of complete strangers, two women, one tall and long-haired and the other chubby and short-haired, woke me up enough to realize that I was not entirely decent.

I was not entirely indecent either, so I didn't apologize or shut the door as I stood in my cotton underwear. At least it was American underwear, which was pretty big, certainly not meant to please the eye, but to cover the skin. I had just got back from Italy, from a research trip, where I could buy only tiny Italian underwear at a shopping mall, or thongs, suitable for carnivals and gigolos. I used to wear that kind of under-wear as a child, growing up in Italy, but as a grad student in the States I first made do with what I could find at the shops, and then I got used to it, actually liked it. Now I was still aware of my underwear, as the tall woman spoke, in a beseeching tone.

Could you help us? We just drove off the road into the ditch!

She straightened with her hand her curly, fluffy, light brown hair. She had a thin straight nose, full lips, and a shine in her eyes. She looked happy even though she was clearly in trouble.

I wish I had a truck to pull you out, I said.

Could we come in and use your phone?

No problem, I said, and led them into the living room, with a large red Persian carpet that felt good under my bare feet.

I went to the bedroom and pulled on my jeans and came out.

The tall woman dialed three times, while I put a log in the stove and stirred the embers, admiring how they still had

plenty of body and glow. The flames licked the log almost in-
stantly, and with satisfaction, I closed the door.

I can't get through, the tall one said.

Try again later. How would you like a cup of coffee?

I'd love it. By the way, my name is Marietta.

I ground some Italian espresso beans (Illy), and dripped a
strong brew, which with a bit of Swiss chocolate wafted an in-
toxicating wakeful aroma of delight and pleasure, to which
hardly any caffeine addict could remain indifferent.

How did you get into the ditch? I asked.

We was drivin' around, and out of nowhere, this fuckin' big
deer jumps on the road. I swerved and ended up in your ditch.

That seems a good choice, better ditch than deer—safer,
too, I think. How's your car?

Just a little banged. The right headlight's smashed is all.

I didn't tell them that just the other day I had hit a big deer
with majestic antlers. I was rubbing my eyes, after a long day at
the library, and trying to defrost the window, when all of a sudden his majesty leaped into my hazy vision. I braked and
swerved to the left since he was already moving to the right.
There was a thump. What did I hit? His legs? His hoofs,
which may have been in the air after a leap? Whatever it was,
the car kept going, and I was sure the deer was alive. I was not
going to try to hunt him. As it was deer-hunting season, someone would get him no matter what, and should I feel sorry for
him now, now that I lost all the light in the car? I couldn't see
the odometer, and I drove shedding such dim light onto the
asphalt as though using lanterns. When I got home, I saw that
the hood was busted. It didn't seem a big deal, but the man in
the cheap body shop said it would be three hundred bucks. I

realize, buck was an unintended pun, at the expense of the poor buck on the road. Since it was an old Sentra, I could get the job done more cheaply if I found the headlights with the assembly trinkets in a junkyard, but all the junkyards I visited along the way were out of the parts.

Anyhow, Marietta's right headlight was out, by a different method, yet the same cause: trying to duck a deer.

I asked, Were you driving back from a party? Were you drunk? Excuse me for asking.

Oh, no, said the other woman, we wasn't drunk. We had only four or five beers each.

That would do it for me, I said. No party?

No, we was looking for my aunt, said Marietta. I kinda remembered where she lived, but we got lost, and kept drivin' along these backroads, and we couldn't figure out how to get out of the maze.

It took you till four in the morning to reach this point? When did you start? (If you get lost, how long can you stand to be lost? Suppose they were looking for the aunt at ten, sort of the last decent hour to start looking for aunts. Six hours of wandering? Doesn't sound right, but what the hell. Let me buy the story, I thought.)

We stopped by to get some cigarettes. Shelly, what else did we do?

By now I had the coffee ready, and I proudly presented it to Shelly and Marietta.

Jesus, what fine coffee. That tastes great! Shelly said all that, but I didn't see her taste the coffee, and she laid the cup down next to the rocking chair on which she was sitting.

Thank you, I said. Why don't you try that number again?

All right, said Marietta, and Shelly said, Do you mind if I go to the car to get some cigs and beer?

I minded but said, No, I don't mind.

Who are you trying to call? I turned to Marietta.

My ex?

That's a good ex if you can call him at four in the morning for help.

Yeah, he's good at some things. But he's a real jerk. I don't like him. I am glad that we're gettin' a divorce.

You are still married? (I wondered at myself. Why should I need to know the details?)

Just on paper. We're separated. I hope never to see him again.

But now you want to see him.

Now, yes. I wish I knew more people I could call, but that shows you the problem; he didn't want me to meet any people. Jerk!

Shelly was back with her dangling six-pack, or rather, four-pack by now, Bud Lite. My stomach turned at imagining the pale insipid taste. Nothing bodied like Urquell or Trappist ale. But that was a snobbish attitude, and momentarily ashamed of being a snob, I didn't mind when I heard the beer pop. Actually, I enjoyed the whiff of the cool and breezy yeast-foam.

Shelly responded, Yes, he's a real jerk. I mean, what can you expect, her husband's a damned cop.

So it's a real husband?

Real cop, said Shelly, real asshole.

I can't get through, Marietta said.

What area code is his number? I asked.

Seven-four-zero.

We are in six-one-four.

Shit, I thought it was a local. No wonder I couldn't get through. I'll call collect.

Don't bother. Just dial direct.

I'd hate to get you stuck with a bill. You're already doing so much for us.

Soon she said, It's me. Me.

A voice was shouting in the phone on the other end of the line, Who?

Me. Gee, don't pretend you don't know my voice.

At four a.m., I don't know nobody's. Where are you? The guy's voice carried even through the receiver so far.

I don't know.

What do you mean you don't know? You've been drinking.

No, we slid off the road in a ditch and can't get out. Can you come over and get us out?

Calm down, Marietta—where are you now?

I don't know, I told you.

I saw it was time to intercede, and I said, Give me the phone, and I'll give him directions. And so I did. I listed all the turns, about three or four, and answered a couple of questions. Yes, their car is in a ditch somewhere around. They aren't drinking.

I'll be there in twenty minutes. Can I speak to Marietta again?

As much as you like.

He shouted something.

I love you too, lilted Marietta and hung up.

That sounded odd to me. She had just said what a jerk he was and how she hated him, and now into the phone, he said he loved her and she said she loved him. Was that like saying, See you later? Good night? Just a greeting? Habit? Or truth? I didn't ask her to explain. But something here was not truth. Maybe she did love him but liked complaining about him on the road. All that divorce and hate rap was valve talk.

Shelly wanted to open another beer.

No, I said. No way. I don't want to be bossy, but it seems you have had enough beer. Drink coffee instead, especially if you are bringing in a cop.

You are right, said Shelly. That's okay with me. She took the beer and poured it in my sink.

I love your coffee, said Marietta.

Have more then. Now, that seemed a better use of the word love to my ears.

I poured her more, with a bit of milk, and she sipped, tossing her hair over her shoulders. Nothing could stop her from having a good time, not even car accidents. That was impressive. She stood up to go to the bathroom, and I saw she had a graceful figure; she moved lightly, sinuously. A strange creature, untouched by poverty, bad circumstances, bad marriage, car accident. She was clearly wonderful. When she had gone to the bathroom, I was facing Shelly, who burped, and clearly was not wonderful, and she said, Sorry.

What do you do, asked Shelly, and burped again.

I am a college professor, European history. Renaissance crime is my specialty.

Sorry.

Sorry for what? Now and then I am sorry to teach European history.

That we are bothering you.

You aren't bothering me. You are in need and I am glad to help.

We thought, when we saw that big tobacco barn, a farmer lived here, so we didn't feel shy about askin' for help. If we'd known—

Come on.

If we'd known—Here you are, a gentleman, European, and you have to deal with us hicks.

Don't give me that. I opened the door in my underwear. That ought to have relaxed you.

Well, no, a farmer would never open the door in his underwear, so we knew at once you was a gentleman.

I laughed. She had a sense of humor. Or did she? She didn't laugh, but seemed doleful. Did she mean that? Were we communicating? Maybe she was wonderful too, with hidden treasures of the mind.

How can you live here and teach at a university? Is there a university around?

No. I drive to Columbus during the week and stay there, and weekends I am here.

I regretted I had told her. Suppose she had friends who were thieves, they would know how to get to my place and rob it. So I added, During the week, I have a house sitter. He likes it here.

Oh, she said. You have another house?

Yes, nothing spectacular. Not even as nice as this cabin. I come here to get my reading and writing done, and to stay away from students, bars, restaurants, and infernal temptations.

Two houses! Her eyes filled with the alarm of envy, I could

tell. She hated me at that moment. Hell, I thought, I better say nothing about myself. Maybe they should say nothing about themselves. Knowledge is harm.

Where do you work? I contradicted my conclusion and asked her, from inertia of the conversation. I couldn't say anything safely in the affirmative, so questions seemed the best way.

Yes, I work, she said.

Where?

Marietta and I build dog houses. We nail them all day long. You want to feel my muscle?

No, thank you.

We have fun at work, said Marietta. She's a hoot. Do you want to feel my muscle?

She lifted her arm and tightened it, and her flannel shirt slid, and I could see gentle slopes of her small and shapely breasts. Did she wear a bra? Maybe not, couldn't see it, and the slopes went on, shedding light into a precipitous darkness in her shirt. The breasts looked larger now than they had let on.

No, thank you. I believe you that you have good muscles.

I would have enjoyed feeling the proffered muscle, even the biceps, but I had already committed to not feeling muscles by saying No to Shelly. It wouldn't be consistent now to say Yes to Marietta. It would hurt Shelly. Or maybe it wouldn't. I had my hang-ups of being considerate, or more accurately, of wanting to appear considerate.

Marietta smiled with a shine on her lips and looked at the stove. Nice how you can see the flames inside, she said.

For a second, I thought that maybe the two worked as hookers, and this was a strange trick. But no, ditching your car would be a hard way to earn a living. On the other hand, how did I know they had ditched a car? I hadn't gone out to see it. But then, why would they call a policeman? No, they can't be hookers. Plus, Marietta seems too airy, untouched, for that. No, how could I think that. That was dirty and insulting of me. Good thing they can't read thoughts. But then, why was I sure that they did call a policeman rather than a thief? Maybe they aren't hookers but thieves, with complex schemes, which work, of course. They could speak in code. I love you too could mean, He doesn't have a gun. Come here and clobber him. But she looks too nice for that, too innocent even.

Would you like a dog house for your dog? asked Shelly. We'll get you a forty percent discount.

So where does your husband live? I asked Marietta.

She sat back in the armchair. On top of the hill, before you turn to 248, there's a white trailer, with many pots of flowers in the windows. You are welcome to stop by.

To see him?

Well, no, there's another trailer, a pink one, and that's mine, way back in the yard.

You think I could just drive in and talk to you all? Your trailer doesn't have the flowers?

No, I have cats. They're always sunbathing in the windows. Why wouldn't you stop by?

If you usually don't even talk to each other?

Oh, we do, I just hope we won't. We have a kid to take care of, so that keeps us pretty close, better than dropping kids off fifty miles away, as some people I know do. I'll need a better car before I get a divorce.

Who's taking care of the kid now?

The aunt. Not the one we was lookin' for, another one, just two hundred feet past our place.

Blessed are the aunts, I said.

The phone rang. The cop wanted the directions to be repeated to him. I found the chains, he said. I'll be there in twenty minutes. Is she all right, sir? Not passing out?

Far from passing out, Marietta was buzzed on coffee, and since she kept repeating how much she liked it, I made her a cappuccino. You better watch out, she said. I may get addicted to this stuff and I don't know anybody else who makes it.

Soon lights showed up in the yard, it seemed less than ten minutes. Why did he say twenty, I wondered. I walked out and welcomed the bony man with a crew cut and a mustache who jumped out of a red pickup.

Where are they? he asked, out of breath.

Inside.

Are they all right? Are they hurt?

Yes, they are all right, just silly.

He walked in, with a big flashlight in one hand. Are you all right? he shouted.

Yeah, we are fine, said Marietta.

You didn't bang the dashboard, or anything like that?

No, we just knocked our heads together. Doesn't hurt.

He walked to Marietta, and said, Look at me.

She did, and he shone the light straight into her eyes and peered.

Man, you'll make me go blind. Cut it out!

I got to look again, he said.

Do her first, I'll take a break, she said.

No, we got to finish this. This is serious.

What did I tell you, said Shelly to me. I understood, she meant, What a pain in the ass this jerk is.

As though he understood that too, he pounced and poured light into Shelly's eyes. He held the flashlight in his clenched fist above his ear in a trained manner, which would allow the flashlight to become a billy club in a second if need be.

I guess you are conscious, he said.

That shouldn't take that much guessing, said Shelly.

You've been drinking. How much have you had?

Oh, nothing, just two, three beers.

That's too much, Marietta. You should've let Shelly drive.

But I don't have a driver's license, said Shelly.

Don't matter. If you drink, you shouldn't drive, let Shelly do it.

But I drank more, said Shelly. I think Marietta had only one beer.

Oh, did you? For a second the cop lost his staccato pursuit stance. Never mind, Marietta, you still shouldn't have drove. You're an awful driver.

I am not that bad.

So tell me, what happened?

We was laughin' so hard tears came into my eyes, Marietta said. Jokes, we know some good new ones. Wanna hear them?

No. Keep going with your story.

Tears made it hard to see—this big deer jerk just leaped out of nowhere, and I swerved.

That was stupid. Don't you know, you must brake and keep your direction.

But then I would have hit him.

Probably not, if you'd started soon enough.

I didn't start soon enough. Plus, he just jumped out of the total darkness.

You shouldn't have drove for the ditch.

It wasn't a highway, I could change my direction, what's so bad about a ditch?

You wrecked the car.

She did fine, I said. Hitting a buck head-on would cause more damage.

Don't defend her, sir. She should learn once and for all. You see a deer, you brake, and keep going straight.

That struck me as insane. She indeed did fine, better than I did or than he would. He probably would have ended up in a hospital if he stuck to his idiotic rules. Where did he pick them up? Do cop manuals print nonsense like that?

If you wasn't my wife, I'd revoke your license. Still might, he said.

Have they been drinking here, sir? he asked.

Hardly. I gave them coffee. You'd like some?

He walked to the sink and grabbed two cans of Lite. You drink this, sir?

No.

I didn't think so.

They brought in the cans already empty, I said.

I didn't know why I lied. He frowned and cringed as though he understood I was lying.

Would you like a cup of coffee? (A cup for a cop.)

No, thank you. I'm going to pull out the car. I'll be back. Please, sir, don't let them drink.

He walked out.

I see what you mean, I said to Marietta. But he is helping you.

I know, it just don't feel like it.

I had to agree with her, and we sat in silence like three convicts.

Pretty soon, the cop was back, with the red car in tow. He shone his light over the damaged area. We all came out.

That's at least two hundred fifty bucks' worth of damage right there, he said. Maybe three hundred.

I was impressed, he was right with his estimate.

Where are you gonna get that? he asked her.

Insurance? Marietta said cheerfully.

No, not with drunken driving. Plus, the rate would jump up. You got to come up with the money.

How?

You figure it out. That's your problem.

Maybe this is the pimp moment, I thought. Now she'll be forced to moonlight, and they'll offer the services to me. Maybe he's the one who designed the whole thing. I chuckled at the thought.

The cop looked at me strangely. Not the right moment to chuckle.

Where's the assembly part? he asked. It fell out somewheres.

Oh, that black thing? I saw it fall out. I'll find it, said Shelly.

They looked in the ditch, shining to and fro, and found nothing, and they came back and sat in the car.

Marietta sat with her hands together, clasped between her knees, as though she was chilled.

Shelly, you drive my pickup, he commanded.

You sure? she said, but climbed in it anyhow.

The cop sat with Marietta, and said before closing the door, Thank you, sir, for your help.

Oh, nothing to thank.

Marietta lifted one of her hands and waved to me briefly and looked away, at the barn. That seemed an indifferent greeting after our conversation. She had seemed much friendlier before, but now, she just waved me off like a fly. She doesn't need me. I am just a middle-aged guy with a tobacco barn, in which there's no tobacco, but only firewood and mountain bikes.

It was five in the morning now. Should I go to bed? No, it wouldn't work, after all that coffee. I made more, and thought, They were sweet, except the cop, of course, but he must be a good guy despite being such a bore. Will I ever see Marietta again? They told me where they worked. Should I stop by and see them at work? No, I thought, that would be silly. Should I stop by at their trailers? No, even if they are separated, somehow that wouldn't be decent, to come by to visit her, and to visit him, that would not make any sense at all. Maybe I'll run into her at the Kroger's and if she's divorced—oh, forget it, I told myself in my thoughts and gave myself sound advice: Don't be an ass.

I was glad I had helped them, despite the policy not to open doors to strangers at night deep in the forest.

The following morning, I saw a cop's car, and the same cop walk up and down the road, looking into the ditch.

I drove past, rolled down the window, and said, Missing something?

Yes, the assembly part.

Good luck, I said.

Thank you, he said, politely, and continued walking back and forth by my barn.

It would have been more pleasant if Marietta had come by to do it, or at least, if she had come with him. Now I had a cop snooping around.

Well, that's all right. It could be worse, I thought.

And of course, it could be.

Now and then I remembered Marietta and thought how wonderful it would be if I could kayak with her, or hike in the woods, or simply drink wine and talk. I was sure she was much smarter than she let on; it would be great to hear her jokes. Each time I began to daydream about her, I reminded myself that it was all pointless, and that was that.

A month later, however, the cop stopped by just as I was doing my email—though "stopped by" may not be the right expression.

I thought I had heard a car, perhaps the mailman, but the days in which I had expected something good in the mail had been long gone, so I kept going through my Hotmail, when suddenly the door bangs open, and the cop, with a gun in his hand, shouts, Freeze!

It looked so ridiculous, a poor cop-show imitation, that I didn't get scared.

Where is she? he shouted.

Who?

Don't play dumb. My wife!

How would I know?

You know very well. Don't play games now.

I never saw her after that night.

Sir, you have been calling my wife. Why?

No.

Don't lie. Are you having an affair with my wife?

No, far be it from me. I am glad I helped you all, but what did I do to deserve this?

His hand was shaking. That made me nervous, and soon terrified. This guy could pull the trigger. I looked up the barrel, then to his eyes. There was rage, tears: a total madman driven by jealousy.

Hey, please, calm down, I said. I have nothing to do with your wife. Haven't seen her again.

Ah, but you may have seen her before, right? I mean, what would she be doing at four in the morning on this road? I don't buy the story she was visiting her aunt. She don't have no aunt anywheres near.

I didn't buy that story either, but who knows where she was driving to or from.

She was visiting you.

Come on. Her car hit the ditch before my place, she was driving in this direction.

True, he said. True. But maybe she was just—

Don't speculate. That was the only time I saw her.

Honestly?

Honestly. Why would I lie?

Because of the gun.

You got a point, I must admit that.

Admit what? You saw my wife?

No, the point that the gun would scare one into saying all sorts of things. Please remove it, if you want to talk normally. Would you like some coffee?

Oh, I have heard about your coffee. I hate city slicker coffee. No, thank you.

I have some Folgers somewhere, if that would make you feel better.

No. He put the gun into the leather at his belt.

Have a seat, I said.

Okay, he said, angrily.

I was already seated. Sure you don't want tea?

No, thank you.

He remained standing, which gave him an unfair advantage, but it would be awkward to stand up now, with his large black rubber shoes close to my feet. Once I stood up from my rocking chair, I'd bump into him, and that didn't seem comfortable. The last thing I wanted now was to imitate the postures of two tomcats, one standing and the other cowering, but that was our geography now. I would have to stand up, or this guy should learn to relax, but how can he relax when he is filled with Marietta jealousy?

You've been calling my wife, admit it.

No.

Sir, I have the evidence. There's a collect call made from this phone to mine, and when I am at work at night, that's her phone.

I never call collect. I have a good calling plan with AT&T. What would be the point? I am not that poor.

You sure? he looked around, and his gaze fixed on the computer. I guess you are right, but that still don't explain it all. And then there's a call from my number to yours, also at night, and I work night shifts, as I said.

I don't remember her calling me at night.

Aha, but you do remember her calling you! he stood on tiptoe, gaining in size.

No, I didn't put that right. She never called here, night or day.

How can you say that, Sir!? I have the evidence, the phone bill.

What's the date? (For a second, it occurred to me that my house sitter may have called her. Who knows, maybe he knows her.)

He said, November 28, 2000.

That's pretty far back. Wait, that was the night of the accident! Of course, she called you from here, don't you remember? She called collect. And then, since you weren't sure of the directions, you called back.

He slackened his shoulders. Boy, yes, yes, that makes sense. Why didn't I think of that?

I don't know, I said. Have a seat?

Now he cowered, lost his posture, sat down.

Folgers?

All right, sir.

He looked totally defeated.

Why are you so depressed? Your wife is not having an affair with me, so you should be relieved.

I just don't know. She must be having an affair, I am sure. She disappears at night. This was the best clue I had.

He really was sorry the clue was failing him. Not that I wanted to comfort him, but certainly to placate him.

Maybe she goes on a drinking spree with her buddy Shelly.

How would you know?

She said so. I regretted that I had said that much. It's best not to know anything about him and his wife, clearly.

I have no idea what your wife does. Sorry not to be able to help. Or rather, glad I can't help you.

I'll get to the bottom of it all yet, he said, more to himself than to me.

Hey, mister, listen, I help you and your family, and I get this in return? Next time strangers in trouble knock on my door at four a.m., maybe I shouldn't answer the door.

Correct, he said. I meant to tell you that. Someone knocks at the door, even if they don't look armed and dangerous, like two women, don't open the door. Instruct them to go back to their vehicle, and you make the nine-one-one call for them. That's better for you, safer. You never know about people.

I couldn't agree more at that point, at least about the last statement.

He abruptly stood up. Thank you for the information.

But the coffee is not done yet.

It's the idea that counts, he said. I appreciate it. He looked me coldly in the eye. I'll be seeing you, he said.

As he walked toward the door, his eye caught the sight of my underwear lying loose. My Italian underwear, light purple, was on the floor near the bathroom entrance. I had always been a slob, I must admit that, and although I hated this kind of underwear, I had run out of clean Fruit of the Loom, and from my last trip I had the clean foreign underwear, to which I resorted rather than to doing laundry, anything but laundry.

There! That's hers! Sir, how do you explain that?

No, it's mine.

I know she wears that kind. It's not men's. Who do you take me for?

It's men's. Italian. We wear it.

Sir, I've had it with you. I don't care if I shoot you, just don't lie to me anymore.

You don't believe me?

Fortunately I remembered that under my jeans I had on a pair of Italian underwear. I let my pants drop, and there it was, a blue pair, smaller than a swimmer's Speedo. My pubic hair wasn't covered, but I didn't care. This could save my life.

Yuck! he said. You a pervert or something?

Yes, sir, a certified masochist, with a Ph.D.

His eyes popped and he backed toward the door.

Good-bye, I said.

He rushed out, laughing. He jumped in the car and honked.

My dog, who usually chases cars, didn't chase his, but only stood there, staring with his jaws open. Maybe he could smell the gun and he knew what it meant, from the hunting season. Why didn't he warn me about the cop's arrival? Same thing, probably; he smelled the metal. Usually he barks. Come to think of it, he hadn't barked when the strange women came. Did they have guns? Actually, he likes women, so he was just glad there were women to sniff. Such is his loneliness; no female dogs in a mile radius.

Later, I retold this story to my former house sitter, John, as an anecdote, and he said, Boy, cops are dumb. You know that in Massachusetts, they aren't allowed to be above average in intelligence?

I remember that, I said, and maybe he is dumb in some ways.

In some ways! guffawed John. Dumb as a doornail.

I didn't say anything. It's the idea that counts, he had said about coffee, and maybe he didn't say it about coffee, but had figured it out. He could see the idea in my head about Marietta. He got the details wrong, but he got the essential idea right. Maybe that's brilliant. Maybe that's the universal brilliancy of jealousy, to see stuff like that. No he wasn't far off. I had committed the Jimmy Carter kind of adultery, in my heart, not the Billy Clinton kind, but, essentially and biblically, what's the difference?

Luckily, I hadn't done anything. Well, of course, I wouldn't have done anything. Maybe she had that idea too, and he could see that? Now, that was even flattering, that a young animal would consider an old animal like me. But forget that kind of flattery. I didn't like looking into the darkness of the gun barrel in a shaking hand of a jealous cop. No, that is not a good situation. I was surprised I hadn't got terrified more then, because the sight of it in my mind even now gives me shivers.

And what does he expect? Of course, with him hounding her around like that, with guns, she must like to fly off, to get a taste of freedom, and maybe she is having an affair somewhere, or maybe only the idea of it, while she drives around and knocks her head with her friend. I don't know, and I don't want to find out.

Neighbors

Marko Sakic drove to his grocery store on the street of Proletarian Brigades in Nizograd. Ordinarily he walked the five blocks to his work, but now he didn't want to face the people in the streets. Croatia had declared independence, and he as a Serb didn't know what that amounted to for him. He wanted to be inconspicuous in the street, but even in his Volkswagen Golf that proved difficult. He nearly backed into his neighbor, a retired math teacher, who had limped from the blind spot, obviously fully expecting the advantages accorded to pedestrians by law and order, as though any law and order had remained. When Marko suddenly spotted the torso in gray, he braked, and stopped a couple of feet before the tilted geometrician, who circumscribed his threats in the air with a knotty walking stick. The teacher had ordinarily been friendly.

Marko had voted, secretly, as most Serbs in Slavonia (northeast Croatia) had done, for the secession of Krajina (the former military borders between the Ottoman and Hapsburg empires). Milosevic in Belgrade and the Serb political leaders within Croatia claimed that if Croatia became an independent country, Krajina should become Serbia to protect the local Serbs from the Croatian army—although there was not much Croatian army yet. If Krajina became Serbia, Marko thought he'd be right at home. He was at home anyway. More so than he'd be in Serbia, where he'd visited only a couple of times, and where he'd been insulted in a bakery for using the Croatian word *kruh* for bread (rather than Serbian *hleb*); to live there, he'd have to change his speech. Moreover, his wife was a Croat and he couldn't rightly say that his two kids weren't Croats—they were after all raised in Croatia and spoke Croatian.

In the streets, he was circumspect, with the new Croatian police, and the red chess board, a Croatian emblem from medieval times, lurking on the walls, beneath new street names (Proletarian Brigades became Toni Kukoc Street). Croatia for Croats! How about others? These slogans stood below pictures of Tudjman, who, instead of looking like a father of a nation, looked like a vengeful law professor.

When Marko walked into his shop, he became cheerful. He flirted with women, and did it not just to sell to them, but because he loved the mutual ego boost and cheer that often resulted from it. (After a good flirtation, he felt handsome, and if there was no customer around, he combed his hair upward; it was still strong and black, with only a few grays above his ears; his blue eyes contrasted well with the black hair and eyebrows.) He loved seeing each customer enter and scrutinize his shelves, and he attempted to guess by how the eyes moved, where the hands were, and how calm they were, whether and what the customer would buy.

Croats and Czechs and Hungarians kept buying in his shop even after the war began, but Serbs who remained in the town didn't. They avoided the appearance of banding together, and if they shopped, they went to the large ill-lit state-owned store in the center of the town.

When the Serbian army advanced in Eastern Slavonia and along the Dalmatian coast, Marko was glad. When a dozen MiG jets flew over the town, he relished the mighty resonant vibrations; the explosions of the sound barrier delighted him. As he stared out the windows, somebody supposedly overheard him saying, "Now you Croats will see whose land this is!"

Later, he didn't remember saying this, although it was possible, since he had gotten drunk out of his mind, but one old friend of his, Branko—a former soccer player for Dinamo Zagreb—came to his shop, and joked,

"Could I have some patriotic beer, Nizograd Pivo?"

Marko laughed. "Maybe you'd like some plum brandy? That's even more patriotic."

"So," said Branko, still smiling, "I hear that you're happy about the Serb invasion?"

"Oh, no, my friend, where do you get that idea?"

"People overheard you gloating when Yugoslav jets flew over the town. And if the jets bombed, do you think the pilots would have worried whether you were here? They assume that most real Serbs have left anyway."

Marko sulked. Yes, Serb militia men did come to him once urging him to join their ranks or at least to move out of town. He'd heard stories in a nearby village about Serb soldiers killing the fellow Serbs who had refused to leave the village and cutting off two fingers from the hands of the surviving villagers so they'd keep showing the Serb three-finger victory salute, always. Villages that had no Serbs left in them could be set on fire and bombed by the Serb army without fear of hurting their own. Still, there were so many Serbs left in town that the idea of bombing struck him as far-fetched.

"So you have any Nizograd Pivo?" Branko said as if repeating the question, and maybe he was repeating it. Marko piled five half-liter amber bottles over the counter.

"Why don't you come over to drink a couple of these?" said Branko. "Like in the good old days. We could play a game of chess and compare our new stamps."

"I'll try," said Marko. Although they had often drunk beer together and compared their stamp collections, Marko knew that this time he would not visit. Maybe there would be a trap in Branko's place—maybe a couple of thugs would knock him down. Sure, they were friends, but this was a new world; what was more important, friendship or patriotism? How could you trust anybody anymore?

Branko laughed in good cheer as though guessing his thoughts. "There are many new stamps now—Slovenian, Croatian—and soon there'll be Macedonian, Bosnian; wonderful times for us philatelists, wouldn't you say?"

★   ★   ★

THE FOLLOWING NIGHT, Marko remembered what Branko had said about bombs not being able to tell your nationality. When the sirens came on, he went into the basement with his wife and two kids, partly because that was the martial law, and partly because he felt uneasy, scared.

"Dad, will nuclear bombs blast the town?" asked the five-year-old, Danko.

"I don't think so."

"So why are we going into the basement?"

"To play war games, to pretend that we are bombed."

"Cool!" Danko said. "But I wish they'd drop at least one."

"Shut up, you rascal," said Dara.

"Why do we all have to play stupid boy games now?" asked Mila, the six-year-old daughter.

"Good question," said Dara. "That's because some boys grow to look like men but remain destructive boys."

"Is there any other kind?" asked Mila.

"Kind of what?"

The kids were bored and they wanted to keep the light on to play checkers. The phone rang upstairs.

"Who could be calling now?" said Dara.

"I'll go and see," said Marko.

"No, don't. It might not be safe."

In the meanwhile, the phone rang the fourth time, and the message machine came on.

"We know you are there. That's all right. But please turn off the light. Or do you want us to turn it off for you?"

Marko turned off the light.

"Sons of whores, those damned cops. They probably think I keep the lights on to signal to the pilots!"

Just then there was an amazing explosion that shook the foundations of the house with the ground, as though a major earthquake had struck, as though different layers of the earth struggled, quarreled, and ground over each other. Shards of bricks shattered their basement windows. Half of a brick flew in and smashed a ten-liter bottle of homemade wine from Marko's little vineyard in the hills. The red wine splashed them all, but none were hurt by the flying glass. The smell of wine was too weak to wash out the smell of fire and explosives and smoke. Before they could orient themselves, there was another blast that sent waves of hot air through the cracks in the basement windows.

"Damned bandits!" shouted Marko. "Damned Serb bandits!"

Dara's teeth chattered.

"I'm not going to forgive Milosevic this," he said. "I take this personally."

"Why, there's nothing personal in this. Bombs dropped . . ."

"There would be if I were personally dead. Or if you were."

An hour later, there was another round of bombing. Half-ton bombs were being dropped on the machine-parts factory.

In the morning Marko, exhausted and jittery, surveyed the air-raid damage. His house had lost one side of the roof, which was plainly blown off, and all the windows were shattered. Half of the stucco on his brick walls had peeled off, and many bricks were damaged.

The house next door didn't exist, and instead of it, there was a hole in the ground lined up with red and charcoal bricks, shattered pipes. Smoke arose out of the ashes, and in that smoke, Marko thought he discerned burnt-out plastic, rubber, and flesh, yes, no doubt flesh, perhaps human, perhaps animal, probably both. His neighbor, the retired math teacher, had lived with his ten cats. Thirty-five years before, he'd taught Marko fifth-grade math, in a reign of terror, which Marko resented then, but appreciated now; in his business it helped to be able to calculate quickly in his head. And as the old man had aged, Marko had liked him more and more, and occasionally they had stood in front of their homes, and chatted, looking across the street at the town market, or into the park with steam rising in the distance from a hot spring. Now, the neighbor's cats, that was a different matter; they raised hell in their mating in February, and they were so needy that they came over to Sakic's doors and windows, and meowed. Mila and Danko, even as toddlers grabbed the cats, and carried them, sometimes by the tail, sometimes by hind legs, and rarely right. Once, an orange tabby scratched Mila's face, and even got her eyelid. As the eyelid swelled, the parents rushed to the hospital atop a hill, and fortunately the eye was intact. So Marko was not about to feel sorry for these cats, but for the neighbor he did.

Fragments of the neighbor's bones were found under the stones and bricks, mixed with fragments of cat bones, and one would have needed a forensic expert to sort out man and cat. So the math teacher's relatives and Marko gathered the bones, and placed them in a little coffin for an infant, and since the cemetery on the hill was too close to Serb positions, it took considerable courage from them to bury the box in the ground. Serbs in the hills could mistake them for Croat soldiers setting up a cannon. Not having much time, they dug a shallow hole, and left the box there, with yellow soil and rocks over it, to await peace, when it could be placed deeper in the ground, and when the mathematician's picture could be found, to be set into a gilded oval frame—like a chick back into its egg—and placed on the glazed tombstone over the bones of man and cat. But for now, nobody had his picture, and there was no time for glazing the stones. To everything there's a season, a time to love, and a time to hate, a time to work, and a time to rest, and now was the time to blast stones, not to glaze them. And now was no time to linger and walk slowly, but to run.

The following night, there were air-raid sirens, but no air raids occurred.

"Let's leave the town," suggested Dara in the dark, and her voice came to Marko together with the fluorescent hiss and firefly luminosity of the electronic clock.

"No way. I'm not going to give up everything I have here. Who is going to give me a shop elsewhere? And who could I sell my shop to now? Now it's worthless." Still, all he could see was the limy clock light, and he spoke to it, as if to a single ray of reason placed in the dark history.

"But let's go to safety," Dara pleaded. "This is horrible."

"Where, to Serbia? No, not after this close call."

"How about Hungary?"

"Hungarian is not even an Indo-European language. You want to live in a place where you don't understand anybody?"

"Yes, that would be wonderful! What did all this soulful understanding here get us? Here all of you have been bragging about big Slavic souls for decades, drinking yourself into blackouts to prove how chummy you were, and where are your chums now? Knifing each other. So yes, Hungary sounds great to me."

"You can't look at it objectively now. We've had a lot of fun, no matter what, in this damned federation of ours. Turn on the radio, let's see what the world says."

"Surely not that we are having fun."

But before the news came on, they both fell asleep, and then woke up when Danko screamed. He crawled in bed with them, and although he'd been weaned a long time before, he probed with his hands to find breasts, and by mistake, he attempted to suck on Marko's nipple, but neither of the males found that comforting, and so Danko groped for Dara's breasts. "What did you dream, sweety?" she asked, but he wouldn't answer.

In the morning, they found out on TV that there was a truce worked out by the United Nations and Cyrus Vance and by the British Lords talking in fine lispy baritones about how unbecoming it was for small nations to wage wars, how tribal and primitive and savage, while at the same time the British Lords supported various air raids of their own in far-flung regions, and while their own enforcements of unity at home resulted in quite a bit of discord and bombing.

And, after the truce, for several days, people walked in the streets, unafraid of mortar fire from the hills. Marko took the advantage, despite the cold November weather, to replace the tiles on his roof, and he got the glass for his windows, and even patched up the stucco.

Passersby teased him, seeing him work like that. "Boy, you are an optimist?"

"What did you say, optometrist? A kind of visionary, you mean? Yes, you're right."

One dusty morning, Marko drove to Hungary, where groceries were much cheaper. He couldn't go straight north to Hungary, but had to deviate west, to Bjelovar, from where the roads north were clear. He envied the Hungarians—all over the place there were loud and bright ads for American and German companies, the roads were freshly asphalted; women bravely wore extremely short miniskirts, despite the cold weather and feverish men's eyes. That could have been us, he thought, if we knew how to get along.

He drove into Pecs, and after buying sausages, cheese, canned goulash and hot peppers, and many other popular items for his store, he took a walk down a fashionable street, and ran into a bar, Playboy Club. He walked in, and five women in bikinis swarmed around him, offering him flutes of champagne. He retreated suspecting they would take his money, basically mug him. Still, where were the men? Well, why would they need the clubs when their women were undergoing a sexual revolution?

On the way back, when he crossed into Croatia, it was dark, and although he thought he knew the roads well, at one point he wondered whether he had crossed into Serb territory. Now, he shouldn't fear, he thought, he could tell them he was a Serb, but he had no papers to prove that. His ID would state that he lived in Croatia. He ran into a ramp barring train tracks, and wondered whether to wait. Perhaps it was an ambush. And then the train passed, brightly lit, with not a single passenger visible on it. Where were they? Lying on the floor, so snipers from the woods wouldn't shoot them? Where were the engineers? Perhaps it was a blinding ghost train barreling across the Balkans like a smart bomb. After the train, the bell clanged and the red-and-white-striped ramp lifted. Was there anybody observing the crossing and seeing him?

He kept driving west on small roads without edge markings, and several times he almost slid off the road. Only when he hit the major roads going to Zagreb, which, despite the war, emanated a pink aura into the foggy sky as though advertising its Eros, did he find his bearing and orient himself enough to go toward the Orient.

When he got home, he slammed the car door and turned on the flashlight to go in through the front, and he saw red graffiti written on the pavement in front of his house, Serbs Go Home. Next to the graffiti were new grenade markings, resembling a large flower, with one bulbous hole and scars emanating straight out—away from the hills from which the grenade was lobbed—like petals. He wondered whether his family was all right, and he rushed inside. They were all playing dominoes in the candlelight.

The pavement sign depressed and scared him even more than the grenade scars. The following day he didn't go to work, but stayed in bed, drank tea, and went to the bathroom to shave (as though that would clean all the trouble out of the way), which he did three times that day (his beard was strong, but one shave per day would do), and he brushed his teeth a dozen times. During each cup of tea, he urinated several times, as though all the icy anxiety in him could be melted and dissolved and pressed out and drained, down into the subterranean traffic of filth and offal, to flow far away. There was no bombing that day, and he got several calls from his customers, mostly Croats, who were wondering whether he'd keep his store open. Most stores were closed, and it was hard to buy food, so they begged him to stay open. And yet, he was not sure whether they really begged him or gleefully and luridly tempted him into a trap, or whether they waited for him to lose his nerve and to flee, so there would be one less Serb in town, which eventually, he was sure, they all hoped would be purely Croatian.

Still, many people indeed needed groceries, and while starving, they would not worry about his Serbdom. And so, in the morning, the next day, he went to work and opened his shop. He had record sales. Although most people frowned, and without saying a word, bought their goods, some expressed their appreciation for his staying open. And some even told him jokes. Branko, his old friend—so old that Marko now remembered how in fifth grade they measured their penises together to see whether they were normal and exchanged basic know-how about masturbation—told him this one: "A Serb, a Croat, and a Bosnian are the only survivors of a shipwreck. They are holding onto a wood plank and freezing. A gold fish swims up to them, and the Bosnian catches it, but it slips out of his hands, and then the Croat and the Serb catch it together, if you can believe it, one holding the tail, and the other the neck, if a fish has a neck. Goldfish says, Fine and gentle people, please let me go. Ordinarily I do the three wish routine, but there are three of you, so each one gets one wish. The Serb says, Oh, please put me in the middle of a tavern, dancing *kolo,* with accordion music and a gravel-voiced *pevaljka.* Done, said the fish, and the Serb vanishes in the wind, straight to a Serb tavern with a wild female singer. The Croat says, Oh, put me on an Adriatic beach, with a jug of *bevanda,* and make the winds blow from the south. And the fish says, I can't guarantee about the winds, because it's the second wish, but I'll put you on your beach. He disappeared in a wind and landed on a nude beach in Croatia, where he was disappointed that there were no naked German women. And the Bosnian says, I'm so lonely. Could you please get both of them back here? Sure, said the fish. Done."

And the whole day passed in good cheer, as though there was not a worsening war taking place. The next morning, Marko walked to his shop, whistling cheerfully. He passed by an old stuccoed house, which in the rains had lost some of the sandy layers, and now, a sign from 1945, in insistent red, appeared, Comrade Stalin Great Friend and Protector of Small and Oppressed Nations. And on a new bank emerged the sign, beneath bullet riddles, Life We'll Give, but Trieste, Never! Again in red. Of course, Tito gave Trieste back to Italy in exchange for Western protection against Stalin. Comrade Tito Loves Flowers and Children. Marko had never noticed these signs before; perhaps the buildings were painted frequently enough to hide the slogans, but now, the unwashable history lurked and jeered. Marko smiled, finding the old printed signs next to graffiti-like crooked and jittery ones—Long Live President Dr. Tudjman and Croatia for Croats—irrepressibly ridiculous.

But he did not smile for long. In front of his shop lay heaps of shards. Perhaps a bomb hit the pavement and the windows were shattered? But when he came closer, he realized that was not the case. Inside the shop, all the shelves where shattered, the merchandise gone. Plum jam jars lay shattered on the floor with jam splashed, dark red, and gluey, like spilled brains. The cash register was gone. He'd taken the money along with him the night before, but the register was worth a lot. The door leading to the storage room was smashed, and splinters lay scattered on the floor.

He kneeled, with his knee bleeding on a small shard, but he didn't mind the pain. He wept. Damnation! This is the end. What's the point? It would be better if they'd killed me, at least I wouldn't have to suffer.

What should I do, what should I think that I should do? How could I think? What's there to think? You can think only if there's something to believe in, something to strive for, a goodness, a value, a gauge for all matters. But here, I can't believe in anything, and I can't think of anything.

But still, he wondered, Who did it? Well, Who didn't do it? Serbs destroyed the town from the outside, Croats demolished it from the inside.

He walked home slowly. On the way, he noticed another shop, also Serb-owned, totally demolished. A work copied out of history books, Kristallnacht.

At home, he told his wife what had happened.

"Jesus, even the Croats are insane."

"What do you mean, even?"

"This is it, we got to leave!"

"Where would you go? In a world like this, what difference does it make where you go?"

"It's not like this in Germany and Austria."

"With our luck, as soon as we got there, it would be like this. They're sick of foreigners, exiles, Southerners; if I had a shop there, they'd firebomb it, I'm sure. Or they'd find some kind of exile camp, more or less a concentration camp, in the outskirts of Vienna, to keep us in for years on cheap sausages and water."

"You are a pessimist."

"Realist. A realist resembles a pessimist because life always leads to death. Life unavoidably ends in the worst-case scenario— disease and death. So how's one to be optimistic?"

"At least we have each other, and we have our kids, and we are all healthy!"

"You call this healthy? I'm sure I have ulcer, cancer, and if I don't this very minute, it'll grow in me. All this explosive cancer all around us can't stay only outside, it will creep in, has crept in, and it's eating me. Don't talk about health."

They didn't tell the kids anything.

AT NIGHT, there were more sirens, and they went back into the basement and sat on crates of sugar and salt.

Danko said, "I hope they drop a bomb on my kindergarten."

Marko slapped him over his mouth with a backhand.

"What did you do that for?" asked Dara.

The boy cried and wailed.

"I'm sorry," Marko said. "That was an awful thing to say, I couldn't control it."

"He's just a kid."

"I know. I am sorry."

"You should be ashamed of yourself."

"Okay, enough of that." He picked up Danko and wanted to cuddle him, but Danko bit him and wouldn't let go. Marko pinched him until he did. Marko's forearm was covered in warm son-spilled blood.

"See, evil has crept into all of us," he said.

"Oh, now the universe is responsible for your bad temper."

"Precisely."

"I'm hungry," said Danko.

"You have no excuse to hit our lovely child."

"Don't talk. Feed him if you want to prove a point."

At least that wasn't a problem. Marko had stored quite a few supplies in the basement, but he didn't have the can opener handy so he climbed up the stairs, to get one, and as he climbed he vaguely remembered that he shouldn't take risks. What if there was an explosion now? Well, now he'd welcome it. God, please, let there be one!

He brought along spoons as well, and so the whole family feasted on refried beans and pickled peppers. They stayed in the basement until dawn, which brought light even into the dusty basement—not enough light for Marko to see the particles of dust drifting, but enough to realize that the night was over. And indeed, there were no more explosions, from the aircraft or from the hills. By now everybody was asleep, the attackers and the attacked, perhaps even God, but that did not prevent the light from growing its indigo blue into a gray haze.

Marko and Dara carried their sleeping children upstairs; Marko the older one.

"Time to sleep," Dara said.

"Yeah, right. I have a day off. Maybe a life off. Plenty of time. I don't even need to sleep. How about sex?"

"Are you serious?"

"Well, yeah, survival of the species is in question. Besides, the kids are asleep."

"Let me think about that."

"About what?"

"Sex." She yawned.

"You'll fall asleep."

"Let me at least take a bath. I haven't had one in days."

"I haven't either. How could it bother us now?"

"Well, it bothers me. You better take a bath, too."

Later, in sex, he quickly ran out of breath, gasped, and rolled over, thinking he was having a heart attack. Damn, can't even do that anymore! Soon however, he regained his breath, and, after she merely touched his abdominal muscles with her nails, his abdomen twitched and his erection came back. He renewed his efforts, and tried to recall a Hungarian in a wind-blown miniskirt, any Hungarian, but he remembered no images, only concepts about images. His wife could appear overweight, but she didn't seem so to him; he found her proportionate, fleshly, voluptuous, and he liked her wild frizzy hair tickling his neck and ears and even back while he clasped her. His amorous efforts didn't last more than several heart-beats, and he rolled over and panted again. He was tempted to be embarrassed, but what would be the point of shame? In his heightened sense of threat, his body didn't wait for anything, in digestion, sex, breathing—everything was heightened. He didn't measure his blood pressure, but was sure it would be at least 200 over 120. Ten minutes later, he measured his pulse, and it was over a hundred, as though he were an astronaut just landed on the Moon, and he might just as well have been one, on a moon of blossoming craters, the dark side of the Moon, which the Earth did not see, and did not bother to see, for where was that Earth with its global villages to stop the current accelerated disasters?

Dara moaned, and he wasn't sure whether she was having a nightmare or whether she had stealthily continued to stimulate herself, to make up for his lapse.

Still, after all the sexual twitchings and gasps and contemplation about various pressures, he grew calm and breathed slowly, feeling safer and safer, or more and more indifferent to whether he was safe, and so he fell asleep, with images from wakefulness dancing in various colorful forms, with falling leaves becoming schools of yellow fish, swimming deeper and deeper, and this sinking sensation was for a time comforting and pleasant. Sleep, wonderful sleep! Marko was aware of welcoming and praising his fuzzed-up consciousness. But not for long—for he was not safe, not even in sleep, where his dreams ambushed him in a kaleidoscope of blood and jam through which he tried to swim, to extricate himself, toward light, but the light turned into shards that cut into his eyes, spilling them. He woke up, sweating and shivering, relieved that it was all just a bad dream—nothing was cutting into his eyes, except the light from the window. He wasn't glued by his blood to the shards of his shop. The pleasure of waking up used to consist in some subliminal awareness that after a nightmare there would be the bright sunny denial—the rays of daylight would melt away the ghosts. He'd frequently had bad dreams, but even amidst them, he was somehow aware that all he needed to do was to wake up, and he'd be safe. And now waking up didn't help, for the more alert he was, the more he realized that the actual threats were perhaps bigger than he had imagined. What if he stepped out in the street and was killed by a Croat soldier? Maybe they'd start shooting civilian Serbs. Who's to say that stealthily they couldn't take them into the woods and shoot, massacre, burn, bury? What if, after he took several steps, a grenade fell, lobbed from the mountain from his own compatriots. What if . . . and it was not much if, to his mind now, but more likely, when. What will happen when a grenade falls. . . .

The phone rang. His wife walked toward it, but he grabbed her and said, "Don't answer."

"Why not?"

"You don't know who is calling."

"That's the point."

"I don't want to know."

The phone rang again, and Marko guarded it, lest a family member should answer. They are attacking me whichever way they can, Marko thought. With light, with darkness, with sound, with silence, from without and within.

"Go get yourself a bottle of beer," said Dara. "You are getting too weird, relax."

"That's not a bad idea, except I think that if I drank one bottle of beer, I'd vomit it; just the thought of it turns my stomach." And he burped as though he'd had a case of beer.

"So, you plan to sit here and grow crazier and crazier? We better go. At this point, even going to Serbia would be better. At least nobody is bombing it."

"True, but you're a Croat," he said.

"They needn't know."

"They would."

"How? And so what?"

"Everybody knows everything."

"There you go again. Let's just pack."

She looked at him with contempt. He wondered whether

she was contemptuous because of his poor sexual prowess. She looked pretty with the light creating a refracting aura through her hair, with tinges of greens and blues. And so the contempt was all the more irritating. She thinks I can't do anything, that I'm too scared to go anywhere. Am I? No, it takes more courage to stay than to run. But look, she's sure that I can't go, and she's just taunting me, out of habit. Maybe she doesn't even want to go, she just wants to create some blame for me.

"All right, by God, let's do it!" he shouted.

She recoiled back from him, in surprise. Perhaps she had counted on his saying no. He enjoyed the surprise. Plus, indeed, a change of any kind might be better than waiting, cooped up, until something irreparable could happen as it already had.

Silently they loaded up family documents, pictures, a few inherited things, such as her cuckoo clock, his grandfather's saber with fancy silverwork, several children's toys (worthless, but precious to the children at the moment), shoes, silverware, children's first drawings.

"Where are we going?" asked Mila.

"We are going skiing in the Slovenian Alps, just like the last year," said Marko.

"That's great!" she said.

"Don't lie to the child," Dara said.

"Now how do you know that we won't end up there, ha?" Marko said.

Danko agreed to go anywhere cold only if he got a bar of chocolate. Marko gave it to him, and the child chewed it and sucked on it.

As they drove out of town westward at sunset, they would pass by his shop.

On street corners strolled the Croatian soldiers. In the beginning, there was only Croatian police, now there was some kind of army, assembled from who knows where. By physiognomies, Marko could tell there were even foreign mercenaries here; Dutch and British soccer hooligans, with tattoos on their forearms and cheeks, and there were Croats from the Bosnian mountains, bonier and taller than the Croatian Slavonian peasants. So did these guys plunder? They were total strangers, invaders in the name of defense. Maybe only some of them did, maybe all of them did, who could tell? Who destroyed the shops?

He thought he wouldn't even bother to look at it. What would be the point? He wouldn't look at it, as though he were leaving Sodom. But as they neared the location of his shop, he noticed several people carrying something, and so he couldn't resist.

Red light from the setting sun flickered and flashed from where his shop should be. When he passed the glare, he noticed that his shop had new glass windows. He stopped and got out of the car.

"Oh, there you are!" said Branko through his pursed lips, which, instead of a cigarette, held large nails.

"What's going on? Who's taking over my shop?" asked Marko.

"I've been trying to call you like crazy, but you don't pick up the fucking phone!"

"So, who has stolen my shop?"

"Nobody, man. We all agreed that it was a terrible thing

that happened to you, and so we are rebuilding your shop."

"How's that? First you tear it down and then you build it?"

"Listen, we are all old townsfolk here. It's the outsiders—true, Croats, but who knows from where—who got into the war to pillage and plunder. They hope to plunder in the Serb villages, but for now, before they succeed to get there, they'll plunder here. You think it matters to them who is who? No, they want booty, war booty. It's business. Your goods are already sold, probably on the way to Serbia, and the money is in some soldiers' pockets."

"You think?"

"Yes, that's right," said another old school friend of his, Ivan, who flunked out of vet school and now ran a large junkyard west of town.

"They couldn't plunder your yard, though," said Marko.

"No!" laughed Ivan. "I chose my profession wisely."

The men continued working.

Marko walked back to the car and told his wife what he'd just heard. Marko turned on the ignition, and they continued driving. They passed by several shops, a bakery, a bar, most of which were Croat-owned. They were all demolished. Some were being repaired, others stayed gaping, wounded, obscene, and some kept smoldering, with wet rancid smoke barely rising above the ground, drifting dustily.

What to say? Was the sight reassuring? Yes, Marko found it reassuring. He was not singled out. And now, he was touched.

"What are you waiting for?" Dara said. "You are changing your mind?"

"Yeah, maybe it's all going to be all right here."

"You find all this comforting? Well, they'll burn down your

shop again. They are just waiting for you to fill it up with sausages and cheese first. Let's keep going!"

Marko drove on, slowly, hoping to come up with a good argument to turn back, not to drive in a loop through Hungary into Vojvodina and Serbia.

Suddenly, after a curve, he saw flames. He stopped. There were two barrels, with the flames providing the light and heat. Checkpoint. But whose? Either way, he didn't want to be checked and interrogated; he couldn't trust anybody. But they must have seen the car, despite his turning the lights off. In the dark, the stars were sharp, wonderfully luminous. Too bad he couldn't enjoy the moment of beauty in the darkness, or perhaps because of the darkness, he in fact did enjoy it? What if it turned out to be his last moment? In the cosmic sense, it made no difference.

"What are you paralyzed for?" asked Dara. "Don't you see who it is? Don't you listen to the radio?"

He stared ahead at the checkpoint, and suddenly discerned that the four soldiers, two seated and two strolling, wore helmets. Blue helmets! The UN had set up checkpoints, to separate the warring parties. He laughed with relief. No need to be cosmic yet. A sign appropriate for a wall flashed in his mind: UN Friend and Protector of Small and Oppressed Nations. He drove, the Nepali soldiers stopped him, and asked him in English, something he didn't understand. One soldier read in the dictionary. "Oruzje? Bombe?"

"Of course not," Marko said.

They searched the trunk. *"Slivovitz?"*

"No," he said.

★   ★   ★

JUST AS THEY PASSED the checkpoint, Marko said, "Boy, it's getting late. Are you sure you want to keep going; you want to look for a hotel in Hungary?"

"Not that I want to, but that's the thing to do."

"I think it's much simpler to go back and sleep in our house."

She yawned. "Well, maybe you are right. And then we could start early in the morning."

And so they drove through the UN checkpoint, where they were asked the same questions, as though in the ten minutes of absence they might have loaded up the trunk with grenades.

On the way back, they saw flames leaping out of the windows of many houses. They realized that the houses on fire belonged to the Serbs who had left and joined the Serb army. Anxiously they drove home, wondering whether the same thing had happened to their house. What were the UN soldiers doing. Observing?

Their house was intact. It was cold, and they had run out of heating oil. They all cuddled in one bed, covered with a thick down cover, and in the morning emerged like chicks of different birds and various eggs from the same nest, shivering in the cold. Marko called up Branko, and soon Branko brought him thirty liters of heating oil.

EVENTUALLY, the Serb army fled from the western Slavonian hills, pushed eastward, during the Croatian army's first blitz offensive. Many people had grown thin in the war, from anxiety and bad nutrition, but some, including Marko, had put on a lot of weight. He used to live differently—everybody used to live differently—people used to walk in the town park, but the war knocked out the habit. They used to walk in the town square every evening, promanading the *korzo*—but they no longer did even though there was no threat of bombing from anywhere. The siege had changed the lifestyle. People now lived like Americans: they watched more television than before (and there were more channels now), and they ate bigger meals, as if the war had created an incurable appetite in the newly independent nation. Branko, too, had put on weight. And so, no wonder, when the two old friends got together in a basement café—during the war, most cafés moved into basements—they didn't feel satisfied with a meal of *chevapi* and onion, and reminiscing about the old days when they had eaten better and wilder, they decided to go into the park, hunting for mushrooms. After all, it was King Bolete season. Considering that they managed to be friends even during the war, now that it was over, they trusted each other completely.

They walked past the railroad tracks and steaming hot springs, past the hospital wing that had been blown by a one-ton bomb the same night that Marko's neighbor perished. Marko was a little uneasy. "Let's not go too far, there could be mines here."

"Not here, further up, outside of the town, yes, but not here. Chetniks never had control of the park."

They walked, staring at the ground, at the colorful leaves, trying to make out round shapes of ceps. They came to a spot, where a cross was raised, with an inscription that read: To Virgin Mary, who appeared to me on this spot and spoke to me when I wanted to kill myself. A flower wreath was hung over the cross. Both men laughed at the sight; there was an inflation of Virgin Mary appearances. Could only one do so much work? The cross was made with old planks of wood, perhaps from an old barn, hammered together with rusty nails, some of which bent because the wood was hard, probably oak, and the man nailing the wood perhaps had an unsteady, hurried, hand. A blue picture of the Virgin, with her head tilted, was nailed to the cross; even the white frame had grown blue in the rains. She had a small, narrow mouth, and raised her fingers on the right arm timidly, not even up to her ear. And as the two friends laughed, and walked further up the hill, Marko stepped on a piece of metal, which squealed against his sole. He looked down, and he saw a round edge, a half-moon, of a mine tilting under his shoe. He gasped in terror, expecting the mine to go off any second. "Run, my friend," he said to Branko. "I'm standing on a mine!"

"Mother!" shouted Branko, and ran several paces, hid behind a tree, and looked at Marko's feet.

"Don't move," he shouted. "I'll run and get help!"

In fright, Marko was unable to move anyhow. The destroying angel glowed whiter. And the wind blew silently, carrying the washed-up piece of paper, with the image of the narrow mouth, above the fibrillating yellow leaves.

And so he stood for half an hour, his heart pounding his ribs and making him so dizzy that he slid and lost his balance. On his way down, his sideburns and ear scraped and broke the cap of a gray-white destroying angel. His nose plunged into moist yellow beech leaves. He drew a delicious breath through the leaves, amazed that the mine was not going off. His hair had however turned completely white and from then on he was doomed to look saintly.

Hail

*L*arge glistening drops descended slowly against a blue mountain cliff in the background. Delighting in the shushing sound of the downpour, Haris remembered one of the early Buddhist *suttas:* "I am free from anger, free from stubbornness; I am living for a night on the banks of the Mahi; my house is roofless, the fire is extinguished. Rain on now, O cloud, if you will!" Maybe that meant, Don't worry and rejoice in the rain; or, attack me now that I am exposed and see whether I care.

And only when the downpour came to his ridge and hit him, did he realize that it was a hailstorm—white ice, the size of sparrow eggs. For a moment he imagined the hail was sparrow eggs that could feed the whole Bosnian nation (except the nation was no longer whole, and never was). You'd collect the eggs and boil them, and eat them in the flimsy shells. To avoid the falling assembly of water stones, he walked under a canopy of pine trees.

He sat in the lotus position, inhaling the aroma of rosin, while his pants grew soaked from the prickly ground. He buzzed Om to end his meditation, but instead of emptying his mind and attuning it to the harmony of the universe, he thought how coincidental it was that the electricity resistance unit was designated by the same sound, Ohm. He thought whimsically that his mind was an ohmmeter, and perhaps the harmony of the universe consisted not of going with the flow of the forces but in resisting it. He walked out bowing to avoid the low tree limbs—the needle rows on the branches resembled spacious garments on the arms of Jesus or some other loosely clad prophet who stretched out many hands as though he had become Shiva—and nearly bumped into Hasan, who said, "You're talking to yourself?"

Their sergeant passed by in a personal cloud of tobacco smoke.

"This business of being Muslim is too hard," Hasan said. "We should get wasted on *slivovitz,* and we aren't allowed a drop!" He trumpeted his nose, whose tip, once released from the grip of the thumb and forefinger, changed from pink-white to glowing red. "A shot of brandy would cure me, I swear. A few jokes would help, too. Can you tell me a good one?"

"Hum. Can't think funny right now."

"If you can't, I'll tell you one. Coming home from Germany, Mujo drives into Tuzla in a new Mercedes, and he rolls down the window and waves to the people in the streets. Hey, what are you waving for? his friend Jamal says. Almost everybody now has a Mercedes. Yes, Mujo agrees, you are right about that, but not everybody has hands." Hasan laughed and repeated the punch line, but Haris did not laugh.

Hasan cleared his phlegmy throat and spat. "Whoever invented war should be killed—it's so damned boring."

Haris took another deep breath, savoring the pines, and exhaled, feeling the hairs in his nostrils tickle. Perhaps he should have pulled out the nose hairs, but then, why would he? They probably filtered out the dust and now enhanced the smells. Snakes smell with their tongues, and who's to say we don't with our hairs?

Hasan stared at him, with his bulging blue eyes, and said, "Oh, I understand. I am not exactly an enthusiast myself. I'll let you in on a secret. I'd rather be sailing, but I was drafted."

The hailstorm was over and the last echoes of it exhaled a lush silence, and with his eyes closed Haris luxuriated in the aftermath beauty of the vanished sound.

But the quiet was short-lived since Hasan continued talking. "How about you? Did they hound you down?"

"I was a pacifist, still am, and I dodged the Yugoslav People's Army draft. But in Sarajevo, the park I used to gaze at from my favorite café disappeared. People cut down the trees and burned them at home in pots and makeshift stoves, smoking up their apartments. The park became a bald meadow, with little tree stumps sticking out, like severed arms, with chopped hands gone, as though the trees had stolen—what, air?—and were then mutilated according to the Koran laws. I thought, you can't take trees from us, and I volunteered."

The sergeant limped back out of his cloud and said, "What are you two jabbering about? Come, join the group."

They followed him. "Our scouts are back," said the commander, a husky man with a black-and-white beard (white on the cheeks and black on the chin). He pointed out two thin men, who looked smoked-out on cigarettes, with sunken cheeks and sparse yellow teeth.

"Tell them what you told me," said the commander.

"Holy smoke," said one of the scouts in an amazingly low voice, "we made it to their position. You can go around the mountain, and there are no obstacles. They have no idea that we are here."

"They don't even have guards posted outside their camp," said the other scout, blinking, while one side of his face twitched. "You can see them down there." He invited the soldiers to the ridge and lent them his binoculars to see the men who roasted a pair of oxen on spits and placed lambs to cook in the chest cavities of the beasts.

It was dusk and a mist arose from the valley and covered up the distant scene.

The commander laid out his plan. One half of the troops would go around the mountain, and the other would attack directly from this side, in two hours.

Haris and his companions walked gingerly for fear of stepping on mines even if the scouts had no trouble beforehand. Not only would the mine hurt whoever stepped on it, but it would also reveal the Muslim position.

They approached the upper edge of the camp. Haris tried to control his breath, to enjoy the aroma of plum trees and roasted lamb flesh, which wafted on the mists, but there was no enjoyment in his breath and no self-control. His heart pounded into his lungs and interrupted his breath, and it skipped beats, and accelerated in a rush, syncopating a strange rhythm he hadn't experienced in a long while, of pure fear. The mist probably made it safer to advance than clear air would, but it added the invisibility and unknowability. No meditation and no mantra could slow his heart now.

All of a sudden, bullets splashed the mud around him, startling him. Guns right next to him fired back into the mist, to where the shots resounded.

"Forward, for Bosnia and Allah!" the commander shouted.

Haris fired into the sounds, and crouched on the ground, and then crawled forward, with mud freezing his elbows and knees, which he didn't mind, nor did he mind sharp stones scraping him since his fear acted as an anesthetic.

They kept shooting and getting closer and closer to the fire, and suddenly, there were men upon them, and they hit one another with rifle butts, bayonets, knives, and fired from close range, and even wrestled to strangle one another.

Shrieks, and swearwords, and prayers, and mothers' and fathers' names mingled with bullets and blood and urine. The two companies of soldiers fell upon each other, as though a medieval battle were being fought, or even an ancient one. The crusaders, however, had used shields and armor as had the ancient Greeks and Persians, and here, bayonets and knives and steel fell directly on skulls, flesh, and bones, which cracked, opened, and poured out marrow.

Haris jabbed a rushing silhouette with his bayonet, straining to spear him. The man fell back and shouted at him, "Fuck your sunshine!" Haris couldn't tell the man's features in the dark, but he couldn't relent; the large silhouette wiggling on the ground—and kicking and nearly breaking Haris's shin—could rise and throw him down unless he kept pressing. And so, not even quite sure that he had his point at the right spot on the man's body, or even whether it was on the man's body, Haris leaned into the dark. He pushed, but the bayonet wouldn't pierce the man, and so he threw his body on the rifle butt and felt the resistance of the abdomen finally give, and the bayonet sank into the fallen man's rib cage. That sinking of the knife, for a brief moment a triumphant slide, suffused him with revulsion. He left the bayonet in the body of strange groans amidst which emerged one more oath, "Your Serbian mother!" And then the man gurgled blood in his throat, and so these were the last words, with which he didn't exhale but asphyxiated.

The throat of the already dead man still gurgled. Did Haris get one of his own? Would a Serb swear like that? Yes, he could. But wouldn't a Muslim, thinking that Haris was a Serb, be more likely to swear like that? And would it be less horrible if the man indeed was a Serb rather than a Muslim?

At that moment he was hit over the head with a stone, and the dank mist of the battle slope lifted to be replaced by warmth spreading through his head. When he came to, white clouds swiftly drifted a dozen yards above him. Haris stood up; he could barely keep his balance. Each step he took hurt his head, wobbling his brain.

He tripped over a corpse with a cracked skull and the brain hanging out of it and quivering and collecting pine needles from the ground. He felt his brain quivering the same needle-pricked way; he touched his right temple, and his fingertips slid through a tepid gluey wetness.

He crawled to the edge of a rock and looked on—down below him lay scattered cattle bones and one rusty tank. He crawled into the camp, and found more corpses of his comrades, from both contingents. He concluded that the two sections hadn't attacked the Serbs, but each other. Where were his live comrades? What if he were the only survivor?

The thought horrified him, but it also appealed to him. If the mountain belonged to hawks, wolves, boar, and foxes, and he were the only human being around, he'd be free to roam, to drink from clean brooks, never to speak again, never to exchange lies and friendly fire of one kind or another; then he could indeed be spiritual. He remembered one of his favorite *suttas,* which he had learned near the felled park, to pass the time, in Sarajevo, years before:

"Having abandoned the practicing of violence toward all objects, not doing violence to any one of them, let one wish not for children. Why wish for a friend? Let one walk alone like a rhinoceros."

He had always loved solitude, and so even amidst the busy city, he hadn't formed strong attachments—at least not to people, but to cafés, yes. The few girlfriends he'd had eventually abandoned him upon realizing that he wasn't the marrying kind, and so for years he hadn't been with any women although he occasionally lusted. But up here on the mountain, he wouldn't be bothered by lust either. If he were absolutely alone, he could be a good Buddhist; he could meditate well.

But he wouldn't be alone on the mountain. He'd be in the company of a hundred corpses whose ghosts would scrutinize him and molest him in his dreams. He had gruesomely killed a man, and his karma couldn't bring him freedom from pain, let alone nirvana. One side of his face went numb, and an ear buzzed. He had a concussion, no doubt, but were some of his arteries severed if the dura mater cracked? If so, he might even want a hospital, but who would trust one in these conditions? A concussion while people were dying would receive the lowest priority, and the hospitals were so shoddy. . . . No, better to die like a wildcat, in hiding, alone. Even outdoor domestic cats usually managed to die out of sight, to bother nobody and not to be bothered by anybody, as though they had attained enlightenment, so why couldn't he?

He limped into the camp, into the debris of CD players, TV sets, cases of empty beer bottles, boots. He found a walkie-talkie. When he flipped it on, it crackled; the batteries were good. He slid the walkie-talkie into his pants pocket.

In the crates of empty beer bottles he found a full one. He pinched the tip between two rocks trying to pry the cap open. The glass cracked. He poured the beer into his aluminum container. Maybe he'd drink some glass.

At the upper rocky edge of the camp, a dozen brown ravens greedily pecked at a man's entrails. Several people from his unit appeared behind them, backlit by the morning orange sun, and walked around the corpse, and the ravens ignored them and kept feasting.

"What a relief to see you," said Haris.

"I thought you were dead," said Hasan, who had a black eye.

"What are you doing here?" Mirzo, another soldier, whose neck was bandaged, said. "Why are you alone?"

"I wonder about that, too."

He stood up and as he straightened his body, he felt a sharp pain around his lower ribs. Did I break them when I jumped on the butt of the rifle?

"It's peculiar there are no Serbs," Haris said.

"Yes, peculiar," the commander enunciated.

Hasan tilted each empty bottle for a few old drops and made sucking noises.

"Stop it, disgusting slob," the sergeant said. "Aren't you scared of their germs? Just imagine all those Serbian mouths slobbering over the bottles; it's like kissing them."

"I'll kiss bottles anytime," Hasan answered. "And germs, I am sure I already have them; they have nothing new to offer to me. And if your spittle is made of beer, I'll kiss you, what the hell."

"Watch your tongue!" the sergeant said, and then addressed Haris, "What's your theory, Haris?"

"Look at them, they are still eating." Haris pointed toward two ravens who played a tug of war with a stretch of the long intestines. The intestines glowed crimson with the sun shining through them.

But he was the only one noticing. His comrades surrounded him and stared at him.

"You aren't answering my question, soldier," the commander said. "Somebody must have told them what we were up to."

"Maybe the scouts?" Hasan said. "They were there ahead of us all and they could have told them."

"The scouts are dead," the commander objected.

"That doesn't mean they didn't inform the Serbs."

"If they had, they would have known better than to go along with us and die. . . ."

"Who could have predicted we'd kill our own?" Haris said.

Haris didn't know what to do with his hands, and he scratched a stone-cut on his forearm. He put his hands into his pockets.

The commander looked Haris up and down. "How come your pockets bulge so much? Empty your pockets!"

Do I have to take this? Haris thought. I guess that's how the military system works: on obedience, not resistance, almost like Tao. He emptied his pockets. The walkie-talkie fell into the grass.

"Who do you need to talk to?" the commander asked.

"I don't need to."

The sergeant ejected green spittle through his yellow teeth. "I heard him talking to himself; he was ratting on us. He hid in a thicket!"

"That's a jump to conclusions. I found the walkie-talkie here at their campground, and naturally, I picked it up. Wouldn't you?"

"And who were you talking with under the trees?" the sergeant asked.

"Oh, those were just yoga mantras."

"Mattress?" the commander combed his beard with his long fingers. "You mean you slept under the trees?"

"No, mantras, you know, Hindu and Buddhist incantations, short prayers."

They were deafened because a Phantom jet flew low over them.

"Rich bastards, drop your bombs or go home!" Hasan shouted.

"Let's see who he's hooked up with." The commander

flipped on the walkie-talkie, and said, "Hey, man, where are you? Over."

"You sound strange. You got drunk? Over."

"I wish. What about you? You got any beer?"

"No, just a lot of whores, plum brandy, and white wine."

"Okay, let's exchange some, I got lots of whiskey from those UN bozos. Bozo booze. Where are you now?"

"What do you think? Over."

"Oh, of course. I'll stop by tomorrow."

The commander flipped off the walkie-talkie.

"So, that's your partner? You warned them, and now they are down, all the way in the valley, probably getting a reinforcement to hunt us. I think it's time to move out of this place."

"But how could we? This is such a good strategic location," said the sergeant.

They didn't walk far—two hundred yards away from the campsite, where most of their dead lay.

Two soldiers tied Haris to a tree and the commander said: "Convince me you didn't do us in. Think up something, make a good story. You have an hour. If your story's no good, we'll bury you alive with those whose deaths you have caused."

At least half of the company had survived. Gradually they appeared from the woods, and from behind the rocks, and they joined in the digging efforts, and some of them bandaged each other, and a couple tended to a man who was dying from many knife wounds, while several stood on guard.

They used shovels from the Serb trenches and fought through the stony land, digging next to the pines and cedars. Haris smelled smoke from so much metal hitting rock and sparking up. They collected wristwatches and wallets, which they combed for German marks; they gathered tobacco and cigarettes. They placed four bodies in each hole. Several men kept glancing at Haris darkly, and later, they threw soiled stones at him. One stone struck Haris in the ribs. Mirzo, when passing by Haris, spat into his face. The sergeant slapped Haris, hitting him above the ear, where he'd been struck down with a rock. Flashes of green light appeared before Haris's eyes, like northern lights filtered through leaves, and his vision oscillated. He couldn't keep his head up, and he let it slump and rested his chin on his sternum. The rope cut into his wrists.

In the meanwhile, men prayed and read from the Koran. Several men wailed, some wept silently, others frowned and paced, and one man, apparently out of his mind, would now and then bellow with laughter, until Hasan bloodied his nose. From then on the man whimpered and sniffled.

The burials went on with somber dignity.

The fact that nearly half the company was being buried was a tragedy, but at the same time, the occasion was a triumph of sorts. The company now controlled the mountain ridge and the river valley roads. It was to be expected to have some losses, and that the losses came from friendly fire could not annul the fact that they did control the mountain from which they could strafe the land and several roads.

Haris's hands, tied to the branches above him, tingled from the lack of circulation. His woolen pants itched him, and the sweating around his groins irritated him, and the more help-less he was to do anything about it, the greater the itching, and he thought that he'd give a finger or two if he could just properly scratch the damned irritation. How far from meditation this is, he thought; if he had meditated better, he would have been able to control his state better—he may have strolled in the battlefield, invisible, intangible, and even if struck down, he would have had the good sense to die rather than to come back to life with a concussion to go through the strange resurrection cum crucifixion. He found support for his sensation of guilt in this recalled verse, "All that we are is the result of what we have thought: it is founded on our thoughts, it is made up of our thoughts. If a man speaks or acts with an evil thought, pain follows him, as the wheel follows the foot of the ox that draws the carriage." He could not recall what evil thought he'd had, but was sure he'd had one. He thought about the verse again, and the wheel that follows the foot of the ox kept turning and returning—to the ox. Now, what did the oxen think that was evil, to be burned on a spit? He licked his cracked lips and his throat hurt from dryness.

The grisly commander walked up to him. "Hey, are you Orthodox, Catholic, or Muslim?"

"I am a Buddhist."

"That's a good one." The commander smiled the way many do upon hearing a joke that's cute but not quite funny. "What were you raised as?"

"An atheist, of course. Weren't you?"

"What was your parents' religion?"

"They were Muslims. But they never went to the mosque."

"Well, then, you are a Muslim."

"No, Buddhist, as I said."

"You swallow fire, walk on nails, put your feet behind your neck, or do whatever they do?"

"I don't mean it as a religion, but as a nation."

"Come on."

"Could I have a glass of water? I'm dying of thirst."

"Buddhist nation, you say, here?"

"You can be Muslim or Christian anywhere, why not Buddhist?"

"You are making fun of Muslims being a nation in our country? I see, there's a Serb lurking in you. That's what they like to do."

"Don't I have freedom of choice of religion and nation?"

"Nobody does. That's fate. And how the hell could you become something so bizarre?"

"Not that I like being a Buddhist, but in my formative years, I read that nonsense and so that's how I think and who I am."

"Well, if you don't like it, change it, be a good Muslim."

"Can't. You said one cannot change."

"But you did—just drop your act. I don't find it a good story."

"I wouldn't mind changing, but I became Muslim in my formative years, late teens, early twenties, the most philosophical years of our lives. Remember in the sixties there were books all over Sarajevo about herb healing, meditation, Buddhism, Hinduism, astral projection, and so on. All that stuff came from Belgrade. They already planned to distract us, get us to fantasize and talk in cafés every night till dawn, while they went to military academies and studied engineering or started smuggling goods from Italy or joined the mafia. You think they read that stuff in Belgrade? No way."

"You are crazy!"

"You call me crazy. You have a better explanation for what's going on?"

"Well, you got a point, but that doesn't mean that any nonsense should make sense. Plus, your giving me this theory about Serb conspiracies won't convince me that you aren't working for Serbs."

The sergeant lit a cigarette and began re-creating his personal cloud, but the commander said, "No smoking."

"What's wrong with smoking now? The Koran says nothing against it."

"The tree might catch on fire."

"In this weather? If it did, it might be a good way to deal with this devil."

"In any weather—look at the rosin oozing from the bark. That burns like petrol. By the way, don't talk back to your superiors."

The sergeant huffed out a blue streak and trampled his cigarette under his boot.

"Well, that was nice, but you used up your time." The commander petted the white sides of his beard. "You could have convinced us that you didn't betray us. All right, try it in five, six sentences."

"Why would I convince you of anything? If that's what you believe, go ahead, believe."

"It's a shame. Now that you have talked about your odd religion, I can see that you could easily do all sorts of unpredictable things; therefore I believe that you turned us in. Sergeant, what do you think?"

"I agree with you."

The commander then addressed Hasan, who stood with his arms crossed. His black eye was even more swollen than before, and it shut.

"Soldier, how about you?"

"I have no idea."

"But you heard him talking stealthily under the trees?" said the sergeant.

"Yes, I heard him, but I don't know if he was saying anything."

"So, see my friend, the jury is unanimous," the commander said. "The trial is over."

"It's no trial, but unfounded opinions," said Haris.

"Don't contradict your superiors!" Sergeant interceded.

"Not even when my . . ."

"When your life is in question, you guessed that right," the commander said. "I don't think it's in question anymore. Mirzo, Hasan, go ahead, shoot him."

"How, to execute one of our own?" Hasan objected. "I think it's enough that we have killed off half of our company. You want to go on?"

"You got a point," said the commander, "but that's precisely why we should shoot him—he caused too much grief."

"I think it would be better, according to our laws, to cut his tongue out," the sergeant suggested. "That's the offending organ—let's just cut it out and move on."

"I kind of like the idea, but no. If you cut his tongue, he'll bleed to death. You'd have to have a way of stopping the bleeding for the sentence to make sense. Plus, I do believe he would be resentful afterward if he survived, and I wouldn't trust him with arms around us. Shoot him."

"I can't, if you'll excuse me," Hasan said. "I am no longer sure he did it. And he's a friend of mine. I admit he's weird, but who isn't. It would be weird not to be weird."

"Don't go all soft and wobbly on me, soldier," said the commander. "But if you don't want to, all right, there are enough angry men who will. Sergeant, go get three or four."

The commander asked, "Do you have any last wishes?"

"Yes, untie my hand please so I could scratch my balls."

"Serious?"

"Yes, serious. Are you? This is absurd. Just because I prayed by myself, I am accused of treason!"

"You didn't pray to our gods, but to foreign gods, which is treason enough. And it's clear what you were doing with the walkie-talkie. Let's not go through that again. You've wasted enough of our time."

"Could you please untie one of my arms? I am dying from the itching."

"All right," said the commander but did nothing.

The sergeant came with three men. The commander ordered them to shoot, one in the head, one in the neck, one in the chest. The men stood some twenty paces away and lifted their rifles.

Haris did not grow terrified. The terrors had spent themselves, and the injustice of the accusations, the absurdity of it all, calmed him. He wanted to lift his head, to stare at the men who could do this, but everybody could do everything, and there was nothing marvelous in that. He drew a deep breath, and it hurt his rib cage, and his head pulsed, and his ears buzzed. Why didn't they shoot? It would be good if they already had, but this waiting broke his tranquility. The pain in his head grew loud as though a waterfall had burst from a mountain next to his ear.

He heard thunder or gunfire and didn't know whether it came from afar, or whether he was being shot. He closed his eyes, and saw himself slide out of the rope, with the skin of his hands torn off. He saw his body on the ground, and had the impression that his eyes were hovering separate from it somewhere in the tree, like owls' eyes, and observing as blood gushed out of his right temple. He heard shouting of men and laughter. So that's what happens in death, your eyes float and look, and nobody can see them, and they can see everybody and everything, and at the moment, he thought he could see even into the valley, from where a smoke came smelling of coal. Or perhaps that smell whiffed over the chasm of years, from his childhood, when his village in the valley outside of Sarajevo filled up with steam and smoke, deliciously smelling of coal and heavy oils, promising arduous journeys to the shores that bear exotic fruits, such as kiwi, which he'd never tasted but dreamed of, and which, if the war ever ended, perhaps the country would import, and he would melt the seeds on his tongue. Or perhaps the smoke came from the guns and spilled oil on the rusty Serb tank below. He was sure that he was well nigh dead, and that concept comforted him, but amidst it all, he gathered a surprising impression that he was drawing another breath, empty, full of purified being and nothingness, perhaps the emptiness of the universe, peace beyond the sorrow of existences and deaths.

He enjoyed the grand vision of departing from life, but something very basic interfered. There was a shout in Hasan's voice, "Stop! Men, stop, stop for God's sake. Don't shoot. Look what I found!"

The men lowered their rifles and turned around.

"What is it now?" the commander said.

Hasan held up a black book with red-colored edges. "A New Testament in Cyrillic was on a scout's body. And look, his ID card says he was no Esad but Jovan. A Serb with a false identity. He betrayed us!"

"So? Being a Serb means nothing," said the commander. "Marko is a Serb, and he's one of our best fighters."

"The soldier has a point," the sergeant said. "Who do you think would be more likely to betray us, this freak or the guy who reassured us that Serbs hadn't bothered to post any guards?"

"Somebody has to be punished. The other guy is already dead; he can't be punished. Men, line up and shoot! What are you. . . ."

Presently shots resounded from all the sides of the camp. Before it became clear what the shots meant, and before anybody had the time to hide, several sniper shots struck the three would-be executioners in the head, and they fell.

Several of the remaining men jumped to the ground and tried to hide behind rocks, and others ran in disarray to the former Serb camp and into the heathers, but grenades and machine-gun fire forced back many of them to their initial position.

Haris observed from his suspended station, with his wrists bleeding. The commotion didn't scare him; he did not care whether he would be struck. He thought it strange that what meditation hadn't managed to accomplish, the concussion combined with torture and threat of shooting did: perfect equanimity, ataraxia of the mind. But then, didn't the Dalai Lama undergo persecution of all sorts? How would the Dalai Lama like to be in his position? Would he attain nirvana like that?

Serb soldiers had some thirty Muslim men under gunpoint. There were at least three hundred Serbian soldiers in the camp. They picked up the Muslim guns and tossed them into a pile, which looked like twigs lined up in a circle for a bonfire.

"Where are your mujahideen?" asked the Serb commander, a freshly shaven man whose cheeks were rosy and flushed with triumph. "What? No Afghanis?"

He looked around, and rested his eyes on Haris.

"And who do you torture here? We saw you were about to execute him."

"Traitor. He was giving information on our positions to you," Mirzo said.

"Oh, was he?" The Serb captain walked up to Haris. "Did you do noble deeds for which they give you credit here?"

"No," Haris said.

"You aren't under their control, brother! Speak freely."

He kissed Haris on the forehead. "You look awful. Have a sip!" He held up a jug of Red Label Johnnie Walker and poured, and Haris, who hadn't had any water in almost a day, gulped.

"There! You can always tell a good man by a good gulp!" The commander cut the ropes to free Haris's hand, with his sparkling knife that resembled a dagger. Once released from the suspension, Haris fell. His arms wouldn't move to protect his face, and it struck the wet ground. He felt like passing out, never to awaken again, and to relax infinitely, but he didn't pass out. He drew breath through his nose, forgetting that it was lodged in the ground, and he inhaled dirt; some of it stayed in his throat, some went down his windpipe. He rolled over and coughed, and each cough shook his brain.

"Oh, my brother," the Serb captain said. "We'll make them pay for this!"

He lifted Haris and gave him water from his aluminum flask. Haris washed out his mouth, spat, and then drank. His nose and his vision cleared. He was struck by how miserable the remainder of his company looked. He felt a tinge of the old triumph, such as he'd felt when he was riding the butt of the rifle and sliding the bayonet into a man's rib cage—the triumph of survival at the expense of the enemy's life. All the enlightenment which he'd experienced tied to the tree seemed to be lifting away as a morning cloud, and what remained were the petty details, gaps among the men's brown teeth and plastic Coca-Cola bottles on the ground, and with these details, old passions pressed his mind.

The Serb captain said, "I can see the flicker in your eyes. Wouldn't you love to shoot them? I won't take that away from you. I'll give you a machine gun and you can strafe them all down. We'll rope them together, and after you finish several rounds, you will have killed every single one of them! How does that sound?"

Haris didn't answer. It sounded, of course, terrible. If he said he wouldn't do it, would he be executed himself? If he declined to do it, wouldn't someone else do it? Weren't the men goners, no matter what? And what is the difference between death and life? The more he thought about it, the more tempted he was to accept the offer to shoot, but a Dhamapada verse came to him and distracted him. "As a fish taken from his watery home and thrown on the dry ground, our thought trembles all over in order to escape the dominion of Mara, the tempter." All right, my thoughts, tremble on. Trembling may be good, it will save men.

"Oh," the captain shouted, "they were about to make Swiss cheese out of you, and you hesitate!"

"To tell you the truth, I don't want to shoot anybody."

"But you will enjoy it, I can tell."

"He's not one of yours!" shouted the sergeant from the Muslim company. "I am the one who gave you the call! Don't shoot me!"

"Nenad," the Serb captain addressed a red-cheeked soldier, "is that your radio connection?"

"So that's what you look like!" the red cheeks boomed. "Stevo, I thought you were dead. The connection went out, and then some strange guy talked to me. I was sure they killed you! Great to see you, man!"

"So you are our hero," the Serb captain said. "Come out, brother, join the party!"

Haris wondered what that meant for him; would the Serbs now shoot him? His breath accelerated. After all, he did like being spared, he did like survival, no matter what he thought and how he philosophized. If he hadn't philosophized, he would have already killed the sergeant, and would be free to live.

The captain offered the sergeant to drink from the jug, which was nearly empty. Pretty soon, the sergeant mingled with the Serb soldiers, hugging them, and laughing all too loudly while Haris stood, gazing vacantly, next to the captain.

"Now then, what do they torture you for? What good did you do after all?" the captain asked Haris.

"Buddhism."

"That's a good one! But you do look gaunt like some kind of monk. Have another sip."

Haris took a gulp of the Scottish invasion. His vision turned a shade darker, as though the shot had toned down the lights in his brain, and the pain in his temple gave him a sudden stab, and he winced.

"Buddhism, ah? You know, I used to be a Buddhist. For a whole week."

"Treason, too."

"I see, you didn't communicate with us, you didn't do anything. Religious fanatics. Damned fundamentalists. You got to wipe them all out, I'm telling you. How else are we going to get along? I mean, I'd understand if they had got the right man to torture, but you? All right, machine-gun them! I'll help you."

I should resist, thought Haris, and tiredly, he lay prostrate on the ground, and the ground felt good and inviting, and he could barely open his eyes.

"You know," the captain said. "That is one thing I liked about Buddhism. It seemed calm."

Hasan shouted, "Don't do it, my brother, I tried to save you!"

A soldier kneeled down next to Haris, and adjusted the train of heavy bullets.

And many voices came, both beseeching and cursing Haris.

He looked over the aim, framing his former companions. The aim and the companions trembled and shook and oscillated darkly into silhouettes. He blinked, and when he opened his eyes again, he saw nothing. He closed his eyes, opened them, but around him was a brown darkness. The voices grew louder and shriller from all sides. Somewhere far away there was a thundering, and for a second he wondered whether the crackling explosions came from his machine gun, and he leaned over and felt the barrel. It was cold, comfortingly cold, and it balmed his bloodied wrists.

A Purple Story

*R*anko had a desktop publishing job to finish before a
friend would visit in the afternoon, but he dozed off in
front of the computer. He attributed his listlessness to a minor
cold that had been dragging on for two months; even during
the visit he yawned.

"Let's go to the mountains and look for mushrooms," said
Mladen, a clean-shaven man with shiny cheeks. "I'd love to
climb Sljeme and look over the red-roofed villages on the
other side of the mountain, like we used to."

"I felt like that even when I was forty . . . like at any moment I'd love to walk up the mountain," said Ranko to his
friend, who was visiting from Austria.

"What should be different at forty-five? It's not a city speed limit, is it?"

"You will see how you feel when you are my age. Your energy level drops."

"He's been talking like this lately," said Ranko's wife, Lana, who was sitting on a Turkish carpet and resting her chin on her knees, in such a way, Ranko noticed, that you could see her thighs. "The war changed him," she said. "He was evading the draft, and he often went into the basement to read books when he thought the MPs might come by. All that hiding and the lack of light made him depressed."

"Nonsense. It's natural." Ranko petted his stomach and sucked air through his teeth, which were remarkably white against his curly black beard and mustache; his long hair was still thick, but mostly white. The contrast between black and white on his face would have been startling if his large hazel eyes had not reconciled the light and the dark. "Did your father play soccer when he was in his midforties?" he addressed Lana.

"No, but he had his war. He was always ill."

"All right," said Mladen. "I have to go now to visit my in-laws but I hope to come back for New Year's—maybe the cold weather will energize you and we'll ski. How would that be?"

"Drinking a few beers sounds more realistic," Ranko replied.

"He just pretends to drink—he doesn't do even that!" said Lana.

After Mladen had left, Lana said, "You practically chased him away with your morose attitude. I thought you loved your friends; you always talk about them, and once they show up, you just want them to leave." She stood up and changed in front of him; she took off her blue midi, and put on a velvety crimson mini. Her figure, although she was past forty, had not changed since that night twenty-five years before when they went skinny-dipping in a fish pond. Their feet had sunk in the warm mud, which seeped through their toes, and waves of gentle touches brushed and tickled their legs. He did not know whether weeds or catfish touched him. Water glistened on her curves in the crescent moonlight. Even now, as she emerged through her skirt, she moved her hips in a sinuous way, like a mermaid. Usually seeing her like this aroused him, but now he only considered her aesthetically, indulging in the visual recollections.

After Lana had gone to teach geography at the local high school, he put on his winter coat although it was a warm day. During his walk to the grocery store several hundred yards away, he was short of breath. In the aisles of soup cans and bottles of spaghetti sauce, he leaned on the cart. His ears buzzed, his vision grew hazy, his heart made strange leaps and gave him a sensation of emptiness, as though there was no longer any blood in the chambers—a sensation of something falling and creating a vacuum within his chest. Could this be an anxiety attack? Am I scared of talking with my friends? The hell with all this introspection, I'll get some wheat beer for them, let them drink like pigs.

He reached for a half-liter brown bottle with his left arm, and his fist tingled as though ants had crawled under his skin.

As he lifted his foot over the muddy threshold of the store on the way out, it seemed that he'd tripped. In his slow fall, before he hit the glazed leopard-skin patterned stone floor, the color of everything around him burst into a purple splash. Am I dying? Is this it?

He woke up in a white room filled with offensive sunlight. His head was wired up to gray electrical machines, and one machine beeped. His left arm still tingled as though he had hit the elbow nerve.

A face like a pizza, round and freckled, floated up above him, like a moon above the clouds. What is this? he thought. A balloon, a kite, oh, a nurse! He wasn't sure he was seeing right: could anyone have such a round and orange-red face? And he was frightened, not of her, but of his mind.

Lana's face showed up too. Her elongated face was white with a tinge of green, her eyes bulging and glowing, her nose more pointed than before. She put her finger on her thin lips, and said, "Shh." She kissed him on the forehead as though to check his temperature, or perhaps to express her love, but why not then on his lips? Well, this was a different kind of love now: not of equals, on the same level of lips, but paternal, or maternal love, from above, reaching down to the forehead, the first place the lips could reach.

As he gazed, she dematerialized into a haze, a cloud in the shape of a stratocumulus, which lifted up, higher and higher. He used to make out resemblances of faces in clouds, and now his vision made clouds out of faces.

He again woke up to the glaring sunlight reflecting off the windows, waxed floors, and glass-covered paintings of poppy fields. Lana told him that he'd dozed off and that it was great to see him awake. He wanted to ask her what was the matter with him, and she, as though hearing his unspoken sentence, said that he'd apparently suffered a stroke.

What hospital is this? He moved his lips but wasn't sure any sound came out. He heard screams from other rooms.

But no matter what hospital, it would be ill-equipped. After the war, the hospitals had not kept up with the new technology. Many good doctors had emigrated. And, being an ethnic Serb, what could he expect? Did that matter? Could the doctors guess by his name that he was a Serb? Of course, they know everything, he thought—or worse, they know next to nothing, except for his nationality.

The following day, a doctor who was a childhood friend of his showed up. "Stroke, they say? Have they examined your heart?"

"I don't think so," he managed to mumble.

The doctor listened to his heart. "You need an EKG. My guess is you've had a massive heart attack."

Without further ado, he gave Ranko a shot of adrenaline, driving a needle between his ribs toward his heart, and ordered that Ranko be transferred to the cardiac unit, where a trusted colleague would take over. Although there was a shortage of space, the friend got him a bed.

RANKO STRETCHED ON A TABLE, and a large tube, like an astronaut's capsule, slid over him up to his chin, swallowing his body. The tube turned around him; an isotope test was performed. "Look at this!" said Dr. Kraljevic, a man with a white beard. "Most of your heart is in a shade, no light, that means the arteries don't work, the blood doesn't flow there. Only about a fifth of it is working!" He talked with fascination, as though glad to witness such a miracle. Ranko watched the illu-minated fraction of his heart in horror.

After several blood tests, the surgeon said, "Sir, have you had an infection, pneumonia perhaps?"

"Something milder than that for a couple of months."

"Have you taken any antibiotics?"

"Not in ten years."

"If you've had a bacterial invasion of the heart, just a few days on antibiotics would have saved your heart muscle. Too bad you didn't come here earlier. On the other hand, who knows whether these idiots would have diagnosed you cor-rectly when they can't recognize infarct."

Ranko could barely move. If he sat up he was out of breath. If he stood up he had needles in his vision. Dr. Kraljevic deter-mined that Ranko needed a heart transplant.

A few days later, Ranko was allowed to go home, to wait. Lana hugged him, gently, as though afraid that he might crum-ble from the pressure. She administered the pills regularly, twenty a day. She played his favorite music on the old phono-graph with a diamond needle: Mozart piano concertos and Bach's *Goldberg Variations*. "Those are bound to be good for your heart," she said. "If they are good for your mind, they must be even better for the heart. Just listen to how steady the rhythm is!"

The music suffused him with a sense of all-permeating beauty that went from his ears even into his bones; he imag-ined the music entering through his pores, into capillaries, and swimming upstream through his blood, effortlessly. It was in-substantial, a spirit, untouched by the avalanches of plasma with blood iron, perhaps exciting the iron, magnetizing it, so

that each particle of iron received, like an antenna, the har-
monies of the celestial spheres encoded and captured in the
Goldberg Variations. Even if his ears were deaf, his body could
hear, and the music would harmonize what's left of his heart.

In the bathroom, while emitting a weak stream, he faced
himself in the mirror: he looked like a flayed chicken. His
hair was cut short, and it stood scattered in many dull,
greasy, weak strands, and was no longer bright silver, but a
dull gray, like smoke around a poorly built bonfire. He was
visibly diminished, carrying the darkness of his heart, which
dimmed his previously luminous self. He had been one of
those people who shone, with smooth skin that not only reflected light but emanated it and big eyes that glowed. He
had been aware of his light; he had been told about it many
times. And now, no doubt, his presence consumed light
wherever he passed. He wondered what it was like for Lana
to be around him.

Lana had found his passivity depressing even during the
war. "Let's go out," she'd say. "Let's go to the concert. Alfred
Brendl is playing Beethoven sonatas. Did you know that he'd
studied the piano in Zagreb in his youth and this is his homecoming of sorts?" Getting no response from him, she had
gone out by herself, and on other occasions with her friends,
first female, and then later, since she was an egalitarian, male.
No, he wouldn't be jealous, he was always a laissez-faire type
of guy. Still, when she had gone out—with her lips vermilion—to meet the male friends in cafés, and orchid fragrances
lingered after her at the door, he was perturbed by her making
herself attractive to others. When she came back, he had an
impression that her lips had lost some of their moist sheen; he

wondered whether the sheen evaporated or stayed on the cigarette butts and gilt edges of porcelain cups, or whether it had visited other lips.

But now she no longer needed to go out; she used no makeup, and she was with him. She wept for him, she caressed him. It was almost good to be ill.

In the warmth of radiator heat, he relished the shades of light slanting through the window. Even just a little bit of light made the room beautiful. Perhaps even just a little bit of light in his heart might make him live well. He thought human hearts were too large, made for the luxury of endurance. Cats, on the other hand, have tiny hearts in proportion to their bodies, and perhaps for that reason they luxuriate all the more in the sunlight. Perhaps the diminishing of his heart had made him a catlike aesthete who could feel each nuance in every motion.

The friends who were supposed to come for the Christmas holidays came in January. Mladen embraced him. Tomo didn't. "Sorry," he said, "I am afraid of germs."

"Oh, don't worry," Ranko said. "I no longer have whatever bugs caused the trouble. I am totally debugged."

"Sorry. You are dear to me, but I am a little afraid."

"That's all right," Ranko said. "I sure can understand that. Anyway, Mladen, how's Austria?"

"The most beautiful place on earth—it would be if it weren't for the Austrians!"

"But look at you, you look lean, ruddy, healthy. It can't be too bad."

"You know how sociable my wife and I are, and yet in four

years we haven't made any Austrian friends. They don't talk to us. And everything is strictly regulated. You know, there's a law that you may not burn firewood that hasn't been seasoned for two years."

"Sounds bad, but it makes sense. Raw wood has chemicals that don't burn clean."

"Maybe, but to have a policeman sniff outside of your house with his dogs to find out what kind of smoke comes out of your chimney, wouldn't make you feel uncomfortable?"

"At least you eat healthy bread. I've had some wonderfully heavy black bread in Salzburg."

"Oh, that bread is expensive. Although I bake it, I am not allowed to take it home. I can't even chew it at work. They watch my hands, my mouth, I swear."

"So why don't you come back to Zagreb?"

"While Tudjman is alive? I don't want to live under fascists."

"What a thankless guest you are," Ranko joked. "They give you asylum, get you a job, an apartment, and you spew all this hatred for them. Seriously, if I were in your place, I would enjoy it all—even the wood police, the bread police, I would see the humor and the irony . . . I swear. I would just love it. Anyway, that's the wisdom of the sick. Cherish everything."

"So you are supposed to get a new heart?" Tomo asked.

"Sure, but they don't have a good system of donors. The heart doesn't live long, so basically they have to take it out from an otherwise healthy body, let's say after a car crash. I am on a long waiting list."

"But there must be hearts around! I think they are waiting

for a bribe, that's all. Those guys never change. And how long do they think you can live without a transplant?"

"One year, maybe a little more."

THE FRIENDS GATHERED several thousand German marks for the bribe fund.

Ranko was touched to see his friends sacrifice for him. "I have good friends, don't I?" he said to Lana.

"Yes, of course you do. You deserve them."

"And such a good wife, too!" He embraced her; with the warmth of her thighs, he got an erection, but then thought, I better stop. In my state, sex could kill me.

So he sat back in the armchair, melancholy again, and literally a little blue in his face, for blood was not reaching it well enough.

"What are you suddenly gloomy about?" she asked.

"Oh, just tired."

"But just a second ago you were happy!"

"I am still happy."

Lana prepared him rose hip tea with honey. As he drank it, with the porcelain warming both of his hands and steam warming his face, he inhaled deeply for the first time in a long while, and he thought, the hell with it, if I die, at least let me make love.

Lana was making a cup of coffee in an aluminum percolator. He sniffed the aroma of roasted coffee, but even that was forbidden to him. He walked behind her and slid the thin cotton dress up her hips.

"I see what you are up to," said Lana. "Are you sure? Oh, I see, you are."

What joy the senses, the skin, could give, he thought amidst slow lovemaking. He savored each tingle. Previously, the tingles of his nerves had threatened him, but now he gained encouragement from them. He nearly swooned, but felt safe, and when he regained his composure, he fell asleep, smiling like a satiated baby.

LANA VISITED THE HEART SURGEON, Dr. Kraljevic, at the Rebro Hospital. Rebro, by a coincidence, means "rib." The Hospital of Ribs—does not sound encouraging, does it? But the surgeon would not accept the bribe. "Oh, no, my dear, that is not how it works. You read the newspapers too much. We'll take care of your husband the best we can."

At home, she recounted the details of the visit to Ranko, and she asked, "What should we do with the money?"

"Send it back," he said.

"We need a car; if you have an attack, I can drive you to the emergency room. That would be faster than calling the ambulance. I am sure your friends would not mind such a use of the money."

THE SURGEON GAVE Ranko addresses of several men who'd received hearts. One of them, when Ranko and Lana visited in the newly bought Kia Pride, was splitting logs. Two streams of steam billowed out of his large red nose in the cold.

"Oh, yes, my friend," the man said, taking off his cap with a pheasant's feather, "the heart transplant, the best thing in the world. Before that, for years, I could hardly walk, and look at me now!" He lifted his axe and split a heavy oak log.

"I'm impressed," said Ranko.

"Oh, it's not that impressive, it's a trick, basically. See, the logs were wet and they froze, so they crack like glass. I tried to split some of them before they froze, and I couldn't. I bet you could. . . ."

"I better not try," said Ranko.

Ranko saw several other hale men who had received heart transplants. One of them played tennis, another rode horses, and the third one went grouse hunting and invited him along. Ranko wondered how one could wish to kill after barely surviving, but then, he was not that man, and he always liked to see the differences; he enjoyed the peculiarities of human natures.

He wondered how many men with transplants he could not see because they had died; the physicians' successes parade on the crust of the earth, and their failures rot in it, as the saying goes. Still, Ranko was encouraged, doubly. First, that his surgeon went out of his way to organize the tour, which meant he was serious in planning to get a heart for Ranko, and second, that apparently one could live so well, normally, with a transplanted heart.

Whenever the phone rang, Ranko and Lana sprang up with anticipation, fear, and hope. Fear, for this might mean the call, the heart transplant, the total anesthesia, cutting open of the rib cage, cutting and cutting . . . and then, perhaps coming back to life, real life. At first they sat close to the green phone. But it was only friends calling. Well, not only. Friends made it worthwhile to suffer the pain of survival. Otherwise, he could curl up and die. Oh, it would be so easy to slip away: in the many moments of exquisite feebleness, as he drifted into sleep and out of it, in the morning, at noon, all day long.

But one day, he did get the call, at six in the morning, the most odious hour of the day to him, when he could not sleep and when he could not wake up. But this time, he was deeply asleep, and the ringing pierced through him. He propped himself up on his right elbow while Lana, stark naked, strangely white, jumped out of bed, and picked up the phone.

"It's for you. Rebro Hospital."

He pulled his pants up so hurriedly that his pubic hair got caught in the zipper; he'd had no time to find his underwear. They were already in the car, on the road. He was short of breath, and had chest pains, as though already feeling the knife cutting through him. He glanced at his wife behind the wheel; her small and pointed breasts were both visible from his angle as she had forgotten to button. He wondered whether that would be the last image of her that he'd carry.

They drove fast, nearly hitting a drunk pedestrian. "Watch out," he said, "I don't want his heart!"

"Why not? It's pickled, well preserved."

She sped up. "If you keep it up," he said, "there'll be too many hearts available!"

Once they got in, Ranko was sent into a room where there was another man, with a bandage over his head and another one over his abdomen.

The surgeon came in.

"So, where is the heart?" Ranko asked, and felt his own producing many extra beats, and some of them may not have been beats, but flutters and even shudders.

"Yeah, we got it, it just needs to be prepared for you."

The surgeon hasn't answered my question, he thought.

Where do they have it? Not in a freezer, though you never know.

"It's not quite ready yet. You can relax. It will take a couple of hours or days for us to have it ready. And you never know, maybe it won't be quite right."

"I thought you didn't wait with hearts."

"Now relax, get a book you like . . . you have a book?"

"No."

Well, then, I can recommend one. *I Served the King of England* by Bohumil Hrabal. Very funny."

"That's been out for years."

"You've read it?"

"No."

"So . . . don't complain. I'll bring it along. Ciao."

A nurse—her face had the pasty color of lasagna, with a flash of red on her lips, like a layer of tomato sauce—gave Ranko a sedative. And so he fell asleep.

Loud moaning woke him up. His roommate was suffering loudly.

"What's hurting you?" asked Ranko.

"What's not hurting me? Even my nails and my hair hurt." His voice was hissy and guttural, as though he'd lost half of his vocal cords.

"What's your illness?"

"Illness? I was shot. One bullet in the head, one in the abdomen." He groaned. "I shouldn't talk. It hurts."

"Who shot you?'

"I have no idea."

"What did they shoot you for?"

"How would I know? All these war idiots with guns on the

loose. A couple of jerks shot me because I took their parking spot. I didn't even see them. They'd waited to back into the spot. I thought I was dead—well, I can't last much longer."

"Keep up the faith. I thought it was too late for me, but I believed."

"Believed in what? I am not religious. I can't believe."

"I am not either, but after my heart attack, even though I was told I had less than a year to live, well, I began to believe in my family, and love kept me going, and now it's been more than a year . . . and I am waiting for a heart transplant."

"Good luck on that. It doesn't sound like fun, but then, if you ask me, I wouldn't mind being in your place. At this rate, they probably need to transplant my brain. Do you know whether they do that?" He moaned again. "And the worst of it is that you'd think the pain would entertain me, you know. But I am bored."

"Let's play chess," Ranko said.

"Not a bad idea, but do you have a board?"

"I'll call my wife." Ranko pulled out his cell phone—they were among the first ones in Zagreb to get one; he needed it in case a heart appeared and he was out of doors, and now it was good for keeping in touch with Lana.

The bandaged man, David, could hardly lift his arm, and so he told Ranko his moves. They played imaginative games, full of sacrifices for combination's sake, as though being close to death taught them not to fear losses but to seek moments of beauty. Propped on his pillow, his face sunken and ashen, David looked exhausted, but now, when he saw a combination, his one eye that was not bandaged opened wider, light reflected from it, color came to his cheeks (or perhaps the blood from his bandage lent the color); he seemed to be coming to life. "I love chess!" he said. "It's worth living for more than love."

"But you just said you love it, so love it is," said Ranko.

"All right, I conceded that, but I won't cede the pawn."

"Do you have any kids?"

"Yes, five beautiful daughters. They are in Split, and, unfortunately, I don't live with them. I drank too much, so my wife chased me out. Here, would you like to see a picture of my youngest? Ouch, where is my wallet?" He couldn't turn. "Oh well, next time."

"I can get it, just tell me where it is."

"Usually I wouldn't trust anybody with my credit cards, but the hospital already ran those . . . I am sure they're maxed. So go ahead, it's under my pillow."

Ranko slid his hand carefully, and fished out the wallet, and soon, he was looking at a picture of the man and his five daughters, all looking like his replicas, in different sizes. His hair was long and black, he was lean, and so were they. "Why isn't your wife with you in the picture?"

"She's the photographer."

"Self-sacrificing of her."

"I wouldn't say that. She spent thousands of marks on photography, and I bought her the best equipment. She fancied herself a pro—she's good, I must admit—but who can be a pro in this country?"

When the surgeon came by, and saw them, with Ranko sitting on a chair at David's bedside, and David propped up, he was startled. The surgeon looked confused for a second, and said, "David, that's just great. Here, I was going to check . . .

oh, never mind. Just great. Still, what are the two of you doing? You should not be exhausting each other! Ranko, please let him rest."

"Chess is not tiring," said Ranko.

"It's a sport," said the surgeon. "Mental sport. David's brain mustn't work too hard now. Who knows what tricks. . . . Look at Karpov, how thin and exhausted he looks."

As they talked, David fell asleep; he snored, a thin, weak snore, breathing shallow.

"So where is that mysterious heart?" asked Ranko. "In the freezer?"

"No, still in a rib cage," said the surgeon, winked, and pointed with his blue chin toward David.

"What? You are going to tear his heart out to give it to me?"

"He should have been dead by now. I wonder how he hangs in."

"Chess keeps him going, he loves chess."

"Don't play it with him then. He's going to die soon anyway—I don't see how he could recover—but you don't want it to go on too long, for his heart might deteriorate, and it won't do you any good."

Ranko watched David, feeling like a predator. He would have liked getting an abstract heart, a heart from a laboratory, even an electronic computerized heart, better than to wait for a friend's heart, for by now David had become his friend. What a crazy thing, to wait for a friend to die, to want it to happen quickly. On the other hand, David was in pain, and maybe a fast death would be the best for him, for both of them. Should he tell David about this? David must know, he must have volunteered his heart.

Should he go over to David's side, and just choke him? That would put him out of misery, and his heart would still be good. Then he could call the doctors. How many minutes did they have after the clinical death for the heart to still be good?

He was ashamed of his thought. But maybe it was his only chance to remain alive himself. The Satan of survival must have whispered that thought to him. Didn't Satan in the Garden of Eden promise immortality, or were there two trees, one with the knowledge of good and evil, and the other, with eternal life. Eve ate the wrong apple. But maybe it was a heart she needed. Maybe there was a tree on which hearts grew. Apples look like hearts anyway. He looked again at David, listened to his troubled and wet breathing, and imagined there was a good heart there, a heart that could beat in his own chest. He shuddered with revulsion at the thought. So it's not only the tissue that rejects the foreign organ, it's the mind, or probably primarily the mind, which suffuses the body. Each time he looked at David's rib cage, he winced. His wince became a tick.

Lana brought him a small stereo system and a few CDs. "You don't mind if I play some music softly?" he asked David.

"What kind?"

"Bach and stuff like that."

"I never went in for classical music, but maybe I'll like it now. I never gave it a shot, was too busy."

Ranko played Piano Concerto No. 4 by Beethoven. David soon fell asleep. Ranko used to love the allegro movements most of all, but now he preferred the adagio. Everything about him was a bit slower now. Even his laughter had a slower rhythm, his conversation did too—it was as though he had slowed the harmony of an orchestra to adagio, to savor each note, to get the feeling out of each string, to let it be . . . to give up.

David awoke and smiled. "Man, that is beautiful. If I could live again, I'd listen to this before falling asleep every night, I swear."

"But wait till you hear this one!" Ranko played Dvorak's Cello Concerto, with Rostropovich.

"That's gorgeous, my God," David said. During the second movement, tears flowed down his cheeks.

"What's the matter?"

"Don't you hear it? It's a funeral march. I heard that melody at my father's funeral—a brass band played it. They missed many notes, but that made it all the sadder, like the world was falling apart, and it was. He fell into the sea while fishing and drowned; probably died of a heart attack before he drowned. I hope he did, though I don't know what difference it would make now."

"Sorry," Ranko said.

"I remember how he taught me snorkeling when I was five—he held me under my ribs, they tickled, I struggled not to laugh, and when I opened my eyes, there was a whole dark heaven below us with yellow and blue fish shooting across like shooting stars and comets. That made the world right for me: a slow heaven above and a fast one below. And I remember how I used to sit on his knee, and he sang about . . ."

Suddenly, two male nurses opened and banged the doors. They grabbed David and carried him away while he swore.

"But wait, he's alive! Where are you taking him?" said Ranko.

"He needs treatment," one of them said.

Are they going to kill him? To bring me his heart? The idea chilled Ranko. Did his friends and his wife pay the bribe after all, a payment which bought David's speedy exodus from life? Do the doctors send people into the parking lots to shoot robust looking men for their organs? Or maybe they could help David after all?

A day passed, and David hadn't returned. A new patient was brought in, this time, another man waiting for a heart transplant. He did not play chess, and he did not like to talk. He merely panted, wiped his sweaty forehead with the back of his swollen hand and kept repeating, Jesus, Jesus. He fingered a rosary made out of gold nuggets, small nuggets, but nevertheless, nuggets, and quickly whispered a Hail Mary.

He was overweight, unshaven, bald, with big ears. Ranko thought he recognized the face from the newspapers. Wasn't he one of the generals the government was supposed to hand over to The Hague?

As though divining his thoughts, the general looked at him fiercely, his thick and horned eyebrows adding to the menace. He buzzed for a nurse to come in, and when she did, he said, "I need a room all to myself. This is a disgrace."

"But we are short on space. Nearly all the rooms are like this, most of them have a dozen people in, and . . ."

"I want a single."

Soon, he was whisked away by a different set of male nurses.

A day later, the surgeon came to Ranko. "You are free to go home." He looked contrite.

"What happened to the heart?"

"Don't ask. It's a sad story."

"How about David, did he make it?"

"He died pretty fast. I don't think he felt a thing—he passed out and away."

"And his heart?"

"It was taken out, and transplanted."

"Transplanted? Where?"

"The idiots should have examined the heart. Instead, as soon as they could, they put it into the man who was in your room."

"But I thought I was top of the list."

"You were. But then, the man needed it more. He was in worse shape than you. And we tested it chemically; his tissue was less likely to reject that heart."

"But I have waited longer."

"I agree with you. I wanted you to have the heart. But . . . higher forces. He was an army general. Anyway, you were lucky."

"Lucky, how? How come they didn't do it in the military hospital?"

"Hearts are hard to come by."

"So how's the general doing? How much did he pay in bribes?"

"He's not doing. He's dead."

"Wow! Why, what went wrong?" Suddenly, Ranko was terrified. That could have been him. He was ready to hate the man, but now he felt some kind of sympathy, such as can be felt for the dead, more terror than compassion.

"The heart was bad."

"Did you do the transplant?"

"No, another surgeon, a military one. There were guards in front of the operating room. Not even I was allowed in during the operation. I was upset about the whole thing."

"Did David's staying alive longer ruin the heart? Did I contribute to it?"

"No, the heart was faulty to begin with. They never properly examined it. It had a perforated septum. Idiots!"

"Lucky? To wait for a surgery like this again?"

"Lucky. You are alive."

"But I won't last."

"Lord knows. If you hang in, we'll find you another heart, and I personally will examine it with isotopes. And you may luck out."

"Now this general," Ranko said, "when was he diagnosed?"

"Don't ask. I know nothing about it." The surgeon shook his head.

AT HOME, even as he poured water into a round samovar, he kept thinking. What happened? He conceived theories. One: the man in the parking lot who shot David was hired by the general, so the general could get a heart. Assassination, not politically motivated, but medically. Heart theft. And they sent in for Ranko as a decoy, so it wouldn't be all too visible what was going on. Now, that's the theory according to which the general is in control. The second theory, perhaps intertwined with the first: procuring the general a faulty heart was intentional, to engineer his death. He died in surgery and therefore did not need to be assassinated, so doubts would not be aroused that Tudjman was behind it. And Tudjman, of course, would not want a well-informed general in The Hague, who could reveal that the dictates for several atrocities came directly from Tudj-man. This is more subtle than what Milosevic did in Serbia, orchestrating a whole series of mafia-style executions, in hotel lobbies, with masked sharpshooters hitting war criminals in the head, through their eyeballs, as was the case with Arkan. But who would know about this, that it may have been an as-sassination? So they knew very well that heart was bad, they wanted it like that. They followed a man with a bad heart to make sure. David was dying too long, too. He did not look like he was dying, but who would know? Maybe his death was as-sisted? These thoughts made Ranko shiver. And maybe David too could have been a witness, and his assassination was a real one, Serbian style. Ranko's mind was going berserk. All these theories, he was getting paranoid.

Ranko was happy at home, drinking his Red Zinger. An-other day in paradise, another day on earth. There's only earth and hell, he thought. Or paradise and hospital.

"Where's your cell phone?" asked Lana.

"I threw it away."

"What for? That's a terrible waste!"

"If there's a heart, I don't want to know about it." He sighed and gasped. Although he was in paradise, he did not feel good.

Ranko drew the curtains off the window and now they both stood before the glass. Ahead of them they saw Mount Sljeme—above the pair of pointed white-stone cathedral steeples and the red roofs of the Gornji Grad, the mountain sprawled and rose above a layer of thin clouds, which skirted it. The very tip was covered with snow, and he imagined it to be so chilly that it could bring him out of his warm, humid, and sweaty medicated haze. What if he died and never touched and smelled mountain snow again? The thought filled him with longing and craving—if he could only be there, just for one hour, that would be as good as any rest of a lifetime. It would be a good way to go. "Let's go to the mountains and look for mushrooms," he said.

"Are you crazy, in this cold weather?"

"Yes, especially in this cold. There are oyster mushrooms, growing out of dead trees, out of beeches, wonderfully new, cool, snowy, crystalline." He wheezed and whispered and moved closer to her ear, and looked at her lobe, where a small crystal earring flickered; the ear appeared to him to be an oyster mushroom, twisted and fanned out, and it even smelled like soiled forest winds in the winter. He leaned closer and nibbled on her ear.

Snow Powder

*L*arge snowflakes floated in the wind like dove feathers. Mirko leaned his head against the windowpane and gazed up the hill into the mountains shrouded in the pale clouds and snow, and he grew joyfully dizzy.

He stumbled to the basement and waited for his eyes to get used to the dark, with a few streaks of light hitting a sack of sprouting potatoes. His skis emerged out of the dark and shone seemingly by an independent source of beige light from within, from the soul of the old wood. Mirko gingerly touched these smooth ghosts of former winters and took them up the stairs while they clanked and fenced with each other. He waxed them with beeswax and shined them with his woolen socks. He walked to the yard gate, an old rusty squeal-making contraption on loose hinges.

Where are you going? You have to do homework and get ready for school!

Mommy, look at all that beautiful snow.

Yes, I understand that. But you got math to do.

I am good at math.

You won't be if you don't keep up.

Mirko ran into the yard and skied between the woodshed and the former goat stall. The town ordinance no longer allowed keeping goats within town limits. Just two blocks away, one could keep goats.

The moist chill on his cheeks and the snow behind his shirt collar gave him a delicious shiver.

Soon, Boro, his younger brother, joined him, and they enjoyed a snowball fight until their fingers turned red and sore. Mirko laughed at Boro because his face had turned into a semblance of a red and green apple—green chin and lips and red cheeks and nose.

Later, Mirko walked to school, with his fingers itching even under his fingernails in the gloves. The first class was his favorite, geography. He knew all the highest peaks on every continent, the longest rivers, the deepest ocean trenches. The topic was Antarctica and the global warming effect. The teacher, Medic, an elderly woman with gray hair and small eyes, which gleamed from a reddish darkness of swollen eyelids, kept talking about how Western industrial nations had been trapping heat within the atmosphere.

Does it mean the highest peak will go down? Mirko asked. Now it's 4,987 meters high.

That's an interesting question, she said. We'll have to figure it out.

But it's made of rock, unlike the North Pole.

Bravo. So it won't go down with the melting.

Maybe it will, he said. How many feet that make the top are made of ice or glacier?

We'd have to look it up.

And if the ice melts all over the world, the sea level will rise, and so that'll cut down the space above the sea level, too, won't it?

You are right about that, she said. Brilliant for a ten-year-old. I am going to give you an A for this.

She opened the grade book and with her trembling and swollen hand she wrote a large A in red.

But that did not make Mirko happy—the world was melting away; what was a grade compared with the world? He gazed through the windows and watched the thickly falling snow. Tree branches were covered with it, the top half white, the bottom brown—darker than usual because it was wet—divided like a flag. He wondered whether there was a flag in that color combination and couldn't think of any. And why wouldn't there be a flag, half white and half black? What would it symbolize? Peace and death? Peaceful death? Deadly peace? Surrender and go to church? None of it sounded appealing.

The evergreens, white and green, made the right color combination for a flag, but not the right shape, with snow-laden branches bending.

The bell rang for the recess. He hopped down the wooden stairs, which squeaked and thudded and sang, as though his feet were fingertips bouncing on worn and untuned piano keys. In the schoolyard, he kneeled and hugged snow into a little heap, which he then squeezed with his palms and rolled. The wet snow made a quickly growing ball after which the cobbled pavement was laid bare, in an ever larger trail.

Suddenly an iced snowball hit him on his right ear so that it rang with a brimming pain, and a high pitch, like that of a struck tuning fork, remained in his ear. He got up to see who threw the ball, but he couldn't. A boy grabbed him from behind, and pulled him down to the ground. Another one punched him and shouted, That'll teach you, you nerd, to show off in class.

Is that what you do, just read books? No wonder you're so weak!

He wiggled to get out from under them.

The bell rang to signal the end of the recess.

The boys got up. Mirko ran after them and tripped the slower one, who fell right in front of the math teacher, a chubby, red-faced man with white hair.

The teacher scrutinized the boys, lit his grainy cigarette with a match, waved the flame quickly out of its life after which a trail of thin sulphurous smoke remained and he went on his way to the classroom without a word. The boys followed, inhaling the incendiary and unfiltered aroma of his anger.

Stand up, you Maric, the teacher called, and blew out thick white smoke, which seemed to make his white hair expand, while his red face diminished almost to the red center of an enlivened cigarette tip.

Mirko did.

Is that the way to behave?

The boy who fell sobbed and wiped his cheeks but there were no tears on them.

Teacher, the two of them attacked me during the recess and I tried to get back at them.

That's a fine way to go. Let me see your homework.

I forgot my notebook at home.

But you did the homework? All right, then you know how to do complex division, expressing the remainder in decimals. Come to the blackboard and let's see whether you've learned anything.

Mirko stood in front of the blackboard, trying to ignore the incessant tuning fork pitch in his ear, and perhaps because of the pitch, he had no stage fright. He solved the problem accurately.

Nerd, nerd! the boys shouted.

Just ignore them, said the teacher and slid his yellow fingers into Mirko's uncombed curly brown hair, and he ruffled his hair in this nicotined blessing so much that Mirko felt static in his scalp, a manifestation of pride, which traveled down his spine and decayed into revulsion low in his abdomen.

Mirko looked into the rows of kids, and saw his favorite girl, Bojana, smile at him. He was blissful as he looked into her green eyes framed by black lashes.

During the break, he followed Bojana outside.

Let's see who can swoosh a better angel, she said.

She fell backward in the snow and closed her eyes, and flapped her arms like a bird.

Her long lips slightly parted and revealed snow white teeth, so it looked as though the snow around her was also in her, especially when she opened her eyes; the whites of her eyes were purely white. There was a wonderful iciness about her.

Your turn! she said. Close your eyes and imagine you are flying to the Lord.

He gladly obeyed, and kept splashing the snow, when suddenly he felt moist tingling on his lips. He opened his eyes, and she leaped away.

I told you to keep your eyes closed! she said. She was flushed in her face.

He wiped his lips and looked at his hands as though there should be blood or honey on them.

It would have lasted longer if you had kept your eyes closed.

Did you kiss me? he asked.

Yes, did you like it? I bet you've never kissed before.

No. Have you?

Yes, just now. I thought it was high time that I have the first kiss. After the age of ten, it's almost too late. You'd have to be embarrassed not to have done it.

She shoveled snow with her open palms onto his face. Now no matter what happens in our lives, we'll always be the first, you know that? We'll never forget it.

Do you want to do it again?

No, not today. It's too early for the second kiss. That can wait for a year.

And she ran away, laughing.

MIRKO RUSHED HOME, skipping steps through flurries, a richer man than before, with more world around him, and a better and greater world it was, just as an orange is bigger unpeeled than peeled. It was as though the world, a peeled orange that had dried and grown bitter, had got back its skin and freshness, a chance to be juicy again. He savored the crunching sound and tried to make a melody out of it by crunching the snow slowly and quickly, gently and roughly. He picked a little snow from an evergreen branch and ate it. He buried his face in it. Snow, heavenly snow.

That evening his father, Zvonko, arrived from Germany. Business at home had been so bad that nobody wanted mechanical watches and everybody got cheap quartz ones from China at street markets, and so he went to Germany once a month for a week, to sell old watches and clocks at antique fairs.

It took me ages to get here, Father said. So many roads are blocked, Serbs had taken so much land, that I felt like a fly entering a bottle through a rotten cork. But you all have been fine?

Thank God, said his wife, Neda. People here get along pretty well. We aren't like those madmen in eastern Bosnia; we don't care who's who.

You think?

Zvonko gave Mirko's brother Boro various coins—several ten-franc pieces, with yellow brassy circles and nickel insides, from a fair in Strasbourg; a five-German-mark coin; a five-Swiss-franc coin with a thick cross on a shield; Italian liras . . . now Boro piled them up into little towers and asked how much each was worth in dinars.

You can't do that in dinars, Mirko said. The dinar is worthless. Do it in German marks.

Good advice, said Zvonko. A German mark is worth three francs and one thousand liras.

Are Italians the poorest if their money is worth so little? asked Boro.

No, they just like a lot of zeros. In Italy everybody is a millionaire.

AFTER SUPPER, the father and his sons went outdoors, and built a snowman. Zvonko used two old irreparable watches as the snowman's eyes.

The following morning, Mirko was awakened by his father's kiss over his ear. That kiss triggered his inner tuning fork. The lights were on. Mirko jumped out of bed to see whether the snow was still there.

Don't worry, the snowman is going nowhere, Zvonko said.

The previous year, Mirko had cried when his snowman melted, and he still kept the shrunken snowman the size of an Egyptian mummified kitten in a Ziploc bag in the freezer. Death of his snowman had grieved him for days. The fact that snow everywhere had melted was bad enough, but that his friend, whose soul was made out of snow, would also melt and vanish, and had, hurt him. But this time, Mirko was not getting attached to the new snowman, even if his watch eyes had stalled the time perhaps from before Mirko's birth, perhaps from before the real global warming effect, when winters were continuous howling snowstorms, and the world a pattern of shifting snowdrifts. Oh, how lucky my great-grandparents must have been, he thought, but then remembered that they had been slaughtered by Serbs in the Second Balkan War, in the winter.

Have you done your homework? his father asked.

We had none.

How nice!

Is it all right if I go to school on my skis?

Do you have a place to hide them?

I'll bring them into the classroom and keep them behind the stove.

Mirko put his ski shoes on and clipped them onto the skis, and with the schoolbag at his back, he started toward the school, but as he rounded the first corner out of Father's sight, he went on, up the hill, through the park, over the trails where he had played Robin Hood during the summer. He found it awkward and painful to go up the hill waddling like a duck, so he took off the skis and carried them, but they separated from one another and dangled and resumed their old fencing match. To handle them better, he got rid of his schoolbag, which he hid in a bush. He climbed high into the hill, reaching the dazzling line of daytime, a storm of light of the rising sun, capping the dark blue below, and he slid down back into the slumbering morning on his skis. He kept his balance, and rode in terror, delicious terror, that he would fall, shatter his bones, fly . . . and he did fly over uneven spots. The cold moist air and granulated snow smarted his face and chilled his ears. To stop, he deliberately fell into a snowdrift, and he climbed the hill again. This time he would go to the top, into the mountain, and he'd ski down for more than a kilometer. He panted as he went up, and ate snow because he was thirsty.

Stoj! a voice shouted. Halt!

Mirko looked around but saw nothing.

He rubbed his eyes, and when he opened them again, he faced several men in camouflage with patterns of green and brown, which visually merged with the sickly evergreens behind them, as though the men too had been eaten by acid rain, or as though the acid-bitten trees had begun to move and chatter and threaten, behaving like mirage soldiers.

What are you doing up here? a soldier said. You got me so startled I almost shot you!

Really? Mirko said. Why would you do that?

Nice skis, where did you get those?

From Germany. My Dad works there.

For those Nazis? Let's make a deal: I'll give you my gun, and you give me your skis and boots, how is that?

No way, said Mirko.

What do you mean, No way? I can take your skis if I like. You are our prisoner, a POW, don't you know that?

Prisoner? That's exciting, Mirko said.

We'll make sure it's exciting.

I don't mind that if you let me ski.

But if we let you, you'll ski all the way down to the village, and you'll tell everybody we are here.

No, I won't.

All right, we'll let you go if you come back with a flask of plum brandy.

What if I don't come back?

Let me show you something. The soldier led Mirko to a cannon on wheels and slid a missilelike bomb into the pipe. See, it even has a telescope so strong that you can see the rings of Saturn at night if you like. You want to take a look? Show me your house in the valley. When you look at it, it'll feel like you are right there.

That one, with the green roof, Mirko said.

All right, we'll have to adjust the scope angle. There. So

now when you go back down there, if you tell anybody we are up here, we can blow you up, is that clear?

You tricked me.

You are a good boy, I have one at home just like you. Nothing will happen to you, just remember to bring the brandy.

MIRKO TOOK A magnificent glide down the mountain, splashing snow left and right; the snow clouds that burst up from under him filled with sunlight, refracting fleeting rainbow fragments.

The following day, it rained, so it was not a good day to ski, but looking up the mountain, Mirko imagined that it snowed up there. Yes, for every one hundred meters, you lose one degree Celsius. You gain snow. He wanted to go up the mountain, but not today. He longed to see Bojana, to smell her cheeks. As he walked, he looked over the minaret and a church dome into the mountain, and for the first time ever, he felt guilty that he was going to school. That was truly irresponsible of him; what if the soldiers up there got angry that they had run out of brandy and bombed the town? They could kill his parents, his brother; their bomb could strike any moment in the streets and tear him to pieces. For a moment, he hesitated; of course, he should rush home and save the town. It would be terrible if they all died simply because he wanted to look at Bojana's face. But it would be almost as terrible not to see her face.

At the beginning of the math class, he was tempted to tell everybody that they were encircled by a Serb army, that any moment the bombing could start, that they were all in mortal danger, and that the only way out of it was to collect plum brandy and haul it up into the mountain. He enjoyed the power of his knowledge. He would not tell them, not just yet.

He gazed blissfully out the window. Having missed a day, he also missed homework. The math teacher checked homework, and Mirko tried the old maneuver—he'd forgotten the notebook at home.

Awfully forgetful at your age, that's no good, said the teacher. Now, at my age it would make sense. All right, prove at the blackboard you did your homework.

He gave Mirko the assignment, to divide 44.29 into 682.91.

Mirko was hesitant. He'd never done a division like that, and didn't know what to do with the decimal points. He remembered the buzz in his ears, but there was none. His knees shook, and to steady them, he tightened his legs and stood up straight and stiffened. The class laughed. They all seemed to relish the fact that he couldn't do the math. He looked for sympathy in Bojana, but she'd joined in the mob lynching by laughter.

All right, do it without the decimal points, the teacher said. You get those out, and the proportion stays the same. Do it now.

Through tears, Mirko couldn't see very well. The class still jeered. He got so flustered that he forgot which way to go, from left to right or right to left.

Get lost, said the teacher. Before you fight with boys, just get lost. Go home and do your homework. No wonder we have wars here, when you all grow up like thugs. Why can't you boys get together to do math? Or play chess? Just ten years ago, kids played chess everywhere, and now, I never see a kid with a chessboard.

Till the end of the class, Mirko stared at the low drifting clouds, his face still brimming and hot. He imagined washing his face in the snow, cooling his cheeks off.

He was sitting close to the tile furnace, in which coal burned; there was a large woven basket full of coal in front of it. The side of his face closer to the stove was hot, and the slight smoke stung his eyes. The tiles crackled, and he wondered whether the heat did it; he knew that it made some things expand, and others shrink. He wondered what the heat did to the rocks, and how global warming would affect the mountains. Would they all grow? Wasn't it true that the tallest mountains were close to the equator? Or was that because of the rotation of the globe? Or both? And why was it that Mars, which was a little smaller and rotated faster than Earth, had a mountain twice as high as Mount Everest? Was that mountain close to the equator of Mars? He got so absorbed in his thoughts that he did not notice when the class was over.

Look at our genius, said one of the boys. What do you think goes on in his head now?

He's probably figuring out what two times two equals.

Mirko heard that but did not bother to answer the provocations.

During the break, he walked by himself. He looked around for Bojana, but he couldn't see her in the crowds of kids.

What are you looking for, my friend? Toni, the best soccer player in the class, asked. Your little girlfriend? Come, I'll show where she is.

He looked where Toni was pointing, to the old chestnut tree. Bojana was leaning against the tree with her back, and Stevo, the class goalie, was kissing her.

Toni jeered. So, what is two plus one?

Bojana saw him over Stevo's shoulder, and then closed her eyes and kissed more strongly than before.

Mirko did not know how to respond. Should he go and fight Stevo, defend his honor and love, defend her? But she was not reluctant; she put her arms behind Stevo's neck and pulled him to her. When the bell rang, Stevo walked ahead of her, not looking at Mirko, clearly not wishing any fight. She walked behind him, smiling, her lips scarlet, her cheeks and eyes full of light, viciously beautiful so that even at that moment Mirko marveled at her and loved her.

You know what? she said. We didn't do it right. We just lip-kissed, which doesn't count. You got to tongue-kiss, deep French kiss, that counts. You just saw my first real kiss! It's wonderful, so much better than lip-kissing, you got to try it one day when you grow up.

Mirko did not respond. He did not walk on, but continued standing and staring at the tree as though he could still see what he should have been doing. He did not go back to the classroom. He left his books there. On the way home, he was out of breath although he walked slowly.

In the streets, soldiers drove in regular cars, mostly VWs. That was something new—by the flags some displayed on their uniforms, it was clear this was the new Bosnian army. Did they know about his friends in the hills? Would there be fighting? He hoped there would be.

AT HOME, he stole a bottle of plum brandy from the pantry, from among the jars of plum jam and pickled peppers. The bottle clanked against the jars, but nothing broke.

His father caught him outside.

You are too little to be interested in brandy. What do you think you are doing?

I need it. If I hurt myself skiing, I can clean my wound with this.

Don't lie, you little thief. I'll teach you to steal!

And his father, who had not spanked him in years, twisted his arms, nearly breaking them, and then beat him with his thick Western belt, which he had pulled out of his blue jeans. His blue jeans fell back to his knees, and he stood in his white underwear, belting his son's back, sprawled over unsplit beech logs, which smelled of oyster mushrooms and soil, the smells being enhanced in the snow through Mirko's gasps and steamy breath.

Cry, you little bastard.

But Mirko would not cry. He ground his teeth; he'd rather die than surrender. It struck him as immensely unjust that he was being punished by the man he was about to save. His father could not know that his son was saving him, but now Mirko would not tell him, out of spite. If Father could not suspect good intentions, if he needed to talk and accuse, the hell with him. Mirko did not cry, but tears blurred his vision, and the silvery logs and the snowman with watchful eyes and the whole sunstruck yard broke apart in shafts of light in the diamond splendor of his pain. The beauty of it all surprised him, and so he even welcomed the scorching licks of ox leather on his skin.

His mother shouted from the house door. Stop it, you old beast! Stop it! She came down the cement stairs in her wooden shoes and pushed her husband away. She carried

Mirko to his bed, and used the plum brandy to wash the stripes on his back.

No, don't do that, Mirko said. I am not bleeding.

Yes, but you are all striped, like a little tiger.

For a day, he stayed in bed, on his belly because of his sore back. He imagined his classmates going to school, playing and laughing. The soldiers probably still walked in the street. Would the artillery men wait for one more day? He expected a grenade to strike any moment, but he was not afraid.

In the morning, before dawn, he was surprised that no bombing had taken place. But if he undertook nothing, the house would be wiped out. He took the nearly full bottle of plum brandy and his skis, and walked out onto the mountain, which in the predawn light looked all blue. Halfway up the mountain, he stuck his skis into a snow covered bush, leaving only the curved tips out. Maybe he'd pick them up on the way back if he ever came back.

By the time he reached the Serb bunkers, sun had cast an orange hue layering it over the blue of the slopes, while the valley still lounged in the hazy indigo. The soldiers were happy to see him with the bottle, which they passed around, emptying the contents within a minute. Good timing, boy, said one of the soldiers. We plan to start blasting your town and we worried about you.

It's so great to see you! said another soldier, and he slapped Mirko on the shoulder. Mirko winced and groaned.

What's the matter? You can't take a little bit of patting?

I am sore, I fell while skiing last time and scraped myself. Let's see your back.

Mirko struggled not to take his shirt off, but then thought

better of it; let them see, let them understand that living at home was hell. He took off the flannel shirt and the sleeveless undershirt, and shivered.

My God, said one of them, that's no skiing injury, that's a regular old-fashioned belting. That's how my father used to beat me, and see what good effect that had on me. Poor thing.

The soldiers gathered and examined the swollen welts.

What did he beat you for?

Plum brandy. He thought I was drinking it myself.

When you go down there again, just buy brandy in a store, all right? You don't need to irritate your dad. Here, I'll give you thirty marks, and you buy me coffee and plum brandy.

I am not going back there anymore. I am joining you.

You want to fight against your town?

Yes, I have declared war on them already. They don't know it yet, but they will.

Well, run away from home for two, three days, just to make them nervous so they'll love you again, but don't overdo it.

The artillery man, who was chewing a strip of bacon, sat him down on his knee and showed him his town through the scope.

At the sight of the school, Mirko gasped. Let's shoot, he said.

What if there are children there, you'd like to kill them?

I'd like to destroy the building. It's Saturday, nobody is there now.

How do you know? Maybe the cleaning women are washing the stairway or something . . .

I doubt it. The stairway hasn't been cleaned in ages; they just don't do that.

Do you want to wait for Monday? That could work better—you could get them all!

No. Let's just smash that ugly school right away.

Maybe you'll have your way. The captain has selected a few targets, the metal factory, the railway station, and yes, the school. The school, he thinks, could already be full of soldiers because of the thick walls. We can aim for the windows, blast inside.

The artillery man called his assistant over, to adjust the projectiles. The captain came by, and nodded. Yes, that's a good idea. We've waited long enough. Go ahead!

Now, my boy, the artillery man said, I've already taught you how to aim the scope—so do it.

Mirko adjusted the scope to the tall black window in the middle of the yellow building, on the second floor. As soon as he saw the window, he recalled all the humiliation he'd endured: the math teacher, the boys who attacked him, the girl who played love games, which were actually, he was sure, hate games. Now he would show her, him, them. They would never gather in that room again, he'd make sure of that. The stove, the blackboard, everything must go. The creeps can gather for school in the basements, below taverns, and enjoy the restroom smells.

The artillery man right next to him breathed heavily, and coughed; his breath smelled of garlic, so Mirko breathed shallow, at least tried to, but couldn't because his heart pounded and he panted from the excitement, desire and trepidation. He trembled, and did not know whether from fear or the cold. His teeth chattered, the ear buzzed, the tuning fork resurrected itself in his ear and chimed a high C, which darkened the yellow valley.

Here, have the earphones, said the man to Mirko.

No, I'd like to enjoy the full blast.

Your eardrums would rupture. Put it on, be a good boy. Do you want music piped in? You could watch your school blow up with your favorite piece of music in the background. What's your favorite music? Maybe we got it? We got Jimi Hendrix, "Machine Gun." I loved that stuff when I was your age.

Explosions, that's my favorite music.

Okay, you got it. You know, we've all been waiting for this moment, and it's just a lucky synchronicity.

What's synchronicity?

You'll find out in due time.

A few seconds later, a powerful blast shook Mirko. The cannon recoiled, emitted fire and smoke, and ten seconds later, there was another blast, a smaller one, at the school. The sound from there came shortly afterward, as a small echo.

Again! he shouted. And that was the loveliest morning he had ever spent. His bones had been shaken, even his teeth, in such a way that his bones felt happy, hale, for a moment at least, until a dread descended onto him. He tasted the dread as smoke and diesel in the back of his nose, thickly descending into his throat and stinging. He looked down into the valley, into the smoke, which grew higher and wider. What if a class had gathered for an extracurricular activity, such as acting or dancing or singing? Did Bojana go to those clubs? What if he had just turned her beautiful red lips into blood? He no longer hated her, no longer wanted revenge. What if he'd just become a mass murderer? Could he go back and live in the town again? Could he walk in the town as though nothing had happened, and worry about decimal point divisions, the quality of snow, and the shine on his skis? Would he walk around wrapped up in a cloud of gun smoke which would never leave him?

No, he would not go back to study at school torture chambers to become a scientist or an engineer in many years. He could become a soldier right away, going from mountain top to mountain top, blasting away. He had found the best job in the world for a boy.

Tchaikovsky's Bust

When I suggested traveling to Russia by myself, my family was in an uproar.

We are all going, said my wife, Joan.

Russia is just not safe for kids, I objected. There's too much pollution. One guidebook suggests taking along a Geiger counter to see how often it goes off while you walk around St. Petersburg. Kids can get food poisoning, the hospitals aren't safe—they reuse needles. And the hotel has lead paint half an inch thick cracking on all the windows.

Oh, don't give me that. We've been there two times, and we just loved walking everywhere—the palaces, the canals, museums, festivals, White Nights—and the kids got so much stimulation that they visibly grew. And if it's so bad, why would you go?

Well, professionally, it's important. I'll meet a lot of writers and artists and get new ideas.

No way, said Joan. You aren't going. I know how Russian women behave. After your trip alone you used to get bunches of postcards in Cyrillic. Who knows what they said.

Oh, that was ten years ago. All they wanted was exit visas.

And they were willing to do pretty much anything to get them?

I don't know. I didn't test them.

No, Daddy cannot go, said my son, Alex. He can't walk straight when he drinks, and there's way too much traffic in St. Petersburg.

That's right, Joan laughed. Too much traffic. I still remember your talking to that slut in German.

I remember hardly a thing.

Case in point.

The mistrust was my fault, no doubt about it. First time we were there, on our first day in St. Petersburg, Boris, our host, could not find a restaurant although he claimed he knew the city like the back of his palm, and we sat at an outdoor bar, near the Bronze Horseman monument. I drank three drafts of local beer, Baltika #9, and got so wasted that I was sure the beer was fortified with grain alcohol. On an empty stomach with jetlag, dizzy from the drink, I fell into a conversation in German with a woman who sat at a table next to ours in such a way that I couldn't recall when and how the conversation started. She was with a boyfriend, but she ignored him . . . after a while, everybody, including Boris, wanted the woman and me to quit talking, but we wouldn't. Hey, man, this is not decent.

I imagine so, I said, but it's nice to speak German. It's been years.

But you are in Russia.

Believe it or not, I am aware of that.

From the beer, I had to make a few runs to the bushes nearby, and Joan, who'd also had a few and laughed with her neighbors at the other table, sought an indoor restroom. And so it happened that Joan's purse was cleaned of all the money in it, some eighty dollars.

Now I told Joan, The woman or her boyfriend emptied your handbag, and stole your money. I think she talked with me for the money.

And what were you talking to her for?

Sheer drunken unconsciousness.

There was more to it than that, but the drunken part, too, is worrisome.

I agree. I'll work at it.

The evening had been enjoyable nevertheless. While we walked back to the hotel, I staggered next to the walls and bounced off them on Nevsky. Even though it was White Nights, at two in the morning it got dark. White Nights, as far as I was concerned, were a tourist fraud, like nearly everything in St. Petersburg. Alex was pushing me along, laughing and calling me a stupid drunk.

And so I now lost the argument. I would take my family along, and be a good dad, and drink hardly at all. And I was a good dad as soon as we got there. I took Alex to several concerts and museums, and I spent my time teaching at Herzen, mostly nonfiction writing. I did not manage to do as much for our daughter, Tina, as I had for Alex, primarily because she was too little to go to concerts and not disrupt them. But she wept to go to a ballet and could not be stopped.

Tina had always danced. Before she could stand, she would hold onto the kitchen table and bob to the rhythm of music on the radio. When she learned to walk, pretty soon she grew to prefer walking on tiptoe. Her heels rarely touched the floor. I don't know where she picked up that style of walking—whether she had seen a tape with ballet dancers, or whether she had stepped on bits of gravel and other prickly debris that now and then found their way to our floor.

I wanted to buy tickets to *Swan Lake,* but the ticket salesman told us that Tina was too little to be trusted to stay quiet for three hours. I could understand that. Tina could throw a temper tantrum in public shamelessly, extremely loudly. So my wife and I explained to Tina that unfortunately we could not see *Swan Lake* with her. She would probably be too loud and talk too much. She said, I will not shout. I will whisper.

Oh, no, you never know what you will say. Sometimes you swear.

Whenever she grew angry, she used a whole array of foul curses, such as I could not decently put on the page. That wouldn't go over big in a theater, I believe. She picked up the swear words from Alex's older friends, not me. At least I believe that.

No, I will not swear, and I will be quiet, she said.

How do you know?

I will sleep. Let me go, I will not talk and I will sleep.

Namely, Alex had fallen asleep at one concert of Bach's *Well-Tempered Clavier,* performed immaculately by Vladimir Feltsman. And so Tina understood that one slept at concerts.

That Tina argued her case so thoroughly made me wish all the more to take her to the ballet. But at *Romeo and Juliet* by Sergei Prokofiev, which I saw with my son, I could not see anyone younger than six at the Mariinsky Theater. Unstoppably she danced around the apartment, hopping, kicking up, and shouting, un, deux, un, deux.

While buying the tickets at the Bolshoi Theater several days in advance, I tried passing for a Russian, to get the Russian rather than the tourist rates, and this time it worked. All of us could go for ten dollars instead of fifty dollars apiece. That was the first time I had passed the test—and I credited my exhaustion after three weeks of being in Russia. I looked ill, and therefore I passed for a Russian. Or, the better and less likely interpretation is that the few words in Russian I had repeated over and over sounded Russian enough.

With trepidation, we set off for the theater. My wife would go with Alex, and I would go with Tina, since we got two pairs of tickets. We started from our temporary apartment, on the Petrograd side of the Neva. We waved down a gypsy cab, with a damaged front window and wires passing above the door to the back. The man asked for only twenty rubles, about seventy-five cents, to take us. The normal price would be forty or fifty, and some cabbies asked for a hundred as soon as they sized you up as a foreigner. That's why I made a point to speak Russian. I imagined that the Slavic accent, from Slovenia, which is pretty similar to Russian, would convince the cabbies that I was not from a prosperous country. I planned to pay him fifty. The man looked tired and sad, with deep creases on the side of his face. Soon, we got stuck on the Nevsky Bridge. The car began to overheat. It grew worse. Damned car, said the cabbie. I worried for him, and his car, and for us, that we would miss the ballet. Smoke puffed out in the front. I did not have to tell him to stop. We got out. I paid him the twenty. He said, I am sorry. I said, I am sorry too. There he sat in the middle of the bridge, in a cloud of his steam, which was surrounded by blue smoke from many cars. The stench from burning rubber of many overheating old cars, the leady smoke, the oil oozing from old military trucks with huge tires that were now used by civilians, turned our stomachs. Yui, yui, yucky smoke tastes yucky, said Tina. We walked across the bridge and looked for the cause of the stalled traffic. The crossroad's traffic moved slowly, but perseveringly, despite the red light. It seemed the traffic from one street would not let the traffic from the other proceed, and at a point the two nearly collided, but one street kept up the pressure and the courage and prevailed over the other in a strange duel of streets. We waved down another cab. *Sorok rublei.* We still had enough time to get a bite to eat. Near the Fontanka River, we went into a small café underground, and placed the order for our food, *bliny* and *palmini.* We ate quickly and rushed off to the theater. Tina rode on my shoulders. Faster, horsie, she said. She was dressed in a red dress. People smiled at her. You hardly ever see children riding their parents in St. Petersburg. You hardly ever see men with children, for that matter. Marina, a guide hired by the conference group, complimented me on carrying my daughter everywhere. That's how I used to sit, on my dad's shoulders, she said. Men these days don't marry, and if they do, they don't want to have children, and if they have children, they get depressed and run away and drink themselves to death—that's current Russian family life. I was happy and proud, a good compensation for the literal pain in the neck that Tina gave me.

We made it to the Bolshoi, ten minutes before the performance, and the ticket controller let Tina and me breeze through. A sign said: No Picture Taking During the Performance. An announcement was made over the loudspeakers to the same effect, but there were so many tourists with cameras hanging from their necks, in some cases like a third breast, that the warning was bound to be defeated.

Tina and I went to a box on the side. She said, Daddy, where are they?

Who?

The ballerinas.

Behind that crimson curtain.

What are they doing?

Putting on their pink shoes.

She shone with anticipation. I looked at her proudly and hugged her.

Daddy, you are covering my view.

The curtains shook as though they would just part. From our side angle, we had to crane our necks to see the full stage, and sometimes, it seemed we'd have to swan our necks. Poor pun for *Swan Lake,* but it did feel like it, although if I didn't stretch my neck, the obstacle to the stage was intriguing enough. We shared the box with a girl, who wore a white silk shirt, a black cashmere sweater over it, and pearls which glimmered in the dark, reflecting the light in a purple and turquoise haze. Her hair was shiny black, falling away to the other side of her face, so her ear and white skin were exposed to me in profile, and sometimes the hair fell to our side like a little waterfall. Before the performance, she leaned her head on her left arm, over the velvet box parapet, and wrote a letter in blue, in slanted boxy Russian letters, yet with a flow of her wrist and fingers. The button on her silk shirt above her wrist occasionally sparkled pink and crimson, no doubt borrowing the deep burgundy of the velvet surrounding us, appropriating it, and disseminating it generously in its own version. Letter writing. Who writes letters anymore? This seemed such a nostalgic view, just as the ballet was, the whole impression came from a bygone era, yet it was here, vividly absorbing me so much that I no longer craned my neck with the worry that I wouldn't see the stage.

I caught myself looking and was embarrassed. Wait a minute, what are you doing? Look at the stage.

I looked at Tina. Pure heaven in her eyes. The innocent delight on her flushed cheeks, the glow. And she was quiet. She whispered something to me so softly I couldn't hear it. It was just warm breath in my ear. More than words could tell. I was happy, she was happy. I sat back a little, and there was again my neighbor's neck.

No matter how old the girl was, clearly she was enchanting. Was she aware of it? How couldn't she be? Her movements, her letter writing, it was all done with such flare that it looked like a performance, but then, why would it be? Did she address the present moment, saying she was anticipating the ballet, while next to her sat a middle-aged foreigner with his little daughter, who was all sparkly in her silk red? And indeed, the girl occasionally stole glances at Tina, and a smile lingered on her face. I was tempted to ask her, in Russian, what she was writing about, but the silence felt subtler than a conversation, and more communicative. She was aware of us, but naturally, my daughter was more impressive than I. Would Tina turn out to be like this in a dozen years, sitting by herself in a theater? Why? Shouldn't a girl like this be shopping, or getting drunk under a bridge with her peers? Under a pier? Didn't this seem to be a waste of youth and beauty, watching reruns of *Swan Lake*? And reruns seemed to be the right word because during the first intermission, Tina said to me, Daddy, this is the best movie I ever seen.

It's not a movie, I said. They are really out there. You could throw a stone at them and it would hurt them, they might scream. They are here.

Oh, she said. There are no stones here.

I mean those people out there on the stage are real. They are not just pretend people.

You mean, they are not just pretend swans. They are real swans? They look like people to me, Daddy.

You win.

The lights came on for the break and I wanted to find Alex and Joan. I was tempted to invite our neighbor along, but she seemed content to pull out her paper and continue writing. What news is there to report?

Russian theater intermissions are unpredictably long. This one went on for more than half an hour. People drank cognac, ate red caviar sandwiches with an amazing amount of butter to go with that, strolled. Some women had fur, although it was warm, but looks are everything, temperature is nothing. There were many young people, unlike what I remembered from such events in the States. And why not? With two, three intermission parties like this, it seemed a fine way to spend an evening. You sat down at a round table, and soon you could be chatting with a stranger. At a different performance, Alex and I met a family from Pakistan who invited us to visit them and go to the foothills of K-2, the second-tallest mountain in the world which for two weeks enjoyed the reputation as being the tallest. It was amazing that classical culture could go along with this leisurely atmosphere in which it was permitted to talk with everybody. Russians knew how to keep up the traditions. I never understood why Russian theater, ballet, and classical music could thrive, but now it seemed, in a flash, clear to me. The intermission! The cognac. The parade. Especially, in the winter, when you can't stroll outdoors, you could come inside and do it. Along the Adriatic Coast, the tradition, as anywhere else along the Mediterranean, has been to go out into the streets, and to walk back and forth in the evening.

But here, things had to happen in public indoor spaces. This was their version of a Mediterranean, and indeed, suddenly, even their temperaments seemed hotter. I had a shot of cognac. Tina and I found Alex and Joan, and the kids chased each other around, after having had a couple of salami sandwiches each. This is fun, Joan said, I love it.

When the bell rang, we walked back to our box. We sat down, and our neighbor put the letter away, and asked, Where are you from?

The States, I said. Chicago.

Do you know any mafia men?

I laughed.

That is what people think of us here now, but you invented it.

Don't blame me. Are you from St. Petersburg?

No, Toko. Oh, you wouldn't know it. It's deep in Siberia.

How much snow do you get? (I asked that question so I could report it to my son, who was crazy about snow, and on Yahoo always looked for the coldest towns, and those with the most snow.)

How come your English is so good? I asked.

I spent a year in Texas as an exchange student in high school.

High school? I was surprised. That would make her older than I thought.

Yes, I am done now, and next fall I'll be studying medicine at the university here. I have just moved here for my studies, and I'll be living with my aunt. There she is—she pointed to the box on the other side of the theater.

The lights dimmed. So, there's a future doctor, maybe a surgeon. So it's not a little girl from Siberia, it's a beautiful woman. She beamed at me as though guessing that I was recovering from the information.

Am I in your way? she said, as I gazed at her profile, straight lines of the nobly tall forehead and thin nose, and the curvy ones of her lips and chin.

No, I said.

I'll clear the view for you. She leaned her head on the parapet and turned her face toward the stage. Her hair fell over the parapet, and her long neck was nakedly clear. True, I could see the stage above her head, and the leaping swan dancer, named Kim, who indeed was spectacular, with his bulging balls and twirling muscles and Jordanesque ability to hover. In the first act the ballerinas had worn long white dresses, but now they came out in fluffy short ones, and as they twirled, you could see that they were no victims of fashionable starvation. They had thighs, flesh. They contorted, tensing alternate groups of muscles into definition.

Ana had taken off her cashmere sweater, and the outline of her body showed itself, like a nascent creature cocooned in a white haze.

Tina was totally rapt. A dimple showed on her left cheek as she stared adoringly. She whispered and gave me a kiss on my ear. She was charmingly grateful for the paradise.

Ana sat back and took up her opera glasses, made of white bone, or plastic that looked like bone. Several minutes later, she offered Tina the glasses. I taught Tina how to look, and Ana helped out, leaning over my legs, touching my forearms. It crossed my mind that it would be wonderful if Ana could babysit. Or was she way too elegant for that? Maybe she was rich. Maybe her father was one of those Mafioso oilmen who had deals with Yeltsin's son.

I borrowed the opera glasses, too. Where should I look? The tensing buttocks of the male lead dancer? No, thank you. How about the female dancer? All right, I don't mind that. Wherever I looked, wonderful legs. What's the point of looking? Of course, sex is too primitive a thought, but then, why are they so pretty, and (s)exposed? Sure, art is a sublimation of sensuality, but this was pure sensuality. And then my neighbor. I touched her shoulder slightly to give her the opera glasses back. She looked for a while, and gave them to Tina. Tina liked flipping them backward, so the stage would look far away.

It was totally wonderful to look at Tina's enjoyment.

Three years old and watching live ballet. Hopefully, this would have no harmful effects. Wouldn't it be terrible if she wanted to become a ballerina? Too much work. Plus, would I like old bastards like me to stare at her crotch through opera glasses?

Another intermission. We walked with Ana. Strangely enough, Tina did not seem to notice Ana probably because Ana was not a ballerina. Tina hopped on tiptoe, twirled, and did one split on the carpet. Several people stopped and laughed and applauded her on the little performance. Tina could capture attention, mine included, so I didn't notice when Ana left. A minute later, I noticed Ana holding hands with a middle-aged silvery-haired woman, a flight of stairs above us, ascending rhythmically, their backs turned to us.

Tina and I found Joan and Alex at a round table. Guess what, Alex, I said. We are sitting together with a Siberian. Much of the winter they have −40°F, and a yard of snow on the ground.

Where is he? Alex asked.

There. I pointed her out in the line. She was presently getting a glass of red wine. She's just a high school kid, I said to Joan, as though apologizing. Maybe sixteen. Babysitting potential.

She's not going to babysit.

How do you know? I haven't asked her yet.

Joan laughed. No, I don't want her to, and I am sure she wouldn't want to, either.

Aren't you impressed by the Siberian snow? I asked Alex. When he didn't answer, I tried another line. Do you like the ballet?

It's okay, but the sword fight was lame. I liked the sword fight in Prokofiev's *Romeo and Juliet* much better. And Prokofiev has a lot of the bass and drums—very exciting.

At the bell, Tina and I went back to our place. You are sure you can stand more of this, I asked?

Yes, I won't talk, she said.

There were hardly any other kids in the theater. In the box next to ours, there had been a kid, but he laughed and squealed, and his parents dragged him out, and he did not reappear. So Tina's self-discipline was remarkable. She sat on my knee, and gazed in wonder as a moving picture of swans appeared against a glimmering lake. And then the ballerinas—Tina smiled beatifically. I wished I could enjoy something quite that much. I cast my glance at Ana's face outlined in clear lines against the fluffy background.

After the overly long end-applause, Ana said, I enjoyed talking with you like I know you for many years. Would you like to give me your email address?

Oh, I'd be delighted to correspond, I said. I sat down with her, and tore the program page, and wrote my email address, hurriedly, since I could feel Joan's and Alex's presence in the back. How did it look, sitting down with her and exchanging notes?

I can write mine for you, too, she said.

I turned around.

Daddy, let's find Mommy, said Tina.

I saw Alex running in the corridor outside our box.

When you email, I'll have it, I said to Ana.

Tina and I walked out and Ana stayed back, placing her

opera glasses into their box. Outside of our box waited Alex and Joan. What took you so long, said Joan.

Wonderful, wasn't it? I said.

Yes, a little long, but lovely, said Joan.

What a bore, said Alex. Tchaikovsky is not as good as Prokofiev.

I agree, I said. Two acts would have been enough.

One would have been enough.

On the main staircase, we ran into friends of ours, who also taught at Herzen, and their son. I had looked forward to getting together with them. We stood in the middle of the crowd walking down the carpeted staircase. Let's have a late snack, said Tom.

I looked to my left. There was Ana, several rows of people away from us, smiling and waving.

I waved to her.

That seemed to make an intermission in our conversation with our friends. Ana waved again, and I did not know how to ignore that.

It took me a second to recover, while we walked to the Idiot, on the Moika, a block away from where Rasputin had been shot and drowned in the river.

Maybe I should have written down her email address as well, just to make sure, I thought. Even as we sat and slurped borscht, and ate the special of mushrooms, potatoes, and cheese, I could not concentrate. Ana's profile superimposed itself over the scene and dissolved it into darkness. Why don't I have self-discipline? This leads nowhere, this imaging of a Siberian cat. Cut it out. But I didn't cut it out. Now, I was not sure whether I could will to cut it out, or whether I simply did not wish to will it since I enjoyed the enthrallment of my visual brain. It was a simple intoxication with beauty; I tried to define it that way. I drank three shots of vodka in quick succession. At the Idiot everybody got a free shot. I drank everybody's vodkas but didn't feel drunk.

It's getting late, Joan said. Let's go home. And we did. Outside, the golden dome of St. Isaac's Cathedral was still bathed in the light of a bygone sun, while amidst the sooty buildings, we were sunk in a gloom, above the Moika, with the bad spirits of Rasputin under our feet, laughing in the dark. No, nothing so dramatic or quite so drunken.

The following day I visited Boris, in his hotel room. I woke him up. He rubbed his hairy chest, stretched, yawned, and then showed me *Infinite Jest*. . . . It's great, he said.

I retold him the rough outline of what had happened at the ballet.

Just forget it, my friend. Don't do anything with her.

I agree. Maybe I should just write a novel.

A novel? A poem, at the most, he said. Look, I am not impressed. That's been done. You yourself have quoted from *Laughter in the Dark*. And such stupid moments are the staple of bad poetry.

I know, it's been done, I said. It had been done even before *Laughter in the Dark,* many times.

So, why bother?

You know, that kind of objection has been done.

Of course, because it makes sense.

See, a theme happens, and it can recur. Look at the *Variations on a Theme of Paganini* by Brahms. You could say it's been done, but I am certainly glad it's been done once again. You never get such obsessions with a beauty?

Sure, they happen to everybody. I fall asleep and they go away. You got to be mature about it. Boris pointed to another metafiction book, which I was supposed to admire. I said, That's been done. I am tired of metafiction.

True, true, he said.

Two days later, after sleeping badly, I walked to Herzen and Idealnaya Chashka, the coffee shop, but before that, I stopped by at the cemetery.

There was a huge line, on both sides of the entrance. I was scared I could not get in, but the line was for the Nevsky Cathedral. What is going on here? I asked, and from what I could gather in the reply, there were bones of a Greek saint from the third century AD, and people lined up, hoping to be healed. Were all of them sick? There were at least four thousand people waiting, some mumbling prayers, others smoking, some yawning. Enough people to start a revolution, or enough to end a revolution.

I passed through one flank of the line, nudging my way, and then through an iron railing gate.

I paid my entrance, the tourist rate, and passed by the cats that I knew. Koshka, I said to the chubby tabby and petted him. On my right was Dostoyevsky's bust in blackened bronze, for his gravestone. Not a cross, but himself. Was he a god to himself? Wouldn't he have preferred a cross?

I walked to Tchaikovsky's bust against the walls of the cemetery.

And there she was, sitting on the rock next to Borodin's grave, and hugging her knees, dressed all in blue. Amazing.

How did she get here? Did she email me? Did we arrange this?

She stood up and as I walked to her, without much ado, she opened her arms and kissed me. She kept looking into my eyes, her pupils seemed to grow larger and larger, diminishing the blue circles around them. Her mouth tasted of red caviar, salty, osmotically touching my tongue, so that particles of me merrily leaped out of my tongue into hers. Actually, wouldn't it be simpler to have caviar? Why are we doing this, I thought.

Suddenly, she began to chuckle and pulled back.

Why, what's so funny?

I always wanted to kiss a Westerner, and I did it!

That's silly. Didn't you get a chance to do that in Texas?

No, there I kissed only Bulgarians. We had a clique going.

And so, how is it kissing a Westerner?

Just like kissing a Russian. No different. I expected more. I don't know what, maybe that you'd taste like kiwi.

I reached with my fingers to touch her blue-black hair, but I couldn't reach it—I kept stretching my arm, and losing my balance, while my vision turned green and blurry. I inhaled deep, and though I could see well again, I did not see her. She had vanished. I turned around and saw her hopping away, skipping her steps, past Mussorgsky, past Borodin, all the way to Dostoyevsky. There was the somber Tchaikovsky's bust of white marble and nothing between it and me. He was not interested in this at all. He kept frowning in his dignified manner, thinking who knows what, pretty notes or Michelangelo's *David,* the perfect torso, maybe lifting him in the air, letting him hover. Wasn't his main inspiration the beauty, not of maidens, but of lads? Amidst the furrowed frown, the furrows may not lead to deep thoughts, but to obsessive, recurring images of a profile, a line of the nose, the curving of the upper lip.

Actually, although the theater encounter had happened, the cemetery one didn't; however, I did walk there. I imagined the futility of an encounter there as I crunched the dusty white marble gravel under my black shoes on the cemetery paths. I did have the salty aftertaste in my mouth. It did not prove Ana's existence. The salt came out of my flesh; I spat a streak of scarlet spittle which stained the white gravel pink. Exhaustion combined with aspirin made me bleed. I closed my eyes. No pictures in my head. No black hair contrasting with pale skin and luminous eyes. I couldn't recall what she looked like. Maybe I should go thank the Greek saint for coming to my senses. I would still have to touch his bones to heal my teeth.

The whole image-obsession thing was part of the ballet swirl and twirl, after which vague impressions stayed with me enough to demonstrate my folly, and vivid ones stay with Tina even now, days later. That was her evening out, not mine. I look at her and admire how lightly she hops, and how she smiles with a dimple, and shines. She dances, shouting, un, deux, trois before she lands in a heap on the floor weightlessly, all feathery, and comes up as a swan.

The Bridge Under the Danube

After a prayer meeting for peace in the Balkans, Milka and Drago Zivkovic were walking home in Novi Sad at quarter to five in the morning through the narrow and elegantly cobbled streets of the East Bank, the Petrovaradin side, where ordinarily the old castle would be lit up. Instead, only tall darkness loomed, hiding the nascent blue light of the eastern horizon. They could barely see the yellow stone cobbles, for people were taking air-raid sirens seriously, turning off the lights.

"Are you sure we should be on the streets at this hour?" Milka asked.

"No, I am not."

"Maybe we should have kept praying till dawn."

"Several people were falling asleep in the middle of the prayers—and I don't think the Rankovices had enough rug space for all of us. So, this is the right thing to do."

"I'm still terrified."

"Even though the Lord says, Fear not those who kill the body but cannot kill the soul? And even though NATO's bombs are so precise?"

"That's the part that worries me. We are supposed to pass by the Vojvodina parliament."

Now they had come almost to the old Petrovaradin bridge. The sliver of the moon resembling a melon slice briefly shone through the crack in the clouds, and the waves in the river showed their blue teeth in response, glimmering.

Milka paused for a second to admire the beauty of the river in the sparse light. She had never seen the river in the natural night light. She turned round; the castle silhouetted itself against the black-blue sky, in an orange tone. The old town looked the way it had two hundred years ago. Would not the world be beautiful without electricity? Why did that Serb from Croatia have to meddle with nature, and find out how to control and transmit electricity? How did Tesla dare play with God's power—wasn't electricity God's? All the same, she was proud to come from Tesla's region in Lika, and wondered whether Tesla believed in God or whether the devil helped him.

"What did you stop for?" Drago asked impatiently. "I thought you were scared, and here, you linger and dawdle in the street. We must . . ."

Just then there was a sudden burst of light. An explosion of sound followed, and the earth shook, the cobbles moved, grinding against one another. Milka felt a terrible pain in her ears and noisy crashing sounds surrounded her, sifted through a high-pitched buzz. She smelled burning, and looked up to see the bridge bursting, crashing into the river, while cement particles hit her face and smarted. Yet the sound of the crash was somehow soft, a distant crackle and a splash, and seemed not to concern her ears at all, which were busy with their own violent sirens. When she wiped the dust from her face, she felt a warm sticky liquid on her cheek. Her blood was recementing the bridge dust, on her. Where did the blood come from? She could not find a cut on her jaw. Blood trickled from her left ear.

But even all the pain was a blessing of sorts; for had they progressed some hundred paces more, their own particles would have been flying.

Dazed, they walked back to the Rankovices, where a discussion was in progress, about whether it was a NATO bombing that made all the amazing thundering, or whether the sky was cracking open for the second coming of Christ. More voices supported the latter theory.

As Milka and Drago entered the curtained candlelit room, the discussion subsided, and the pious gazed at the entrants who were grayed by the concrete dust, caked in blood, and paled by horror. The candles, deprived of air, which was almost entirely consumed by sighs and sweat, eked out a dark and hissing light, revealing the couple's faces, from below.

The gathering prayed again, quietly, in whispers, and with each human gasp, the candle flames winced, and one of them sputtered, giving up its ghost as a thin trail of black waxy smoke. But perhaps it only seemed to Milka that the pious whispered; her ears would not allow the voices to get into her in any other form than the low whisper. Whispering prayers sounded more intimate than voiced ones, and she thought, from then on, that she would whisper to God. He ought to hear well; he could hear thoughts, so the voice was simply for those who prayed, and the whisper would be for her.

Milka watched the tormented gathering, all of whom had their eyes closed, and beneath the eyelids, she could see how the eyeballs moved and twitched. There were Hungarian and Croatian natives of Novi Sad, but most of them were Serbs from Croatia, as was she. They used to gather to pray for safe conditions to return to Croatia.

EVEN BEFORE THE WAR in Croatia started in 1991, the Zivkovics' three sons had joined the Serb paramilitary forces to the chagrin of their pacifist parents. The sons had given up the Baptist church a long while back, and to compensate for their turn-the-other-cheek kind of upbringing, they became brawling barflies, or more accurately, hornets, who secured no profession, relying instead on the idea that they could take over their father's carpentry business, but in Yugoslavia's recent economic decline, hardly anybody ordered furniture to be custom-made. Like most Krajina Serbs, the Zivkovics had signed the Referendum, the secret plan to annex former Austrian Military Borders, Krajina of Croatia, directly to Serbia. The Referendum was to be a pretext for Milosevic to occupy Croatia "by popular request."

In Bukovo all the signs were exclusively in the Cyrillic alphabet, something that you wouldn't see even in Serbia. At night, in the late summer, songs in broken voices came from the taverns: *Dajte nam salate, bice mesa klacemo Hrvate.* "Give us salad with a lot of chives, we'll be slicing Croats with knives."

At first when the skirmishes between the Croatian militiamen and Serbian paramilitary backed by the Yugoslav army came, the Zivkovics hid in the basement, praying for Serbian victory. The Yugoslav forces took over the town and Serb paramilitary filled the Catholic church with explosives. The steeple blew open, and the belfry tilted sideways, with the bell hanging out the window. There were rumors of mass executions and graves in the mountains, but nobody dared to go there for fear of mines, and the Zivkovics did not believe the rumors, taking them to be a result of the Balkan fervid imagination, such as had bred oral tradition with blood epic poetry. But in the winter, Milka tiptoed into the woods to gather kindling wood, and as she pulled at a thick branch, she realized that its loose bark was the frozen fabric of a pair of jeans; the fabric gave and her hands gripped a sheathed and footless human leg, sticking out of the elevated soil. In horror, she ran home, and didn't dare to mention what she had seen, not even to Drago. She often had the nightmare of seizing the shin wrapped in frozen jeans and after a while she wasn't sure whether she had indeed seen the leg; however, in the spring, with putrid smells coming out of the woods, she could not doubt it. Soon the smells disappeared; the maggots and wolves did their job. From then on she knew that evil festered in the soil, and that only worse things were to come.

Supposedly, Krajina would become Serbia, and soon there would be tourism, mountain inns, hunting. Instead of the prosperity promised by demagogues, poverty resulted. Belgrade had enough difficulty keeping a modicum of Serb economy going under the sanctions. Quite a few Serbs, unable to take the ever worsening poverty in the region, sought exile in Sweden, New Zealand, Canada, and the United States, and many moved to Belgrade. There were rows of bunkers, underground tunnels and ammunition storage spaces, and several hundred tanks, which created an impression of invincibility at first, but after soldiers had not seen salary in a long time, their morale slackened. Many troops went into Bosnia to burn Bihac and help hold the town under siege until the inhabitants starved to death. While the troops were so diverted (they couldn't reoccupy their former defensive positions effectively), the Croatian army attacked in August 1995 and overtook the depressed Krajina in three days. Now, Serbs ran out of their homes; many of them feared revenge; most had relatives in the army. Even retreating Serb soldiers urged the civilians to flee for their lives. Croatian soldiers provided free gasoline and cans of food for the departing ones, an act of dubious generosity.

And at night, Milka and Drago heard broken and hoarse voices sing in the tavern, "Give us sweet herbs, we will broil bitter Serbs."

Empty villages and towns had lost their people and were filled with ghosts, and many people from the valleys claimed that they could hear ghosts fighting with scythes, with much clanking and howling. And there was howling of wolves, among the last wolves of Europe, who now increased in population; because of mines, people no longer hunted, and the population of deer, partridge, and rabbits went up. Wolves grew to be so numerous—and they had become used to eating human remains—that they threatened anybody alive in remote villages.

Milka and Drago were among the last inhabitants to leave their little town, and soon they caught up with the columns of refugees, becoming a part of this exodus on a biblical scale. As they passed through Karlovac, and on to the Autoput, they were pelted by jeering crowds of Croats, with eggs, tomatoes, melons.

The exiled Croatian Serbs hoped for a martyrs' welcome in Serbia. Instead, they were shunned as peasants; their speech was corrected in shops because it was *ijekavica (biyelo,* for white), the Croatian way of pronouncing, rather than *ekavica (belo).*

Many Croatian Serbs quickly changed to *ekavica,* but the elderly, and among them the Zivkovics, claimed that it was too late for such changes—the way they grew up speaking, that way they would die.

In Novi Sad, administrators assigned them to move into a small whitewashed house with mossy tiles from which a Croatian family was presently being evicted into Croatia. Because of overpopulation, three families moved into the three-bedroom house; they all shared one little kitchen with a wood stove according to a schedule, and one leaky bathroom. One of their neighbors was a wizened man who groaned, afflicted with stomach cancer, while his wife helped him and swore colorfully; she seemed to spend more time tending a couple of white goats next to the grassy ditch in front of the house. General poverty had made goatherding common even in the cities. Another neighbor, a teenaged mother with a toddler, spent several hours every night gasping and crying out in faked and unfaked orgasms; a stream of men visited her, and every morning, her pimp, on his way to the tennis club, stopped by in a yellow BMW, which had probably been stolen in Bosnia. He shouted at her that she should be ashamed to be worth so little—couldn't she fetch a better fee? He banged her head against empty cupboards, which drummed like timpani. The rest of the morning, the toddler cried. So between the sounds of pain from one quarters and pleasure and pain from another, the Zivkovics suffered from insomnia, and they slept usually only in the afternoon when the house could be quiet for a couple of hours. Since they had no employment, in a way it didn't matter when they slept, but, still, they found the atmosphere in which they lived sorrowful.

The beauty of the promenade along the Danube and over the Petrovaradin bridge was one of the few consolations they could find. Thousands of people would go out to walk, *na korzo*. You could not tell there was trouble in the world if you walked here—you'd see sharply dressed young men talking on cell phones, and slim young women in provocative miniskirts; in the meanwhile, two million displaced persons roamed in the former Yugoslavia, from forests to refugee camp tents, to distant relatives, to overcrowded quarters. Serb police went from house to house in Kosovo, confiscating guns and beating the civilians, and prohibited Albanian Kosovars from attending schools. No, you could not tell that any of that was going on, and that many refugees were in Novi Sad as well, nor did those refugees who visited the *korzo* in the evening want to think about that; they, too, enjoyed the breezes and the sensation that the world could be and should be a carefree place, where one could look elegant. And indeed, even in their late fifties, Milka and Drago looked fine. She had black hair and strikingly light hazel eyes, so that warm light seemed to be coming from her; her complexion was smooth, assisted by a touch of plumpness. She walked erect; it was because of chronic pains that she could not tilt forward. She wore Russian river pearls, which, because of irregular sizes, sparkled most unexpectedly, in purple, green, and white hues, playing with the light from her eyes, and adding to it.

Drago still had all his brown hair, gray only slightly on the sides; his black mustache shone. Occasionally he flashed his natural teeth in a smile. He brushed them thoroughly three times a day. He did twenty push-ups every morning, and when he stood, his abdomen lined up with his chest and thighs; he frequently irritated other men by petting them patronizingly on their stomachs. They both sang in the choir: she a sonorous soprano, and he, a warm bass. In short, no matter what the circumstances, they kept their physical pride, and the bridge *korzo* helped them. Milka sensed that Drago looked at the young women—and it did not bother her: it was good that he, nearly sixty years old, had such youthful zest in him. She drew satisfaction from seeing the young and the superficial; and she wished that she could keep enjoying the surfaces—but under the surfaces of good looks, vice lurked, just as under the sheen of the river during sunset, perch-pike tore other fish. Yes, worries would soon come back, and she'd think about her sons. She heard rumors that they were massacred by Muslims and Croats outside of Prijedor, or that they joined Arkan's forces and grew rich on looting, and now didn't care to remember their poor parents.

The parents often prayed for their children. They prayed even like this, "Lord, please let that not be true that our sons perished in Prijedor last September"—expecting that God would revisit the past, and in case the sons were killed indeed, perhaps resurrect them even before the second coming of Christ, and let them in the new version of the past and present, come to Novi Sad and receive the word of the Lord. In this cosmology, anything could happen in the future and in the past; the two were of the same fluid that could go backward and forward, the way water in the oceans can flow in different streams, north and south, at the same time, depending on the depth and warmth—and some water even goes up into the sky, while other water falls down and sinks underground to surface and evaporate again, and just so perhaps the blood of the murdered sons could rise out of the dust and envelop the bones to become the living flesh. In an evangelical vision, time travel could be even swifter than in the theory of relativity, and death and life become nearly interchangeable concepts. Nobody is dead for long, and nobody is alive for long.

Naturally, such cosmology could be stressful too, and it was the bridge promenade that could relieve them. But even before the bridge went down, the evening *korzo* closed because of American threats of bombing. People stayed at home in fear, chagrin, and boredom.

THE MORNING AFTER the bridge was downed, the two tormented souls stumbled in the blue light of dawn. Pink light in the clouds brought little relief, and people lined up along the river and wept for the old bridge as though it had been a living soul that now lay broken, slain and sunk. Elderly people remembered the lives of the bridge, for Germans had destroyed it in World War II as well, and at the end of the war, whipped German prisoners rebuilt it, and perhaps it was the POWs' sins and hatred and millions of hissed swearwords that had doomed the bridge.

Winds blew from the northwest plains, chilling the sleepless crowds. A bald man rafted people, like Charon, for a small fee, to the western side of the Danube. He was gloomy, as though indeed he were rafting across the River Styx, but there was no need for that, except for a certain theatrical expression of pathos. The Zivkovics went to Most Slobode (Freedom Bridge) up the river, walked across, and they continued on the west bank for two more miles, past the Staro Sajmiste dormitories surrounded with piles of papers and garbage, and past the medical school on Hajduk Veljkova. The glass entrance to the medical school lay shattered, perhaps not from any direct hits but from the powerful explosions to selected targets, after which waves of sounds and wind—intermingled with waves of vacuum—had rattled the glass so much that it crashed all over the marble staircase. They trudged past old socialist project buildings near the train station. Usually, there were smells of diesel fuel wafting, but not now. The rail tracks had been blasted in many places, and the traffic was close to nil. NATO wouldn't bomb the train station with people sleeping in it; on the side tracks, the refugees—Serbs from Bosnia and Croatia and lately, Kosovo—formed their wagon villages.

That night the Zivkovics listened to the BBC and Croatian reports on the shortwave—nearly a million Albanians languished in the squalor of makeshift camps. Stewardesses on the planes transporting Kosovars from Macedonia to Turkey wore gas masks so they would not breathe in Kosovars' germs. The Albanians were handled as untouchables.

"Do you believe all that?" Drago asked.

"Why wouldn't I? I think that at this point everything is true." She closed her eyes, and she could still see the afterimage outline on her eyelids—the massacred man's leg sticking out of the land. "Yes, all the evil is true." Her hand twitched as though she were still touching the dead purple leg.

"In 1990, newspapers lied to us that Croats were slaughtering us when nothing was going on."

"Yes," she conceded, "it started with lies, but the lies became the truth."

"This Albanian thing could be Western propaganda so they'd have an excuse to bomb us."

"Oh, leave politics to politicians."

"The Bible says, Give to Caesar Caesar's. You can't really paraphrase this as Give to Milosevic Milosevic's, or to Tudjman Tudjman's. They have stolen everything from us, so why should we give them anything?"

"You think Caesar was any better?"

"Yes, they fought wars heroically back then. Armies met in open fields, and whichever side won, won."

"I don't believe that. I think even then, armies avoided each other, and went from village to village, burning, plundering, raping, and murdering. And then they wrote something else on the walls and in books."

Exhausted, she grew bored with the conversation, and while he recounted some ancient battle or another, she lost track and slumbered. Despite weakened ears she woke up to sounds of orgasmic crying from next door—with a note of sinking helplessness in the woman's voice. She held her breath. Drago was breathing quickly; he cleared his throat, which had gone dry. He touched her breasts, but she rolled away from him. Is it possible, that he was excited by another woman's sounds? And now he'd want to make love to her to those sounds, perhaps imagining the neighbor? No, those terms of lovemaking did not charm her. She rolled away even though the wooden bed frame edge cut into her arms and legs. She fell asleep, and when she woke up, she walked barefoot to the bathroom, quietly tiptoeing so as not to disturb anyone, and on the way, she was startled to see Drago kneeling—not in prayer, as she had sometimes seen him, but in front of the key-hole, peeping into the young woman's bedroom, where the bed squeaked.

"Ah so, you old swine!" she whispered loudly.

Drago leaped up, and walked back into their room, attempting to hide his erection.

She followed him.

"Aren't you ashamed? At your age? At any age? Is that the way to behave?"

"I was curious from all that noise."

"You were more than curious."

"But we haven't had sex in a month. . . ."

"Why would we? There's too much trouble to worry about it."

"Well, my body. . . ."

"Oh, shut up, you pig. Go to her! You want her, go to her, get her diseases, wallow in filth, die in pus!"

She turned away from him in disgust. After all the tragedy to suffer such a base indignity! That was worse than . . . than what? Well, the hell with it, she thought, let me sleep. Let it all go to hell. But how dare I think so blasphemously?

She couldn't fall asleep, while Drago apparently did, and

who knows what he was dreaming; he kept gritting his teeth. Watching him in the blue moonlight, she thought, And he dares to quote, Fear not those who kill the body but cannot kill the soul. Some demons may have infected his soul with base lust. Where? At the Petrovaradin bridge *korzo?* Or have those murderers on all sides singing their blood ballads darkened his mind? Now she grew afraid for him, for his soul. Should she pray for him?

In the morning, sleepless, Milka walked to the bathroom where she had forgotten to go before, and out walked the pimp, with a black eye, smiling sheepishly, and lifting a bottle of champagne. "Wish me well," he said, "I just got engaged!"

"Sure, I wish you well," she muttered.

When she walked out of the bathroom, the old man—all bluish-white, even his eyebrows and eyes, ringed with cataracts, were bluish-white—crawled on the mud floor toward the bathroom, groaning.

Milka wondered where the old man's wife was; wasn't she taking care of him? She looked outside, but there was no wife and no goats there.

Milka helped him, and lifted him. He was incredibly light, hollowed by his disease, and he kept burping. She seated him on the stool, and afterward she carried him to his room, and she washed him. The old man cried, without strength of breath in his voice. In his agony, the blue old man struck her as saintly, and she wept for him in deep sorrow, and her tears mixed on his caved-in chest with the warm water that foamed out of the sponge. She prepared him chamomile tea, but he begged her for sharp Slavonian sausage.

"Why, that will hurt you!"

"Oh, I am beyond being hurt. I will die soon, and all I can think of is *kulen*. Who cares if I can't digest it. I can't digest anything. I want the taste, and then I can die."

She went into the pantry, where she hid sausages and *kulen,* and gave the peppered crimson *kulen* to him to eat, and the old man chewed slowly, his eyes watering, and tears, perhaps of joy, flowing down his sunken cheeks.

She made thin slices for him, and he chewed, and chewed, and fell asleep with a smile of peace on his face.

TWO DAYS LATER, on the first Sunday after the destruction of the bridge, Milka dressed for church and placed the river-pearl necklace over her green velvet dress, but Drago lingered in bed, with bags under his eyes swollen, and his eyes small, as though bees had stung him. "What are you waiting for?" she said. "You better go to church and repent. I expect to hear a prayer from you. Your brain needs to be cleansed in the blood of the Savior."

He surprised her by not arguing. He said, "The old man has been moaning for months. How much longer can he go on? I couldn't sleep; his fear got to me."

And so, the couple trudged for two miles to the Baptist church; everything seemed to be two miles away, and the long blue buses with a large joint in the middle (so the body of the bus could make the curves) were nowhere in sight. In the church, after a song in the choir where both of them sang their souls out, the old and tall condorlike minister held a sermon about the end, when nation would rise against nation, brother against brother, and the earth would quake as never before. And he quoted Jesus's words from Matthew, chapter 24, verse 9,

"You will be hated by all the nations on account of my name." He paused and in silence stared at the congregation, while his eyelids drew over his gray eyes and lifted again. He repeated an octave more deeply, "You will be hated by all the nations on account of my name."

A partial confirmation of the prophecy came swiftly. Shards of glass splashed over the congregation, cutting several cheeks. People ducked on the floor, probably imagining there was another North Atantic Treaty Organization bomb blasting. Several bricks flew in, and shouts followed. "You American spies, we'll show you your god today!"

"Damned *novoverci* (new believers)!"

A machine gun fired a round into the ceiling. Something resembling a hand grenade fell into the baptismal hole and did not explode but did make a splash, which startled Milka with its coldness. Wet, she trembled on the floor, and smelled urine—fear with its indignities.

The minister locked the door. The church was under siege by a mob.

The minister asked, "Does anybody have a gun here?"

One woman shouted, "A small pistol."

"That's not enough," the minister said. "Let us then pray."

In the middle of the prayer, he pulled out a cell phone to call the police, and he kept dialing.

But someone else must have alerted the police already. Just as the front door seemed ready to collapse from steady pounding, the police dispersed the crowd with tear gas.

A policeman shouted through the cracked door, "You can leave now. Everything's all right."

But the people, who were used to believing so much, could

not believe this, and they still stayed inside; someone whispered, "It's a trap. They organized the whole thing to begin with."

However, when they peeked outside, the police seemed quite earnest. They were beating back drunken hooligans, one of whom fell on the ground with smashed-in teeth, bleeding from the mouth.

As Milka walked out with Drago, she thought, Maybe Caesar did provide after all. Or somebody's prayer worked. Whose prayer could have done this? Who could pray that good? Or maybe God didn't need prayers; he acted when people could not take more misery, so they could get refreshed, so the new misery would hurt doubly once it came. And she censored herself for thinking so.

But as they walked away, even the police taunted them. "How can you go to Clinton's church?" That's what the locals now called the Baptist church. They didn't reply, but walked on, into darkening and narrowing streets. The sun must have just set, but as it was cloudy, dank darkness arose from the ground, as though darkness were a substance, a vapor that carried smells of the Danube, deep clay smells, with ghosts of rotting fish eggs that never came to life.

Several blocks later, four tall men with crew cuts caught up with the Zivkovics, and talked with them. "Where are you from?"

Milka noticed that one of them had an emblem with SSSS (CCCC in Cyrillic) which stood for *Samo Sloga Srbe Spasava*—"Only unity can save Serbs"—traditional Chetnik sign.

"Oh, don't ask, from Lika," Drago said. "Serbian Krajina."

Another man, in a black T-shirt, even though it was a cold day, said, "That's where my roots are. We got to stick together a little bit better, don't you think?"

And another one, wearing a black leather jacket, said, "Why don't you go back?"

"How would we? The Croats burned down our house to the ground so we wouldn't come back."

"You should have fought them," the SSSS guy said.

"It's easy for you to say, but we are too old to get involved. Besides, we are pacifists."

"You should've gone to the States, *novoverci.*"

ALL THE WHILE, the Zivkovics were hastening their pace, but now the men surrounded them and stopped, and when Milka tried to walk on, they pushed her back. "Wait a minute, Old Whore, our conversation is not over yet."

"Clinton and Gore and Albright, they are all Baptists!" shouted the fourth man, clutching a metal pipe. "Have you shaken hands with Clinton?"

The voices came quickly, and Milka couldn't follow who was saying what; she did not look at the men, whose faces were contorted by aggression. Perhaps they were on speed besides being drunk on brandy.

"You, I am talking to you," said the SSSS guy, pushing Milka back. "Have you sucked Clinton's dick? Why didn't you clench your teeth then, ha?"

"This is a religious war, Baptists against the Serb Orthodox!"

"You shine with your flashlights on our bridges and rails so the Vandal pilots could aim better?"

"Where do you get such an absurd idea?" Drago asked.

The SSSS man punched him in the nose, and blood covered Drago's lips. He wiped them, and suddenly kicked the SSSS man in the groin, and the man writhed on the ground, but the T-shirt guy hit Drago on the jaw.

Milka cried, "Leave him alone, he has a heart condition."

"He has a head condition. This should clear it!"

A brigand slammed Drago with a metal pipe above his left ear. The force of the swing brought Drago down onto the cobbles. The guy in the T-shirt kicked Drago's thighs.

Milka tried to push them away, and to guard Drago, but the SSSS guy, now up and shrieking, punched her under her sternum so hard that she stood there, stunned, and for several seconds her vision was all bright gray, without any detail, and when her sight came back, in it swirled many limbs and sticks and boots, bursting and splashing. When she came to, still standing, the brigands were gone, and at her feet lay Drago, with blood covering his forehead.

Still dazed, unsure whether she was seeing right, she strained her eyes. Near his head glimmered rays of purple and red, her spilled river pearls playing with the crimson light of his blood.

She kneeled down, and leaned her good ear on his chest, waiting for heartbeats. His chest was warm. She thought she heard a faint beat, but perhaps it came from within her ear, from her own blood? She felt for his wrist pulse with her thumb, and again she felt weak beats. Were they her own? She put three fingertips against the tip of the radial bone, and with disbelief she felt his steady beats and then she heard him draw a wet breath. My God, she thought, how can we live through all of this? She was almost disappointed that this was not the end of suffering for her husband, but perhaps just the beginning. What would come next? How to find a doctor? There must be one. They were after all a block away from the medical school. The work ahead of her terrified her, but what choice was there? She looked around, expecting to see the desolate street, but instead beheld an old woman in a brown scarf who walked out of her yard with a bucket of water, a bottle of pharmacy alcohol, and a towel. She came to them, and without a word, kneeled next to Drago and began to wash his face. Drago opened his eyes and smiled as though to say, I didn't know life could be this good. Or perhaps, I did not know I was alive.

And Milka felt fortified, too, with the new knowledge that it was possible to survive almost anything. And as the NATO aircraft explosively penetrated the sound barrier above them, she was not startled; she wondered whether that was the sound of the wrath of God which might neither destroy them nor protect them, unlike the love of God, which came through the old woman, who did not seem to hear anything—she did not respond to words of thanks and questions about whether there were doctors on the block, but her knotty gray hands kept washing Drago's tranquil face, hair, and neck, as though he were a baby.

59th Parallel

I waited for the A train around five in the afternoon, at
Columbus Circle, comforted that it was Saturday, hence, no
rush hour. You'd imagine that, in the wake of 9/11, New York
City subways would be less crowded than usual, that at least
the paranoiacs of the city (no doubt a large population, of
which I might be considered a member) would not be in the
subway, which seems like a target. For a month after the attack,
I observed the multitude of bags every morning and wondered, What's to guarantee there are no explosives here, no an-
thrax, no plague? The police who stand around the entrances
with their billy clubs, chewing bubble gum, don't actually
check anybody going in. They are here not to prevent anything, but to act once a tragedy occurs, postmortem. Despite

all the talk about limitations on freedom, you can still walk in, unchecked, unidentified—unlike in the old Yugoslavia, where I once lived, and where the police "randomly" checked passersby, demanding they produce their IDs. (This might be the case in the United States soon, which should make us feel much safer—or much more threatened, depending on which line of thought you take.) Anyway, for a month I imagined explosions and choking smoke, but now such thoughts hardly cross my mind. What crosses my mind instead is that such thoughts don't. Strangely, there is a sensation (perhaps thoughtless, perhaps thoughtful) of safety here.

On Friday, the subway was so packed that you could see the backs of people flattened against the doors as you waited on the platform. I glanced over at an Asian man, thinking he would be as amused and exasperated by the sight as I was, but he didn't respond to my attempt at eye contact. Well, I thought, in Tokyo, they even employ subway-pushers, to push people onto the train, so to him this must look normal. But after I had this thought, he burst out laughing and asked me, "You feel like getting in there?"

I mumbled a reply. I had moved on to pondering something I'd seen coming down the stairs from Fifty-seventh Street: an old man lying on the floor of the submezzanine. One of his legs was dangling down the stairs, the other stretched out in front, culminating in an old hiking boot whose sole was detached so that his filthy toes, with curling blue nails, protruded. His beard was gray-brown, so was his hair, so were his clothes, so was his grimy, unwashed skin. But his penis, which he was stroking slowly, was all white-pink and gleaming, the only part of him that looked young and clean.

When he noticed me, he slowly packed away his penis and coiled his body sideways to sleep. Who knows from where he drew his inspiration? There must have been a mind in there to form images, or maybe he did not need images.

And in the subway train just a day earlier, I'd seen a beggar who screamed, "People, I am starving! I need to eat. I ate garbage out of a Dumpster, got food poisoning, and they had to rip my stomach open. See?" He pulled his shirt up to show us an unhealed scar. People gasped. He reeked; incredibly filthy, bending, drooling. I gave him a dollar, but was careful not to touch him. Another man walked in wearing only underwear and socks, although it was the middle of the winter, and said, "Ladies and gentlemen, I have nothing to wear. Please give me some money so I can buy a pair of pants."

But somehow the homeless don't go into the most crowded trains. Maybe they are squeamish about contact with the clean.

SATURDAY, I boarded the A train at Columbus Circle, relieved that it was Saturday, and hence no rush hour. Nothing seemed unusual, except that everything seemed totally normal and usual. I got on behind a redhead whose hair was flaming orange-red. Although I did not stare at her, her hair burned itself into my field of vision; you could see her while not looking at her. There were hardly any seats on the train, except for one between her and a big, hefty guy. He even breathed heavily. I dislike sitting between two people, because although your asses may not touch, your shoulders usually do, especially when the people are men.

Just that morning, I'd sat between two huge guys and had

to lean forward because, had I sat up straight, I would have been squeezed like a tube of toothpaste. Eventually, I thought, The hell with it, and I did sit up straight, and though our shoulders were crushed together, none of us would relent.

But this is not the real macho game played on the subways. The really macho guys sit with their legs spread wide apart. The wider your spread, the more of an alpha male you are. You're making a statement: I don't give a shit about your ass. I am going to claim my space. I don't give a shit if you rub your leg against mine. I am not a homophobe. That's your deal, not mine. I am a real man, and I have my space, and nothing—I mean, nothing—will move me. You can rub your leg against mine if you dare, but I bet you won't, because you aren't as tough as I am. Usually, a guy who spreads his legs also lets his eyelids droop and leans his shoulders back in his seat.

That morning, though I resorted to a shoulder squash, I was not going to rub legs with those guys, so I crossed mine in a retreat of sorts. (Although now my foot was sticking too far out into the crowd, threatening to trip anybody passing by. But that was fine; this would be my form of rudeness.) When I crossed my legs, the guys sat up even straighter in psychological and sexual triumph: they were alphas, and I'd revealed myself as a beta simply by being squeamish. Squeamishness is a beta quality. Tough guys don't mind touching legs; they don't squirm. I sat between them like an intellectual who does not have much use for his body, not a prime male fucker who is proud to display his balls and now and then slides his pelvis forward with pride: the balls have got to swell, spread, pop merrily out into the world.

That morning's ride fresh in my mind, I regarded the open

middle seat with distaste, forgetting that the flaming redhead probably would not play leg games with me. She was not a guy (a big plus on the subway, from my point of view) and seemed slender. But the other seat was occupied by a guy, and a real space-hog at that. I looked at the seat and then down the train: Should I walk down to the next group of seats? Maybe I'd find something on the aisle, where I could face away from my neighbor. I know that does not sound particularly friendly, but why would I feel friendly in a crowd of strangers, on those awful, hard orange seats, which hurt your ass even more than your eyes? After months of grinding my sciatic nerve between my bones and that hard plastic, I sometimes lose sensation in my feet.

So I was about to give up on the empty seat, which was almost as orange as the redhead's hair. I was not going to be squashed like that again today, not even to sit next to a pretty girl. And she was pretty, judging by the way she carried herself (I was trying not to stare), erect and yet at ease. She crossed her legs, and the crossing of her long, delicate legs caught my eye. I was turning away when I heard a voice:

"Would you like to sit down?"

She was addressing me, in a slight lisping accent. She had full, stung lips.

"Sure. Thank you."

How considerate, I thought. Not that this was an invitation to conversation. She was reading a book of phrases, in French and English, I guessed. People love France. Let her go to France. *C'est la vie.* Why should I care? I used to travel a lot, study German and Russian, and what good has it done me? Maybe she was French and was actually studying English. I

would not look. I didn't want to be rude, or, rather, to be per-
ceived as rude.

I was careful to hide the cover of my magazine from my
neighbor. Not that I had any reason to think that she would
glance over at my reading material; in fact, she seemed so ul-
tracivilized that she didn't need to be curious about her neighbors. She read her dictionary. I read about a Unesco grant, and
about awards for the best novel for readers aged ten to twelve.
Now, why ten to twelve? There is a huge difference between
ten and twelve. When you are ten, you can enjoy *Snow White*.
When you are twelve, you are too busy jerking off to care.
Should I write a letter explaining that to the international
body? No, fuck them.

I whipped out my magazine, *Poets and Writers*. I know, totally lame, but it's all right for the subway in the evening,
when I am particularly scatterbrained. Obviously, a dictionary
would be even better. The redhead had chosen well. With a
dictionary, I'd need to concentrate for only a few seconds at a
time; why hadn't I thought of that before? I'd read John Dos
Passos in the subway the other day, and when I was leaving, I
saw a man in a business suit reading a shaggy copy of Dos Passos's *42nd Parallel*. In the mornings, I read the *New York Times,*
elbowing my neighbors unapologetically in a form of beta revenge. Why is the paper so large? There should be a narrow
subway edition. Hell, if papers can have evening and morning
editions, they could have subway editions. Of course, some
people develop that amazing accordion technique, whereby
they fold the pages vertically in half and manage to whip
through the whole paper without bruising anybody. Now, they
are the truly civilized, brilliant in every respect. I envy them,

but I don't entirely admire them, for I find something terribly fascist about that organization of body and space; I imagine that most of these people work as insurance actuaries and IRS agents.

I READ ON. The heavy man on my left got up and left. Although there was no longer any chance of body contact with the redhead, since she had a rather vertical and elongated style, I moved away from her, into the newly vacated seat. Now it was 125th Street, Harlem. More people than I expected got on. It occurred to me that someone might sit between us, and that I would prefer to be next to her for some reason. Or absence of reason. So, quickly, I slid back to my original seat and launched a conversation: "Are you planning to go to France?"

"No," she replied simply and laconically. (You might think that *no* is always simple, but sometimes it's not, so I say it now: her *no* sounded simple.) Her eyes were a very light hazel, but not green.

"You are learning French, though, aren't you?"

"No, Italian. I like French, though."

"Will you travel to Italy, then?"

"I don't think so. I like Italian but not Italians, if you know what I mean."

"No, I don't," I said.

"I hate talking to Italians. They are obnoxious and they give me a headache. Half an hour of talking with an Italian, and you might consider suicide or homicide."

"Not in my experience," I said. "By the way, are you Russian?"

"Yes."

"I am Croatian. I speak some Russian. We could try speaking it."

"You are a writer, yes?" she said, ignoring my offer.

"How did you know? Oh, the magazine, of course." Though I had tried to hide the title, she must have read enough to figure it out, even though I never got the impression that she was looking over.

"What do you write about?" she asked.

"Half of my writing is about the wars in the former Yugoslavia, and the other half is . . . well, I don't know what it's about, and I don't really care."

"Pardon? I didn't catch what you said."

"That's all right. It was not particularly articulate."

"So, what is your writing about?"

"Yugoslavia. Wars. Emigrants. Disappearing places."

She closed her paperback dictionary and put it in her black purse.

"So, what's your occupation?" I asked.

"I was just starting to work in real estate, but 9/11 wiped that out. There are more real estate agents than buyers in Manhattan now. I am a concierge at the Iroquois Hotel. Nothing to be proud of."

"Oh, that's on Forty-fourth Street."

"How did you know? You are the first person ever to know the place."

"There are lots of fancy hotels there. So, do you go to the Russian Vodka Room?" I asked.

"No way. That's where the Russian losers hang out. They all come from Brooklyn and lie about what they do."

"How about Uncle Vanya's?"

"Horrible food."

"And the Samovar?"

"Awful, just awful. That place is lost in time. They even have a white piano, and people weep when they sing World War II ditties."

"You know, Baryshnikov owns the place, and the piano is his."

"So? It might as well be at Brighton Beach, with all the misfits who want to feel they are still in Russia."

"Where *do* you like to go?"

"I don't like to go out. It's enough that I have to spend so much time on this subway. What a nightmare."

At that moment, a thin man in rags at the other end of the coach began wailing as though his entire family had just been wiped out. The more you listened to him, though, the more you realized that he was out of his mind. He was screaming and weeping, but also laughing softly in between his screams.

"I agree," I said. "The A line is a total pain."

Now she was preparing to get off. She wiggled in her seat and double-checked her leather purse, clicking it shut. Her fingers were amazingly long.

"Well, it was nice talking to you," I said. "Maybe we could exchange emails?"

"I'll see you on the A train."

"Why do you say that?" I said, a little put off.

"Why would I not say that?"

"It's a big city."

"Not so big. We have already seen each other on the A train."

"When? I don't remember."

"I used to be blonde. It was a mistake to color my hair red. It looks silly."

"It looks all right to me. I don't remember you as a blonde, though."

"You looked right at me one day."

"I don't remember."

"You don't? Trust me. You looked right at me. If you think about it a little, you will remember."

Boy, is she comfortable, I thought. An American would never so calmly observe such a fact. She would either accuse you of it, or ignore it, or be triumphant about it. But this woman seemed merely factual and casual about it. And I thought, Does that mean that I am more memorable-looking than her? I doubt that. Apparently she has a better memory than I do. But she is making up excuses for me. Why? Maybe she's vain and can't believe someone wouldn't remember her. No, it doesn't seem like it. It's just a fact she remembers. It has little to do with me; she remembers when people pay attention to her.

"I don't remember," I said. "But I'll think about it."

"It was a pleasure to meet you." She stood up and offered me her hand and even curtsied a little. The homeless man at the other end of the coach howled louder.

Maybe I should stand up, I thought. But why should I? She does not want to exchange e-mails, and I am not into subtlety. Apparently not, if I ogled her. I did not remember ogling any pretty women on the A train. Overall, I tried not to pay attention to the damn crowds. I didn't want to be a stupid lech. I was sure I had not seen her.

"Pleasure meeting you, too," I said. "When did I see you before?"

"About six weeks ago. Good-bye."

As soon as she left, I remembered. She was with a bearded man, and they talked about getting their real estate licenses. She said it was a must, that real estate was the way to go; there was so much money in it. She was dressed in a black skirt, a little above the knee, and her hair was blonde. Her full lips were vermilion, in stark contrast to her wan skin, and she had a graceful way of moving, like a former skater or ballerina. She seemed aware that I was looking at her. In fact, she looked back, but not brazenly, because she was also calm and seemed to communicate neither like nor dislike, irritation nor pleasure.

At one point, the man with the beard took her hand in his and clung to it. He hugged her, wrapping his arm completely around her. One of his fingers bore a broad gold ring. He was desperate to possess her, I could see, but he did not possess her. I knew then that she was aware of me. She should not have been aware of me while her boyfriend (I assumed he was a boyfriend, or perhaps even a fiancé) hugged her like that, with such fervor and happiness. But then I thought, No, she is not interested in me, nor in her boyfriend, for that matter. She is simply aware. And right then I thought what a misfortune it was that a conversation between me and her was totally impossible.

And now, miraculously, we had talked. She wasn't too surprised that I did not remember her, though the certainty with which she said, "You looked right at me," implied that I should have remembered. And now I did remember. I remembered how she'd walked onto the train, a little uncertainly, a little gingerly, like someone stepping onto ice. And when she modestly brought her knees together, as if to close herself in, it looked so elegant that I thought, She must be Russian. Americans don't do things that consciously—or self-consciously. And then she cast a glance at me, held my gaze a moment. It was a conversation with no words spoken.

She had left the train now, but the door was still open. I could have rushed out to tell her that I remembered, but I didn't need to. She'd already figured out that I would remember, and that we'd meet again.

Or maybe we won't. Just the fact that my desire to have a conversation with her was fulfilled is enough. It does not need anything to follow it. It's not much of a plot, but that's fine; I don't need plots. In a way, after 9/11, it's nice not to have a plot, or big events; I've written so much about war and murder—and crime and sex, for that matter—that it's a relief not to have any of that. The fleeting encounter was fine—finer, to be sure, than listening to that madman bellowing at the top of his lungs as though he were dying and his family were dead.

WHEN THE TRAIN reached my stop, the madman got off, too. I went home and opened the windows and heard him crying out in the street. His bellowing was so tiresome and wild that I could not concentrate on my Dos Passos book—a scene on a train in which a hobo struggles to sit up straight, fearing that he will cough to death if he lies down—so I closed the windows, even though this made the apartment too warm. What a loud, awful, obnoxious racket the man was making. Him I would remember; his cry I would recognize.

Ribs

On Saturdays the mail usually came around eleven in the morning. Starting at nine, Mira waited for it, drinking Turkish coffee and washing the dishes from the previous week; if it weren't for the mail, she wasn't sure her garret apartment would ever be clean. During the week, she taught high school history, which, with the new Croatian regime, she had had to relearn.

At quarter to eleven she walked down the dusty stairs, which were worn and indented in the middle even though they were made of thick oak boards. The lightbulb in the windowless stairway had burnt out and no tenants had bothered to replace it; nobody in the building seemed to know who the landlord was. The state had owned the building, but probably someone in the government had "privatized" it, not to look after it but to collect the rent.

No mail in the yellow box by the house gate with chipping gray lead paint. She looked out into the street: nobody in a gray uniform walking with his big leather bag—actually, no pedestrians at all. She peeked into the neighbors' mailboxes; they were empty. So there was still hope for today's mail, and even a bit of hope for what she was really waiting for: news about her husband, who had been drafted nearly a year before. She hadn't heard anything from him in more than six months. He was not reported as MIA. She could get no information about him from the government offices.

When he was home, she didn't enjoy his presence—they had been married for twenty years, and how wouldn't she get bored with someone who didn't like to read the same books, or even talk? Still, there was something terribly threatening in losing him, and in not knowing whether in fact she had lost him. Were they still a family? It was not up to them to decide, but up to the state, and probably not even the state, which wasn't much in control in the drift of the wars in the Balkans. And so now and then she looked up at the framed black-and-white picture—Zarko, bald, with a thick black mustache and raised eyebrows that looked like slow accents, ^ ^. His eyebrows made him look skeptical and disenchanted. Wistful. The eyebrows roofed large eyelids with purple veins. And what could he see better by raising the eyebrows? Why do people raise them? To correct farsightedness? She had not studied him much while they were together, but now she could not help it. He was a tram driver, and he had dreamed of becoming an independent painter, but he'd given up because he couldn't sell paintings, and acrylics were too expensive. He didn't like oils because, he claimed, they took too much time, and painting with them, with attention to timing and the order in which one applied the paints, resembled cooking too much. The picture on the wall was taken while he was still a tram driver and he had already given up his art. But the disenchantment couldn't be explained so easily, in commercial terms—that would be too Marxist, she thought. He must have given up on image making because his eyes had failed to see something that they had yearned for; his mind had failed to capture whatever it had hoped, and that probing gaze perhaps expressed alarm at the emptying of his vision, at the dissolution of the things seen, observed, into a meaningless vastness. But there was something that perhaps grieved him more than his stalled art: an accident. One day when his tram had been pulling out of a stop, the doors, which closed automatically, caught a boy's leg. Zarko did not see that. Perhaps he had been too abstracted to look in the rearview mirror. People screamed. He did not hear the screams in time. Perhaps he had been too self-absorbed or dreamy to realize that the screams were directed at him. So he did not notice that the boy, with his leg caught in the door, fell on the asphalt. The train dragged the boy's body. By the time Zarko responded to the screams, the boy had fallen under the wheels, which crushed him. After that, Zarko quit driving trams and worked as a ticket salesperson at the international counter at the train station. Who knows, Mira thought as she sipped more of her muddy espresso, what he lived for. Why could he never express his longings, misgivings, sadness? And why can't this country get any better coffee? On all her trips abroad, she found much better coffee—in Vienna, Milan, even Hungary. Why was Croatia and the former Yugoslavia in general bent on importing the worst, stalest coffee in the world? Perhaps it wasn't stale upon arrival, but stayed in storage places for months.

She drank her third cup of espresso, or depresso, and walked down. There was one blue envelope, from the ministry of defense, but it was addressed to her son, not to her. She opened it.

Pero, her nineteen-year-old, was just barely getting up. He had stayed out late; although he didn't have any money, he frequented bars and cafés. It seemed most young people spent their time sitting in the tiny jittery chairs of cafés all over Zagreb. Terrible lifestyle, but there were no jobs and the universities were in disarray—during the war, the brain drain had intensified: many of the Serbian faculty were sacked, and many, Croats and Serbs alike, had gone abroad. The replacements weren't always qualified; they got jobs through political contacts and temporary political correctness, which, at the time, was nationalism. So the quality of education fell sharply, and Pero claimed there was no point in studying anything. Mira loved her son, but she hated his sloth and his lifestyle. She wished him to work as a laborer or anything for a year, simply to work, not to lounge around watching bad TV and reading American books in awful translations.

Pero was up, stumbling around the sink and squeezing an empty toothpaste tube.

You know what this means? she asked Pero, who was baring his large teeth in front of the mirror.

He read the notice.

Sure, they'll probably want me to go to Bosnia to fight in the idiotic war.

That's right.

Shit, I'm not going.

How do you think you'll accomplish that?

I'll run away, abroad.

But your passport's expired, and you can't get a new one without a release from the army. And what would you do abroad?

Maybe I can walk across the border at night. Nobody guards their borders the way they used to.

He spat white toothpaste into the sink and forgot to wipe his mouth, so although his face was red from anger, his lips were white, like a clown's.

Mira's cousin, who was a physician, wrote a note to the effect that Pero suffered from hypertension, 200 over100, but the recruitment office director, according to Pero, said, We could send you to a hospital for a week and check out your condition to see whether you are malingering, but that would waste everybody's time. So what if you had hypertension? If Serbs and Muslims invade Zagreb, wouldn't you still have to defend yourself? And so what are you going to do? Die of a heart attack? Come on, you look pretty healthy to me. Who gives a shit if you have high blood pressure. You'll have it at home, too. Walking in the woods will do you some good. Go home, get your underwear, and off we go, in three days.

And Pero did go home, with a bottle of brandy.

Mira was beside herself. Wasn't it enough that she'd lost her husband? For what? For some kind of fake country, which

served as a pretext for a few robbers to get rich while everybody else got poorer?

How would she live if she lost her son? What would she
do? Write letters? Go again to Mothers Against War and
shout? She had done that; she had protested with Mothers
Against War because they were the best-organized protesters,
a group of several hundred women who marched peacefully
in Zagreb, Osijek, Rijeka, and several other towns in Croatia.
On one occasion, she took trains through Hungary to Serbia
with several other mothers and joined a similar Serbian organization. Together the two groups gathered in front of
Savezna Skupstina (the parliament), carrying enlarged pictures of their beloved sons and daughters, for there were
daughters in the war as well. They threatened to storm the
parliament, but the police stopped them—not by force, but by
informing them that nobody was in. The politicians were all
watching the soccer match, Zvezda vs. Dinamo Kiev. And
Milosevic never came to the parliament anyhow. The cops
said, Your best hope is to get attention from the camera crews
so they'll broadcast your protest on the news, or get journal-
ists interested so they will put your pictures in the papers.
And as the mothers stood, ignored by the media and politicians, they talked about their children and husbands in the
war, and soon Serbian mothers started blaming Croatia, and
Croat mothers Serbia, and the peace-loving gathering ended
in fistfights. Mira got a black eye in the brawl. If it hadn't
been for the police, the brawl would have been much worse
for the outnumbered Croatian mothers. They ran down the
steep cobbled streets, twisting their ankles, to the train station,
and crammed into a couple of compartments with a few quiet

soldiers who were on the way to Novi Sad. The soldiers were courteous, offering them homemade poppy-seed strudels, and it was hard to imagine that they might be drafted murderers on vacation.

No, she was not going to join Mothers Against War again. She took a tram to the recruitment center and asked to speak to the director. He was too busy to see her. She waited till the end of the shift and followed him out to his black BMW. He went alone, unescorted—pretty remarkable, she thought.

Excuse me, sir, could I talk with you for a second about my son, Pero Ivicic?

Why, everybody wants to talk with me about sons!

But he has high blood pressure, couldn't you let him stay home?

That is not my job. If the recruiters said he must go, he must go.

How much money should I give you to change that?

You want me to go through the records stealthily, to take his out? That's awkward. I am not bribable.

Are you serious? I thought everybody took bribes.

How much are we talking here? he asked while he unlocked the door with a beeper remote.

Eight hundred marks.

He scoffed. At this rate, you may indeed arouse my sympathy.

I don't have any more money. My son is all I have. My husband hasn't come back from central Bosnia. Perhaps you could find out about him?

That's not my job.

What is your job?

He laughed. I could let my colleague who deals with stuff like that look into it. Anyway, what was his name?

Is, I hope. Zarko Ivicic.

Zarko Ivicic?

Please, do have someone let me know where my husband is.

But about your son, I can't do anything. We need soldiers; we don't have enough to cover all the fronts. You know what our country looks like, like a banana, with borders everywhere and territory nowhere. That's all we have, borders, impossible to cover.

He took a look at her. What is your son's name? Sorry, I am no good with names, it takes two, three times before I can remember them. And your name?

Mira Ivicic is mine. Pero is my son's.

And Zarko Ivicic? He sighed. Okay, I will remember.

He again took a look at her, up and down, as if to determine her proportions, and he said, If you'd like to talk more, let's have a cup of coffee at Gradska Kavana.

The Kavana was an old establishment in the center of the city, with marble floors, high ceilings, and newspapers on sticks, which tremulous old men with yellow fingers and white hairs read slowly, their blue lips moving asymmetrically. Crimson velvet curtains hung in round vertical waves over the windows, and even where they did not cover the windows, no light came in from outside. The low awnings blocked the sunlight, and inside the lightbulbs, imitating candles in chandeliers on wheels, dissipated only a feeble orange light from up high.

They sat in a corner and a waiter in the traditional white-and-black outfit came over.

Mira put her hands on the marble surface of the table and was struck by how chilly it felt.

Two cappuccinos, the director said.

She was already wired enough from her morning coffee and the alarming news, so she knew the cappuccinos would be overkill.

She trembled from so much coffee and fear, and now the uncertainty of what would be said. The stern man was handsome in a rough way—his five o'clock shadow made his protruding chin and the space above his upper lip blue. And with his somewhat graying hair and blue eyes, and the blue smoke that enveloped him, he was thoroughly blue. She wondered whether his blue jacket and blue shirt lent their color to his eyes and hair. When she picked up her glass of water, her hand shook, and the water rippled and almost spilled over. She clutched the glass with both of her hands to drink. She had not been with a man in a year, and there was something disarmingly erotic in the uncertainty and the threat that this man posed. The fact that the erotic sensation seemed trivial in the face of more important matters, such as her son's freedom, only enhanced the vague but irrepressible flutter of her senses.

If you sleep with me, I'll be nice to you, I'll help you, the director said.

Why would you want to sleep with me?

Do you need to ask? I find you attractive.

If you want sex, you can easily find it. I can give you one thousand German marks—I think I could borrow two hundred—and for that you can have ten whores. I am not one of them.

I get offers of bribes all the time, so bribes don't excite me. People offer me women.

Women are people.

Of course, of course. People offer sex, too. But that's different. I am picky.

Should I be flattered?

I'd say so.

To be treated like a whore?

Oh, don't put it so roughly. As a beauty, a high-society girl, let's say.

And you are the high society?

I am afraid so. He laughed. Anyway, I don't mean that either. You could see me as a friend.

I don't know whether I could trust you.

Of course you don't know. Who can trust anybody these days?

She felt his shin sliding against her outer calf. His hairy legs above his sock tickled her naked skin.

Without thinking, she slapped him. The sound resounded and her palm brimmed with heat.

Feisty, aren't we? he said. I like that. Fire! What sign are you?

The go-to-hell sign.

She stood up and left.

Hey, hey, he shouted after her, I was just being playful!

But as soon as she was several blocks away, she considered: what's worse, her sleeping with a creep or her son's getting killed in Bosnia? No-brainer. She'd perhaps have a pang of guilt and discomfort for the rest of her life whenever she thought of sleeping with the director, but at least both she and her son would have a good chance for a longer rest of their lives. And she could dispel the discomfort by thinking that her self-sacrifice saved her son, gave him a second birth . . . so she might even gladly remember how she had helped him. After several blocks, she turned and walked back to the Kavana, but the man was not there. She sat down nevertheless and ordered a glass of white wine.

When she got home, her son was awake. He was not going out. He sat at a drafting table and drew images of woodpeckers, something he loved to do whenever he was ill, as a child. And now he looked all miserable and sallow, his spine bent over the table.

Where were you? he asked her.

What do you mean, where was I?

You were gone so long . . . and I will be leaving soon.

That's just it, I went to the military offices to see whether I could bribe them so you wouldn't have to serve.

They are open this late? And?

Believe it or not, the draft director would not be bribed.

Incredible. How much did you offer?

A thousand marks.

But that's too little. Offer five thousand.

Where would we get it?

SHE COULDN'T SLEEP THAT NIGHT. She kept imagining the director. If he hadn't approached her so crassly and blackmailed her with sex in exchange for her son's freedom, she would have agreed to sleep with him. But this way, he degraded her, himself, and sex, and so it could only be a sordid event. Except that her son would be free. But the sex itself would be sordid and utilitarian. Was that a subtle distinction? What difference should it really make how he approached the subject?

She had been sensually awakened on many occasions—and some days continuously. The war and the occasional bombings, especially in the beginning, when she spent several months in Osijek in eastern Croatia, had suffused her with a sensation of thrill and weakness that affected her eros. The war had sunk the country into literal darkness, with power outages, and into savage energy, which she felt everywhere. In the streets people looked at one another aggressively; sometimes she felt almost naked in front of men's gazes.

She dressed impeccably, and when her budget didn't allow for the best new dresses, she made them herself. She walked to shop at the distant farmers' market and to her work, a couple of kilometers away, so she stayed slim, and her motions displayed a certain ease and grace since she was used to moving, walking, working, but nothing she did was strenuous. In her midforties, she felt even better than in her twenties, and she noticed that men stared at her body.

In the other room, her son groaned in his sleep.

In the morning he looked thoroughly miserable. He was smoking. He had quit. Perhaps he had pretended to quit, and now the pretenses were down.

After breakfast, consisting of two eggs over fried onions, he vomited.

He had only two days left before his departure.

She called in sick to work; she taught in the afternoon. A teacher calling in sick—a fine example. But why shouldn't she? She was underpaid. And she did feel thoroughly sick.

She called up the director.

So you changed your mind? Delighted.

Well, would two thousand marks do it?

No. No money, only us.

If we sleep together, who's to say that you will be motivated afterward to do anything about the draft? What could I do in that case? You might lose interest in me after the first time, wait—don't interrupt, I know men can be like that.

Inconceivable. Anyway, I can't keep talking like this on the phone—my secretary is here, colleagues.

They met in the apartment of a friend of his in an old, crumbling yellow building which shook whenever trams passed. As they sat on the sofa and drank Riesling, a small chunk of mortar from the ceiling fell on the coffee table.

Jesus Maria, she said, this building must be at least two hundred years old, and if it reacts like this whenever a tram passes by, I wonder how it manages to still be here.

Good question, he said, and drank more. It's too bright here, he said, and drew the roller curtains that were on the outside of the window. One of them got stuck, and stood diagonally across.

Do you know, he said, you haven't even asked me for my name?

Why would I? Don't you think I would know it from the office directory?

Well, there I give only my initial and my last name. So what is my name?

True, she knew only his last name. Petrovic, she said.

No first name? That doesn't matter to you? See, I take interest in you, ask you for your name, personal questions, and you don't care. So who wants to exploit whom, you tell me?

You have a point, she said. But, you know, to me, you are just you. We don't know anybody in common, we probably won't either, so we don't need names. It's just I and you.

Not quite. Anyway, my name is Branko.

Oh, pleased to meet you. She ironically stretched her hand and held it limply in his. His felt hot and dry, and that meant that hers must have been clammy. Playfully, he brought her hand up to his lips.

They undressed. She emerged from her dress and, with a swing of her hips, shook it off and let it slide down her legs. The drop of the cloth created a motion of the air, which stroked her coldly. Her knees touched each other, and so did her ankles, and her hip stayed tilted. She thought she was perhaps unconsciously affecting a mermaid posture, but now she was self-conscious. The more the cool draft, obviously no longer from her skirt but from poor windows, touched her, the more she was aware of her skin, even her hairs. She hadn't yielded to the American pressure to shave her legs. Coca-Cola could have us by the throat, NATO could blast the hell out of the region if it wanted, but Gillette and Sharon Stone would not get to her, would not possess her hairs and scrape her skin with blades. She had light brown hair, hardly visible, but certainly feelable—they were tiny feelers, antennae for the motion of air and skins. As far as she was concerned, they were an erogenous zone, an erogenous prezone, and to her mind, there was nothing more sensuous than the moment before two skins touch, when the hairs already have bent to the warmth of the oncoming skin. The warm air moves the hairs, a subtle force spreads through the coils, the cuticles, evolving electricity. The pretouch communication of skins should enter its own time, its own sphere of slowness: and if skins could stay at slightly less than an aroused-hair-length of distance for minutes, she could have a most fabulous excitement of the senses, transcending the erogenous zones, local and provincial orgasms; all her hairs would add up the microthrills into a gestalt, in which she would be more than the sum of her parts; she would be herself, in and out of her body, astrally projected, brought out to the surface and beyond it, but not divided from herself and the world.

But the moment was not this subtle, she remembered; she was in this position for her son, she was going to sacrifice the integrity of her bodily aura and self, but as she considered her senses, she was not sure there would be any sacrifice. She perhaps hated and feared the man in front of her, but that did not interfere with a nascent thrill. Through her fear of the man her senses were alarmed and aroused in a diffuse way. Once the fear failed to produce flight, it became a sexual breathlessness. Perhaps her mistrust of the man was an aphrodisiac.

He undressed too, and pulled down his red boxer shorts. His legs were muscular, with big calves and quads, clearly a soccer player's legs, and his hairs were plentiful. Whether she liked him, whether she hated him, it didn't matter; she yearned for a conflagration of the senses, muscles.

They approached each other, but there was no moment of electrical discharge from their skins, for they fell into a grasping embrace. She liked squeezing tightly against him, feeling her muscles press through his to the bone. Her breasts pressed into his ribs. His hands, emanating the aroma of sunny tobacco fields, roved; one clasped her thigh, another the back of her neck. They fell onto the bed.

He kept touching her, massaging her breasts and thighs, and yes, she enjoyed it, but she longed to be spread out, invaded, she wanted a momentary surrender, the thrill of losing control, of defeat, mutual defeat, but the man withdrew, sighed, and a blue cloud seemed to come out of his forehead although he was not smoking.

He looked humiliated, and she felt safe, and that safety disappointed her. The situation had become banal. No threat, no conflagration. And she worried about Pero—would this count?

I am not with it today, he said, hoarsely, without clearing his throat. My daughter is in the hospital, with pneumonia. I am worried and guilty.

How could it be your fault? And what are you doing here?

Not that it is. But you know—maybe I could have kept our house warmer. Maybe I should have been buying oranges. I forget these things, and so does my wife.

So what are you doing with me?

Good question. You know, I wanted it, I thought about it, and I still want you, but the timing is bad. Sorry, he said.

You don't have to be. Why would you be? This still counts, doesn't it? You will let my son off the hook, won't you?

She was confused. Here, this man presented himself as a bully and exploiter, and then not only couldn't get it up but turned out to be a worried family man. Perhaps he only wanted to talk with her. Maybe he needed the pretext of sexploitation just to talk.

He drank warm Riesling from a thin green bottle. Funny, I keep thinking of my childhood, I don't know why, he said.

I don't know either, she said.

Was yours happy?

Oh, please, of course it was happy. I was in a bucolic Zagorje village, surrounded by barefoot kids, lots of cats, dogs, ducks, horses, what more would you want? What do you want from childhood? To explain your current troubles? That's passé even in psychotherapy. She wasn't sure about that, but she felt like saying it, perhaps because she was not ready for soulful confessions and lives explained and disguised. Not now, anyway. What happened to the good old sex?

For my part, the director said, I think childhood matters, if it's an unhappy one. I grew up in Stuttgart, on a hill, near an American military hospital, in a wet dark gray building, and my father was a *Gastarbeiter,* a mason. He hated his work. He was damaged anyway, from the Second World War, because he was in the Croatian army when the war ended and he spent a year in Communist prison camps. His weight went down to half of his previous weight, he was skin and bones when he jumped off the train and fled to Italy. He was damaged, full of anger, and he made sure not to be alone in that. Every night he got drunk and beat my mother, me, and my brother, with fists, shoes. . . . And I still felt sorry for him when he died. Fell off the building and broke his neck. Strange, after him, my mother went through a transformation. Her nerves were damaged, of course, and now it was she who beat us every night.

How lovely. And that drove you into work for the Croatian military?

Oh, please, it's not that simple.

He was sitting on the edge of the bed, next to her feet, while she lay back, leaning on two pillows, with her breasts exposed. She did not wish to cover them; the cool air felt good, and being naked in front of the man, even though they could not have sex, gave her a sensation of airiness. Perhaps it was even aggressive, to display her femininity to him, keeping his masculinity in question.

Actually, I lied, he said.

You made up your childhood traumas?

No, not that part, but the present. My daughter is all right. She is not ill. I don't even have a daughter.

Why would you lie about something like that?

Good question. I don't know. Maybe to justify myself. I mean, my lack of arousal.

There's no need to justify. There's always Viagra.

Hey, don't put me down. I . . . this happened for the first time.

With his head bent down nearly to his knees, he formed a letter C which was threatening to become a zero. What a metamorphosis of a power figure, all because of a stalled erection, how ridiculous, she thought. In a way, in his bent position, if he got an erection, he would complete the circle for a zero. What's in this for him? Strange what moves men, she thought. But now that he looked so vulnerable and sorrowful, he came to life for her as a man; he was not just a sex-driven bureaucrat who held the fate of her son in his power. She felt a momentary sympathy for him.

We can always give it another try, she said, and poked with her toes the side of his body, above his hip, near where his kidney should be.

He wiggled uncomfortably.

Just hours before, he had been playing cat and mouse with

her, as the cat, and now he was becoming all mousy and she catty. She laughed.

Actually, he began, and withdrew even further to the very edge of the bed.

You aren't interested at all? We can keep massaging, don't worry about sex. That's erotic and fun too.

No, I don't mean that . . . you interest me. Sex interests me, believe me, unfortunately. But there's something more urgent. I should have told you about it right away, but I didn't know how, or whether I should, and actually just because I do like you, I can't avoid telling you. I still probably shouldn't tell you.

What? You are talking in circles. If there's something to tell, go ahead. I can take it. What's it about? You have some terrible VD? So we can go out and buy condoms. Thanks for being considerate.

Not that simple. It has to do with your husband. We were together, in the same company in Bosnia.

Is he alive? She jumped out of bed.

Branko Petrovic did not say anything.

Do you know whether he's alive?

I'll get to that point. I'll tell you what I know.

She covered her breasts with her hands, and then the motion struck her as absurd. She let her arms hang limply.

We all, as members of the Croatian army in Bosnia, participated in the action in Stupni Do. You know about Stupni Do?

Who doesn't? That's pretty horrible! In that massacre?

We went house to house looking for arms and hidden Muslim soldiers, in basements, but there were no arms and no soldiers. I am sure our commander knew that there were no soldiers; he wanted terror, that is all. You know, it worked for Serbs, to massacre a village or two, and rather than to hide the fact, to broadcast it, so people from the whole area would flee. Our officers imitated the Serbs, no doubt. The commander did not explain that to us, just told us to go door to door and shoot, because there were soldiers in hiding. I swear, then I didn't know what we were doing, not at first, anyway.

How wouldn't you know what you are doing? Were you shooting old women? What's there not to know?

Our men kept shooting their way into all the houses, killing whoever we ran across, in the gun smoke and tear gas. Sometimes we threw hand grenades into the basements without checking who was there. We were in a rush, before other armies could come to the village. We set many houses on fire.

You did that? My husband, too?

We all did some of that.

Some of what? My husband killed randomly, just like that? Mira was horrified. She had seen footage of the remains of carnage on satellite TV at a friend's place. The footage was not shown on Croatian TV at the time. If he did that, maybe he should not come back.

Yes, I am sure he killed one or two people. We were all shooting in a terrible rush because we didn't have much time, and there were the Brits not too far away, and the Croatian officers were pushing us. It was absolute frenzy, you couldn't think straight.

And that's some kind of excuse?

No, nobody is talking excuse here. But your husband did something noble, stupid but noble. He protested as a couple of soldiers beat and threatened to knife a ten-year-old boy. Zarko wanted to stop the beating, and an officer shot Zarko, point-blank, in the face, with a semi. Strafed his head off.

Jesus. You saw that?

Yes, that's the point. That's why I hesitated to tell it.

So, he's dead?

I am afraid so. No way could he live.

My God! You are sure? I mean, there was smoke, and you all rushed . . .

That's why I am here. To tell you.

You could have told me right away, at the Kavana.

It's not that simple to tell. I had to get to know you a little. I had to trust you. It's sensitive information. I am putting myself in your hands, you understand that, by letting you know I was at Stupni Do? You could turn me in. Nobody must know I was there.

Why are you telling me that? Would you like me to turn you in? You think you might go to The Hague?

No, of course not. Yet I don't want to have power over you, with your son's fate, so I am equalizing the playing field here.

Is he buried? Where?

I think he was burned down with the Muslims. We ran out at that point. I didn't see. If you want to find him, you'll have to go down there to Bosnia, and perhaps some of the bones could be identified as his.

You are lying. You lied before.

No, I wish, I wish I were.

Horrible. Horrible, she said, but the word struck her as too weak. She wanted to attack the man, but that seemed futile. She was still naked, sitting on a smooth floor of large wood planks and hugging her knees. She imagined her husband and the boy. To him it may have been the same boy who died under the tram tracks, the ghost of his guilt, and he got a chance to expiate for his absentmindedness and dreaminess, to stand up and save the boy. And that, after throwing a grenade at civilians in a cellar. How could one live after all that anyway? Maybe he died happy. Did that matter? Was that the end he had envisioned with his wistful gaze?

And the boy, did he live? Was he saved?

I don't know.

And, you, what did you do? Did you try to save my husband, to save the boy? she asked.

Nothing, what could I do? He was putting on his pants and tightening his belt, so that his middle-aged love handles spilled over it.

Couldn't you protest too, and if enough of you protested, nothing would have happened?

I doubt that. There were enough deranged soldiers there, drunk, drugged, that even if three or four of us protested, we would have all been shot down. Not only that . . . we would have slaughtered one another.

Would not that have been better?

How?

So what do you suggest I do now? How do I bury him? What use is it?

No, I'll tell you how. But I don't want to help you with all that. Nobody must know that I was there, in that action, you understand? I don't want to end up in The Hague.

Why not? Maybe you could help with the whole thing. How can you live with yourself, your conscience, if you have one?

That's for me to decide, to judge, not for you, not for The Hague. I am the only one who knows what went on for me, inside me. Nobody can judge the soul of a man. But don't worry, your son is safe. He is not going to be drafted. He will not have to join the army, I'll see to that. But if you tell anybody about our conversation, he will have to go. And he will go to the worst position, front lines, you understand?

You are even threatening me?

No, I am not threatening you. Just letting you know.

Or as you put it, to level the playing field. What game are you playing? To you this is a game? Are you having fun?

No, I am not playing a game. Playing field, just a cliché. I couldn't express my thoughts precisely. I am not expressing myself well when I sound like I am threatening you. No, I am not threatening. We are together for sex, perhaps love.

But you said you weren't here to sleep with me but to tell me the secret.

That's not exactly what I meant. I had to say what I said to clear the air, so you would know, so I would know that you know. Now that we share all that, we can move on, go deeper. You are the only one who can understand me.

She sat on the edge of the bed. He sat next to her and put his hand on her knee. She slid away from him and imagined Zarko's head falling off in the smoke, with the blood spurting out of his body. Could the head have fallen off the body? Or did Branko exaggerate? And now, there were these persistent fingers, like an assembly of hard toothless snakes, creeping up her belly. How could she be in the mood for physical intimacy now, with all these ghastly images assailing her senses? She was dizzy.

The director undressed again. Now he had an erection, and he proudly showed it.

Just like that? All you needed was a good confession, with some blood, blood of my husband, and now you are ready?

Mira sobbed, kneeling at the side of the bed.

Leave me. I can't do it, not now. Maybe tomorrow. Go.

Hey, hey, he said. Not so fast. I can't leave you here. This is not your place.

AT HOME, she explained to her son that he would not have to serve in the army. He was surprised, delighted. So, you found more money! Great. Where?

I can't talk about it.

Why not? A state secret?

Something like that. Yes, a state secret.

She looked at him and considered telling him that she had found out about his father, that he was dead, but she could not bring herself to say it. Not now. She would have to gather strength. She could have presented the case as good news and bad news, which do you want first? No, she would bring only the good news. But there was relief in knowing so finally about her husband. He is dead. Nothing to worry about anymore. Her son would be alive. Two problems were solved. She could relax. She was so exhausted that she fell asleep without undressing. And she had dreams. Mira, get up, how can you sleep? Zarko's image spoke to her, made all out of blue clouds, with small black clouds for eyebrows. Get up, look for my bones, bury them. You can't leave them out in the charcoal mud of Bosnia. I need to go home, to the village of my birth, to my soil. You must do it. I will not let you rest until my bones are buried.

She woke up in fright, rose, and paced around. Her son was out. He was probably having a good time in a bar. She turned on the lights and listened to Mozart's *Eine Kleine Nacht-musik.* The predictable, all too predictable turns of the melody did not comfort her. They were predictable, of course, because she had heard them too many times. She drank a warm Staro-cesko Pivo. She wondered, is that really my husband talking to me in my dreams? How come he didn't talk to me when I did not know he was dead? So this must be just my mind talking to itself. But the vividness of the dream spooked her, and she couldn't get rid of the notion that it was her husband's ghost talking to her directly. The way she was afraid to fall asleep when she was a child, that was how she was afraid to fall asleep now.

She kept the lights on and remembered the nightmares of her childhood. She had told Branko her childhood was a happy one, and in a way it was, but she had certainly had hor-rifying dreams of the house catching on fire with her parents and siblings burning to death. Probably it was simple to ex-plain: her father smoked ham in the attic, and the wafting smell of smoke and flesh entered her dreams. And so she had slept with the lights on, even though it angered her mother who claimed that electricity was too expensive. So she won-dered why she had so categorically claimed a happy childhood to Branko—perhaps simply to avoid a boring and predictable conversation. Now she fell asleep. Zarko spoke to her again in the dream, from an evergreen tree on fire. It was a Christmas tree with sparklers, and once the fire caught on, he spoke, be-seeching her to gather his bones.

In the morning, she was exhausted and unhappy, and she

decided that she could not deal with her husband's bones until she felt better. At the moment, she did not feel sorry for her husband. She hated the nuisance. How could he be so pushy in death? She hated him. Served him right. Let him be dead. What difference did it make how he was dead? Bones scattered or not, rot or ashes, who should care? Once you are dead, you aren't you.

The following evening, afraid of one more terrible night of sleep, she agreed to get together with Branko. Her son had gone with friends on a trip to the coast, so she invited Branko home. They drank Dingac, red wine, which darkened their lips and overcame the taste of tobacco and coffee. They kissed languidly and probed each other's bodies. In lovemaking, perhaps because of sleeplessness and the long abstinence, she experienced strong electrical currents and tingling in her head, with flashes of light in her vision, even though she kept her eyes closed. She floated in the currents of electricity as though she had ceased to be a creature of flesh and bones, and so as not to drift off into the ethereal space, to ground herself, she clasped Branko, and dug with her nails into his back with such force that he gasped in pain. Blood trickled down his hairy back.

Afterward, as they relaxed and drank more red wine, he said, Wow, that was passion! On one side of the body, great pleasure, on the other, pain!

I feel so calm—calmer than I ever remember, she said. Discharged. Empty. It's great to feel empty. I never knew that.

And who is that? Branko pointed toward the picture of Zarko.

Oh, Zarko, my husband, former husband.

Boy, has he changed! Branko commented. When I knew him afterward, he'd lost most of his hair, and he grew much thinner.

Must have been stressful for him. And you, have you changed?

Not in the war, but if we keep going at this rate, I too will lose all my hair and much of my skin.

She playfully stroked him with her nails, over his naked belly, and pretty soon they were making love again. It was windy outside; a strong draft slammed a window shut. Even a door closed although she did not remember leaving it open. Although she was naked, she felt more naked still with the blowing of cold moist winds, which seemed to undress her further, to strip away an invisible layer of her heat and her vapors, her salts, so that she was completely fresh and open, invigorated and free, desiring and loving the cold electrical currents under her skin. While escalating her breathing in her excitement, she looked from under Branko's armpit, and in the dim light, she had an impression that someone was sitting in the armchair across the room. She should not have counted on her son being away. Or was she not seeing right? Meanwhile, the armpit closed, she shuddered, and as she closed her eyes, she saw lights, akin to northern lights. Beautiful. Maybe she was seeing other things, she thought. Still, she opened her eyes as Branko shifted and caught a glimpse of Zarko in the armchair, gazing intently, with his eyebrows arched even more than before, thicker, sadder. She closed her eyes. Why would the ghost of her husband now torment her even in wakefulness? The lovemaking did drive her out of her senses. But this was not the kind of hallucination she welcomed. And was it a hallucination? Probably, what else? He was dead. Why think about that now? She wouldn't. She closed her eyes and relished the waves of intense thrills in her flesh, with northern lights pulsating in the rhythm of her heart and sex.

She opened her eyes again. The same eyes were still there, glistening in the dim light of the indigo aftermath of a purple dusk. She screamed.

What is it? Branko said.

He is here!

Who is?

Zarko!

He can't be, he's dead.

Turn around. Look. Tell me, am I hallucinating?

Branko turned around, heftily.

Keep going, she heard her husband say. I want to see how it ends.

Oh, is that you? she addressed Zarko, and covered herself with a pillow, and then she said to Branko, There! Sitting with a gun and pointing it at us! He's going to shoot us! Don't shoot!

Don't freak me out! Branko said. You are insane. Look into my eyes—are you there? Insanity scares the hell out of me.

There he is. Say hi to him. Say you are happy he's alive!

Branko quickly got dressed and rushed toward the door. He tripped. Mira saw Zarko's foot tripping him.

After Branko's exit, there was silence, other than the faucet dripping and a distant train rambling on the uneven rails.

She closed her eyes, trying to close her mind. She was terrified of her mind. How would she sleep now if Zarko ruled her dreams? Her mind was no longer hers, she thought, but his. If she fell asleep, he would run amok in her mind, terrorize her, slash and burn, as though still in Stupni Do, shooting, unless he ran into a young boy, but there were no more young boys. Even their son had just ceased to be a young boy and was now a draftable man, a soldier, nobody to inspire mercy. There was no young life, new life, to stop the madness and to redeem them. She felt old, spent, and yet, at the same time, she still tingled from lovemaking, and wished she could vanish in another wave of it, a bigger one, more overwhelming than the last one. And just at that turn of daydreaming, she heard a snore.

She turned on the lights. And there, she could clearly see, was Zarko, sprawled on the floor, with his mouth open, and sleeping. To make sure that her mind was not deceiving her, she touched his body, his ribs, like a doubting Thomas. There were ribs, she could feel them under her fingers, and she was sure there had to be a hole, somewhere—she would find it.

Insights,
Interviews
& More...

Meet Josip Novakovich

Jeanette Novakovich

"I CAME TO NEW YORK when I was twenty out of sheer curiosity," says Josip Novakovich. "I came from a provincial town of a provincial country, and my lust for the cosmopolitan world was irrepressible." A native of Daruvar, Croatia, Novakovich studied psychology, philosophy, and religion at Vassar, before going on to earn a master of divinity at Yale. Philosophy in some way cleared the ground for his career writing fiction: "I was impressed by what Willard Van Orman Quine said, to the effect that there are two philosophical landscapes—that of the desert and that of the jungle. Logical positivism and minimalism he likened to the desert aesthetics. I thought my tendency was toward the jungle, and when I looked around, fiction was even more jungle-like than any philosophy—nothing reduced to abstractions, but everything rendered in detail, in an abundance of life. After reading many boring philosophical texts, I was astonished by how alive the language of fiction was. I read fiction for months, then sat down to write some. Even now I delight in how irreducible and nonabstractable people are. Each one is different, doing and feeling things in his or her own peculiar way."

After earning a master of fine arts in fiction from the University of Texas, Novakovich married and began teaching at the Nebraska Indian Community College. In the early 1990s, after receiving numerous grants and fellowships—including one from the National Endowment for the Arts—and getting his stories published in journals such as *Ploughshares* and *The Paris Review,* he traveled to Sarajevo and wrote extensively on the Yugoslavian civil wars. A book of essays, *Apricots from Chernobyl,* and two short story collections, *Yolk* and *Salvation and Other Disasters,* followed, and Novakovich won numerous awards, including an American Book Award from the Before Columbus Foundation, a Guggenheim Fellowship, and a Whiting Award. *Kirkus Reviews* named him one of the best short story writers of the decade and *Utne Reader* placed him on the list of ten writers who are changing the way we look at the world. Novakovich's next book, *Plum Brandy: A Croatian Journey,* a collection of personal essays, recorded his journeys to find his roots, some to his native Croatia, some no farther than Cleveland, Ohio. In 2004, his first novel, *April Fool's Day,* was published to great acclaim. "Novakovich knows how to tell a story, and his prose has an easy, elegant velocity," wrote Maud Casey in the *New York Times Book Review.* "Strange, lyrical beauty abounds here." ▶

66 'I delight in how irreducible and nonabstractable people are. Each one is different, doing and feeling things in his or her own peculiar way.' 99

Meet Josip Novakovich (*continued*)

If Novakovich's work is possessed of both Balkan and American sensibilities, then it may stem from his movement between the two cultures: "I have remained in the States, but I visit what's now Croatia quite a bit," he says. "For two years my family and I experimented with reverse immigration—before it grew fashionable under the Bush regime to do stuff like that. My kids went to schools in Zagreb, and I spent half my time in Croatia. I grew tired of bad coffee and clouds of cigarette smoke and pollution and the complaints that are the usual mode of conversation there. I imagine I will never be free from being drawn back to Croatia, though, or from the impulse to flee it once I am there. That exilic impulse is part of me wherever I am—I'd always like to be elsewhere. It's a symptom of a cultural schizophrenia—my bicontinental disorder. It's quite expensive to treat it—lots of airfares."

In his books Novakovich has cultivated a unique and infectious brand of humor that runs through even the darkest subject matter. His eye for the absurd is crucial to his perception of the former Yugoslavia's recent tragedy: "Before the war people joked and they joke after the war. I often say that the war took place because we lost our sense of humor. We joked wonderfully and then suddenly began to take offense at the ethnic content of our jokes. We took them seriously and our humor failed. The war was a direct result of that failure. And I don't mean that as a joke, either."

With *Infidelities: Stories of War and Lust,* Novakovich continues to mix the comic and the grotesque, the playful and the brutal, and,

"'I will never be free from being drawn back to Croatia, though, or from the impulse to flee it once I am there. That exilic impulse is part of me wherever I am—I'd always like to be elsewhere. It's a symptom of a cultural schizophrenia— my bicontinental disorder.'"

in doing so, confirms his reputation as one of the best short story writers working in Croatia or America. He has taught at the University of Cinncinnati, and now teaches at Pennsylvania State University. Novakovich makes his home in the woods of Pennsylvania with his wife, two kids, and five cats. ⌒◡

A Conversation with
Josip Novakovich

On some level I want to entertain as though I were telling anecdotes to my friends. No matter how grim the subject—heart transplants, wars—there's space for comic relief. In a terrible situation, you may be thinking something that doesn't make sense at all. You may be recalling a stamp collection you had as a child, or you may be distracted by an image of feminine beauty. Many of us use whimsical thoughts to distance ourselves from events going on right in front of us, and in my stories I explore the subjectivity of our minds—or the quest for mental independence and freedom.

In most of your stories, a lot seems to happen. Why is that?

Stories to my mind are like dreams and nightmares. Unless you wake up too soon, a lot tends to happen in dreams, even if it doesn't always make sense. Our fears and desires take shape, express themselves, in events. Although in real life it's rare that one would, let's say, take revenge on someone, there are wish-fulfillment revenge stories all over the place. Same with sex, murder, etc. On the other hand, although there is a lot of lust in my stories, there isn't that much sex. I suppose I am repressed enough not to launch into outright erotica. Moreover, with my friends, I have noticed that the stories of

> 66 Many of us use whimsical thoughts to distance ourselves from events going on right in front of us, and in my stories I explore the subjectivity of our minds— or the quest for mental independence and freedom. 99

erotic failure are far more entertaining than the stories of success, which may arouse jealousy. Lust is a metaphor for many forms of unfulfilled longings, one that provokes imagination most easily. My characters long for a good meal, drink, even trees, freedom.

Why do you write in English even when your fiction is set in the former Yugoslavia?

I live in English and therefore I write in English. I acquired the writing habit in English when I went to college and graduate school—two years at Vassar, three at Yale. After five years of writing in English, whenever I sat down to explain anything on the page, it came out in English unless I checked myself. Moreover, Croatian had been changing under political influences then and I wasn't there to follow all the changes. My form of Croatian became antiquated, and editors in Croatia considered it a political statement, Yugo-nostalgia. English has an amazing speed and fluidity. When you see ten parallel translations, the English is usually the shortest. It certainly influences me to express myself efficiently, unlike in Croatian, where the main virtue used to be syntactical endurance—long and convoluted sentences. Under communism, we wrote strange sentences indeed, with many dependent clauses. I still occasionally enjoy the linguistic slalom that writing in Croatian proves to be. ▶

> 66 Lust is a metaphor for many forms of unfulfilled longings, one that provokes imagination most easily. My characters long for a good meal, drink, even trees, freedom. 99

A Conversation with Josip Novakovich
(*continued*)

What do you gain by writing in English as a second language? What's lost in translation?

In fiction, you can make something ordinary extraordinary by "defamiliarizing" it, which is usually an artificial process. But if you move out of your native realm, the process becomes unavoidable—ordinary details strike you as unusual. Looking at the former Yugoslavia not only from a distance of four thousand miles but from another language gives me freedom to notice the stories, to play with them, and to transform them into a reality of their own. It's no longer Yugoslavia, or Croatia, in a literal way, but in an expressionistic painterly way— a country of my own making, perhaps more surreal than real. On the other hand, the surrealism expresses very real fears and longings.

As for drawbacks: On a concrete level, I can't translate many jokes which depend on the language. I used to be good with dialects— in fact, often when answering questions in class, I used to joke like a stand-up comedian, using a mélange of dialects. I can't do that in translation. If I have a couple of peasant soldiers, what should they sound like? They can't sound like English professors, and if they talk slang, well, they can't sound like Kentuckians or Bostonians. So I have to write in some kind of informal but not slangy language. And if I write about immigrants, I should best write in both Croatian and English, in a Cronglish of sorts, but who would understand me? Now these problems perhaps keep me from sinking into meticulously realistic writing. They keep me inventing.

> ❝ In fiction, you can make something ordinary extraordinary by 'defamiliarizing' it, which is usually an artificial process. But if you move out of your native realm, the process becomes unavoidable— ordinary details strike you as unusual. ❞

Why did you write Infidelities?

I didn't write the stories with a mission, although some of them are pervaded by my antipathy towards wars. These days it has become important once again to make the basic and obvious points that war is a horrifying mess and that usually there are no victors, only war criminals and victims. It seems each generation needs to be disillusioned afresh. This is true both in America and in the Balkans, where after several years of war we grow exasperated, sometimes staying peaceful for twenty or thirty years before new frustrations are exploited by a new set of warrior demagogues—whether domestic or imported.

Is your style of writing about the war common in the former Yugoslavia?

People there no longer want to read or think about the war. They find the topic repulsive. When my friends found out I was writing about the war, they said, "Why about that? Anything but that! We thought you had a sense of humor."

   Most writing about the war has been journalism. I've found that to understand what people go through, I have to resort to fiction. I can't walk up to someone and ask, "What did it feel like to have your parents shot in front of you?" I asked my brother-in-law what it was like living two hundred yards away from Serbian tanks. His house had a howitzer hole in its foundation. But he didn't answer— instead, he preached to me. So, to better ▶

" These days it has become important once again to make the basic and obvious points that war is a horrifying mess and that usually there are no victors, only war criminals and victims. It seems each generation needs to be disillusioned afresh. "

9

understand his experience, I wrote a piece of fiction. I am still not sure I know what it was like for him, but I understand what someone may have gone through in such a situation—perhaps what I would have experienced.

I wrote "Ribs," another story, after spending some time in Croatia. The Croatian army had burned down a small Bosnian village, killing its inhabitants, and I wondered where the soldiers would go after something like that. Maybe a good husband became a criminal? If so, how would that play itself out in real life? How would it be real life any more? So the story becomes somewhat surreal in response to that, and the missing husband returns as a ghost at the end.

Now, what about the erotic elements in the stories, and in the title of the collection?

During war, life doesn't stop, but the essential elements become even more essential. Erotic impulses surface, perhaps as an expression of a survival impulse, or longing for beauty amidst of the excess of ugliness. In New York City, we had a sensation of war for at least a month following 9/11. I was in the city then, I watched the towers go down, and I rode the subways, paranoid, imagining that we'd all be blown up. Amidst the tensions, everybody looked around suspiciously and alertly, expecting the worst, and strangely enough, all that gazing resulted in an eroticized atmosphere. People claim that romance flourished all over the city in that month. I wouldn't know much about that—for me, it was all mental, in the observations, which

> 66 During war, life doesn't stop, but the essential elements become even more essential. Erotic impulses surface, perhaps as an expression of a survival impulse, or longing for beauty amidst of the excess of ugliness. 99

could become flirtatious. So, out of such observations I wrote "59th Parallel." I was reading John Dos Passos at the time, mostly on the subway, and I paid tribute to his *42nd Parallel.*

Where do your diverse protagonists come from?

For a while, I wanted to cover the war from many points of view, ethnically, and in terms of gender. I have one story from a child's perspective, "Snow Powder." This grew out of my son's love for snow. He was born in Fargo, North Dakota, in the middle of January, and he grew up with the mythology of cold weather. As a child he always wondered how much snow we were getting, and how much more there would be at a higher altitude. I transported him into the mountains in Bosnia and the rest is a fantasy. Many boys dream of destroying their schools; I know I did when I was eight or nine. I read reports of schools being bombed, and I put all these elements together as an expression of what a boy might desire, with the war as fulfillment of such destructive dreams. I also explore, I imagine the infantile aspects of a military thug's love of destruction. Alcohol is famous for throwing one back to earlier stages of psychological development, and drunken bands of soldiers might indeed behave like a band of dangerous boys. At the same time, there are child warriors all over the world, who can be particularly cruel and brave.

"Spleen" is the first story I've written in the first person from a woman's point of view. It seemed to me the best approach ▶

A Conversation with Josip Novakovich
(*continued*)

to get close to the experience of what a woman in exile, a victim of attempted rape in the war, might go through. I set the story in a real Cleveland neighborhood where immigrants from Bosnia, Croatia, and Serbia live in close quarters and there can be suspicions of who did what a decade ago in the wars. What happens if you see someone you think wronged you? In this story, more than in any other, I interweave the themes of war and lust. The element of fear and curiosity between the woman and the man strangely enhances her erotic impulse, and she becomes almost suicidal or homicidal. *Eros* and *thanatos* are closely linked there.

How did you come to write "Stamp"?

I chanced upon the materials for "Stamp" while researching World War One at the New York Public Library. I wanted to skip reading the accounts of the assassination in Sarajevo, but somehow I got waylaid there. It seemed strange that the whole gang of assassins had tuberculosis—since I had tuberculosis as a seven-year-old, I tend to be drawn to the subject. One would-be assassin slept with his chains under his covers, lest he should lose body heat, and I transferred that detail to Cabrinovic, another would-be assassin, who really did come to feel sorry for the children of the Archduke. Imagining what he thought provoked me to write the story. Once you get into a person's thoughts, no matter how strange his actions are, you can trace those thoughts until the actions seem reasonable and even plausible, in a *Crime and Punishment*

> ❝ Once you get into a person's thoughts, no matter how strange his actions are, you can trace those thoughts until the actions seem reasonable and even plausible. ❞

kind of way. Cabrinovic seems to me to be a Dostoyevskian character.

....

How does a collection of stories become a unified book?

Unity of purpose can be difficult in a story collection, and that's where editorial insight comes into play. Terry Karten, my editor, checked my impulse to include additional stories. I had several others with more sex or more war than the average story in the collection; on the surface they might belong, but they didn't add anything new to the book. I didn't have a sense of measure or of overall composition, and that's where Terry, a totally insightful editor, rescued the project. I believe it's a unified work—there's a Gestalt of a dramatic book. ᑐ

Josip Novakovich on
April Fool's Day

APRIL FOOL'S DAY is a very personal book
for me. I wanted to write an obituary to
Yugoslavia, in a personal form, so Ivan Dolinar,
the main character, is Yugoslavia personified.
The country was a strange one, and I play
with the sensation of paranoia, the power
obsession, and the sense of uniqueness that
plagued the country. In addition to my
memories of totalitarian socialism, I explore
particularly the moment of dying there. The
initial impulse for the novel came from my
desire to write a good death story, having read
"The Death of Ivan Ilych." I witnessed my
father's death when I was eleven, and for a long
time I found it too painful to recollect the
details of his dying, and then, tired of that pain
and fear of death, I took a different approach:
comedy. Even so, after a while, I forgot that I
had set out to joke and in a long stretch of Ivan
Dolinar's dying, I tried to imagine what it
would feel like, where that moment of death is.

In Minneapolis, Minnesota, a paraplegic
came up to me and told me he had read
nothing more convincing about dying than
my novel. He had been clinically dead, having
jumped into a river and broken his neck, and
having drowned. After he was resuscitated he
remembered the moment of losing his life, his
thoughts, his wonder whether he was alive or
dead, the consciousness still hovering around
even while he lost all sensation of his body. He
wondered how I knew what it all felt like. I
said, I didn't. I simply tried to guess,
imagining the details and potential thoughts.

I believe that imagination can compete
with journalism, and as far as reaching for the

subjective experience of others, fiction has a huge advantage: you are free to plunge into other people's minds, envision their thoughts and sensations. You don't have to be accurate, and you can be more expressive. A fiction writer's own pain and doubt—say, a moment of being under the knife in a hospital—can translate into other sorts of pains and doubts, such as what you might experience in crime or war. My father died, but he continued to torment me in my dreams, where he was alive almost every night, not in a physical way but in some other, ghostly way. So it's easy for me to slip into telling ghost stories.

Praise for APRIL FOOL'S DAY

"In this harrowing and hilarious novel, Josip Novakovich's wry Croatian Candide is our sympathetic guide through the recent history of the Balkans, and through the pleasures and sorrows of an ordinary and extraordinary life."   —Francine Prose

"No one portrays the lunatic grotesquerie of life—and death—in the Balkans like Josip Novakovich. *April Fool's Day* is both brutally ominous and bizarrely joyous. The only book I can think of to compare it to is the Czech classic, *Good Soldier Schweik*."
                              —Melvin Jules Bukiet

"A compulsively readable novel, enlivened in every sentence by the author's warmly sardonic style. Novakovich has the storyteller's gift."   —Phillip Lopate

> ❝ I believe that imagination can compete with journalism, and as far as reaching for the subjective experience of others, fiction has a huge advantage: you are free to plunge into other people's minds, envision their thoughts and sensations. ❞

Josip Novakovich on *April Fool's Day*
(*continued*)

"In *April Fool's Day* you will find the heartbreaks of love, the ironies of politics, descriptions of war as horrible and humane as any in *The Things They Carried* or *All Quiet on the Western Front*. Also, genuine wisdom: Josip Novakovich is a laughing, weeping and very entertaining philosopher. We are lucky to count him as a fellow citizen of our melancholy planet." —Matthew Sharpe

"*April Fool's Day* is terrific: so funny, so desolate, so brave, so grim, so hilarious, back and forth, sentence to sentence. Novakovich's wise fool seems the perfect voice for this absurd tale of a most starkly real time." —Jane Hamilton